She'll reveal the s

Dominic came an[d] reached up to take the [...] down on the floor. His [...] locked onto me, and we stared at one another intently. He lifted his hands and tugged the pins which held my hair in the remnants of a bun. As he removed each one, the weight lessened from my head as my tresses fell down past my shoulders.

"Oh, Jillian," he sighed. "Would that I could paint you, for you are so beautiful."

His eyes were like liquid amber as they bored into mine. I wetted my lips.

"You are like Athena," he said softly, "with your gorgeous velvet brown hair cascading down your back." He threaded his fingers through the mass at my shoulders. "I want to capture you in oil, Jillian. Then you will become immortal."

His face came closer to my own, and I could see the flecks of bronze in his eyes, the thick fringe of dark lashes, the hint of whiskers darkening his complexion. Drawing nearer, he released my hair from his hands and slid them down to rest on my shoulders. Gently he pulled me towards him.

Praise for
Jude Bayton

"THE SECRET OF MOWBRAY MANOR is an elegant historic suspense that does a beautiful job reminding us that when you scratch the surface of dignified family, you don't have to scratch hard to find blood. Jude's bold and crisply defined characters felt tangible. I loved getting swept up in the stunning settings, and the mystery and angst locked me in. I couldn't put it down. The juxtaposition of dark vs. light and good vs. evil gets cleverly flipped on its head. I went from trying to solve the mystery to just hoping that the noble heroine Kathryn isn't killed before she can uncover the secret and find out what really happened to her friend."

~Amy Brewer, Literary Agent

The Secret of Hollyfield House

by

Jude Bayton

This is a work of fiction. Names, characters, places, and incidents are either the product of the author's imagination or are used fictitiously, and any resemblance to actual persons living or dead, business establishments, events, or locales, is entirely coincidental.

The Secret of Hollyfield House

COPYRIGHT © 2021 Deborah Bayton-FitzSimons

All rights reserved. No part of this book may be used or reproduced in any manner whatsoever without written permission of the author, except in the case of brief quotations embodied in critical articles or reviews.
Contact Information: author@judebayton.com

Cover Art by *Diana Carlile*

Print ISBN 978-1-955441-00-1
Digital ISBN 978-1-955441-01-8

Published by redbus llc

Dedication

To my wonderful daughters-in-law, Emily Wessels Bayton, Natalie Curran Bayton, and Jessica Sutherland FitzSimons. Without you, there would be way too much testosterone in this family.

Acknowledgements

Alicia "Ally" Dean—a fabulous writer, an amazing editor and the dearest of friends.
A huge thank you to my Brit ladies—Lynne Bayton Imeson, Danii Imeson & Sheila Dawn Smith—your help was invaluable, and to my American ladies—MJ Hawe, Nestora Germann, and Susan Brown, who kindly read the first version of this book many iterations ago.

Chapter One

Wednesday, May 6, 1885

IT WAS A DAY MEANT FOR walking and picking wildflowers. Discovering a dead man lying in the shallows of Lake Windermere had not been part of my plans. At first, I thought a sheep, or large farm animal must have become entangled in the thick green rushes. But as I neared the water, to my absolute horror, I registered human eyes staring vacantly up at the heavens. Foamy spittle oozed from his gaping mouth and there was the appalling buzz of flies in a feeding frenzy atop the bloody wound on his chest.

What little I had consumed for breakfast rumbled in my roiling stomach, and I turned away to be violently ill. My breath came in ragged gasps, and my heart pounded. I looked around frantically, desperate to see another living soul to call to my aid. But I was out of luck. There was no one else about. I did not wait another moment. I took off at a run to get the village constable.

TWO HOURS SPENT AT the police station, and I still could not accept my gruesome discovery. *A body. Dear God, I had seen the body of a dead man.* I baulked at the recollection and knew the vision of that poor creature would be forever imprinted on my mind. My hands still shook, though the constable had already brought me two cups of sweet tea laced with brandy.

How I wished Uncle Jasper were here. Though a messenger was dispatched to our house to fetch him thirty minutes since, I had warned them not to waste their time. My uncle would still be foraging out on the hills, while here I sat with my head consumed with images of the dead man, the blood, the flies. My stomach churned once again, and I forced the scene from my thoughts. Who was the poor fellow? The constable had not yet identified him, and I certainly could not, for I had only lived in Ambleside the better part of a month, and hardly knew a soul.

"Miss Farraday." Constable Bloom was back, his face pink with exertion from climbing the steep staircase of the police station. "It seems your uncle, Professor Alexander is nowhere to be found. Is there someone else who can collect you?"

I shook my head. "No, there is not." Mrs Stackpoole, our housekeeper, was visiting a friend for the afternoon. I sat up straighter. "Constable Bloom. I believe myself recovered enough to go home."

But he wasn't having it. "Now then, miss. Let's not hurry. You've had a nasty shock an' I wouldn't want you to go off in a faint or anythin'—"

"Thank you," I interrupted. "But I assure you I am well enough. I feel I would be better off at home—if you please."

The policeman reluctantly nodded.

OUTSIDE THE CONSTABULARY, THE fresh air was a welcome balm to my rattled senses, and I filled my lungs. The sun burned bright in the May sky, and I tilted up my face to capture its warmth. After a moment, though, I began to feel rather odd. Most likely the culprit being the brandy in my tea, drunk on an empty stomach. My head spun, my vision blurred, and I teetered off the pavement and stepped directly into the street.

A carriage flew past my face, the wheel rims so close to my body that I instinctively lurched backwards, losing my balance. I tumbled to the ground, landing on my back with enough force to knock the wind from me. For a moment I lay stunned, until a stranger hurried to my assistance and gently helped me back to my feet.

"Are you hurt, miss?" The kindly man asked, keeping a tight grip of me.

I was unable to speak. Nothing felt broken, but my back and head had taken a blow. Strangely enough, the dizzy spell had abated, though my head now throbbed like the dickens.

The carriage came to a quick halt not far down the street and a liveried coachman rushed back to assess the damage.

My rescuer turned on the driver with a scowl. "Good God, man. You should pay attention where you are going. This poor woman could have been killed!"

"...She stepped right out in front of me," the driver protested, his face white as a sheet. I began to say something but was distracted when the carriage door swung open and a passenger alighted, heading in our direction.

She wore a striking sapphire blue travelling suit, her mass of blonde hair artfully scooped up into an elaborate bun, underneath a matching jaunty felt hat. With eyes blue as forget-me-nots, her expression was one of genuine concern.

"Oh, dear." She came to stand before me, inspecting my face as an artist studies his subject. "Are you all right?"

"Yes," I said unconvincingly. "At least I shall be once I catch my breath." I still felt winded, and my legs trembled—though it was hardly surprising after the morning I had already endured.

"Come." She grasped my arm firmly and glanced at her driver. "We must go somewhere close where the lady may rest and perhaps take refreshment." Dismissing the stranger with a polite thank you, she led me a short way down the street into a tearoom before I could protest. In truth, I was rather relieved to sit. I was queasy, and my spine was sore where it had taken the brunt of my fall.

The lady gave our order to the hostess as she took me inside the establishment. We settled into our seats and, before long, a waitress brought over a tray with a pot of tea and a plate of hot, buttered crumpets.

"There now," said the young lady. "This should set you to rights, I'll be bound."

I did not respond but watched her pour me a cup for which I was most grateful. I eyed the crumpets. Perhaps they would help settle my nausea. "May I?" I enquired boldly, glancing at the food.

"Certainly, please help yourself," she said.

I did not hesitate. I took one bite and at once my upset stomach decided it was ravenous.

"Goodness, you must think me so rude," the lady said as I ate. "Here we are at tea, and I have yet to even introduce myself. I am Evergreen LaVelle. May I ask your name?"

I swallowed and dabbed my lips with the serviette. "Jillian Farraday, miss."

She gave me a pretty smile. "Are you new to Ambleside? I do not recognise you."

"Yes. I am recently moved from Devon."

"Indeed?" Her blue eyes sparkled. She looked like a porcelain doll, smooth and delicate, not a hair out of place. I shuddered to think how I must appear.

"I have never been to Devon," she continued. "Pray, tell me. What brings you to our Lake District?" She removed elegant white cotton gloves, set them upon the table, and then helped herself to a piece of a crumpet. She placed it delicately in her mouth, and I became uncomfortably aware that in comparison, I had devoured mine like a rabid dog.

"I moved here to work for my great-uncle. He lives in Ambleside."

Miss LaVelle's eyebrows raised. "Indeed, what is it you do?" I believe she thought me his maid or housekeeper.

"I am a secretary. Uncle Jasper is an academic. He does much in the way of research on lichens and flora. I transcribe his studies which are sent to various agricultural colleges in the country."

There was an immediate change in her countenance. I had apparently been elevated in status.

"Would that be Professor Alexander, by chance?" She took another sip of tea.

"Why, yes. Do you know him?"

"Not really—but Father does." Miss LaVelle placed her teacup back in its saucer and her expression grew thoughtful. "Miss Farraday, I am sincerely sorry about what happened with our coach. Are you sure you do not require a physician?"

"Positive, thank you. I shall have a few aches and pains, but I will recover." I did not mention what I had witnessed earlier that morning. *Those* wounds would scar.

She was not mollified. "But I feel dreadful about this. You will at least allow me to take you home in the carriage?" Her pretty eyes glittered with an idea. "And you must come for luncheon on Friday. That way, I can ensure you are fully recovered."

"Oh, that is not necessary," I stammered, shocked at her invitation.

She reached into her reticule and retrieved a small, embossed card. "Please." She touched my forearm and gave a mournful smile. "I should so enjoy speaking with you again, and it would be far more comfortable at Hollyfield. Say you'll come."

I hesitated. I had no desire whatsoever to do as she asked, but something in her face made me reconsider. Surely she could not be lonely? I was uncertain. Yet as I examined all the reasons I should decline, I heard myself accept both her card and her invitation.

THAT EVENING, WHEN UNCLE Jasper finally returned from his trek across the hills, he discovered me in the kitchen with Mrs Stackpoole, the housekeeper. I cradled a mug of beef tea between my hands, which she had insisted upon making after hearing my shocking news. I still could not shake the image of the dead man from my mind.

The day had stayed warm, yet with the sun gone, the evening brought with it a slight chill, so we sat before the stove warming ourselves.

"What's this, then?" Uncle Jasper put down his satchel and pulled off his boots in the mud room. He strode into the kitchen, leaving a trail of dried dirt from his thick wool socks. "Good evening, ladies. Am I late for dinner?" Sparse grey hair on his head stuck up at awkward angles. His face was ruddy from a day of wind and sun, and his round glasses threatened to slip off his snubbed nose.

"Professor, do have a care. I have just this day swept the blasted floor." Mrs Stackpoole shot to her feet, throwing a disapproving glare in his direction. She put the kettle back on the stove to boil.

"Forgive me, Mrs S. My mind is elsewhere. I have been on a decidedly important ramble." He took a seat. "Do you recall the missive that arrived before lunch?"

"Of course, I do," she flustered. "'T'were me who gave it to you when I was on my way out."

He looked at me for the first time. "Well, let me tell you, Jilly, it was of vital import. My dear, I have been invited by Lord Mountjoy, to participate in an evening of lectures presented by none other than the Royal Pharmaceutical Society. I am to give a detailed talk on the substantial variety of lichens and mosses found here in the Lake District." His face beamed with pleasure.

I smiled. It was difficult not to, for he looked terribly happy. "I am pleased to hear it, Uncle. Congratulations." Though I had not lived with him long, I was already attached to the old man. He was my only living relative, after all.

His bushy eyebrows drew close together. "I have only until the twenty-first, so I shall have great need of you these next two weeks, Jilly. It is imperative my notes are up to date and in perfect order."

Mrs Stackpoole came to the table and placed a cup of tea in front of him along with a thick ham and cheese sandwich. Her capable hands crept onto her broad hips and she shook her head in disapproval. "Never mind your blasted fungi, Professor. When you stop to take a breath, you might ask your poor niece how she fares after the rotten day she's had. The poor mite has had a nasty shock as well as a tumble."

Uncle Jasper paused, pushed his spectacles back up his nose and took a large bite of his sandwich. Once he had swallowed, his pale blue eyes fastened upon my face. "Well, go on Jilly, speak up. What has happened?"

I set down my tea and sighed, dreading the telling. "I took a walk this morning down to the lake and had the misfortune to discover a dead body floating in the water."

Uncle Jasper stared at me, momentarily lost for words. Then he set his food back on the plate and reached over the table to take my cold hands in his. "Oh, my goodness, surely not, dear girl. A body? Good Lord. You have told the police?"

"Yes, of course. I ran to the village as fast as I could and fetched Constable Bloom back there with me. Then he took me to the police station until I was well enough to come home."

Uncle Jasper searched my face. "My poor, poor dear," he said softly. "That must have been horrifying. 'Tis rare for something like that to happen here, but with a lake as large as Windermere, sometimes drownings occur. Especially when there are tourists visiting."

I shook my head. "No, Uncle. This was no accident. There was a deep wound in the man's chest. Constable Bloom says the man was stabbed." As the words left my lips, my voice wavered. And then much to my consternation, I began to cry.

Chapter Two

THAT NIGHT, MRS STACKPOOLE PREPARED an Epsom Salt bath which gave soothing comfort to my sore back after a long soak. As I climbed slowly into bed, she brought me up a small snifter of 'medicinal' brandy to help me sleep.

By morning, my mental state was much improved, even though I had woken from bad dreams more than once in the night. My body ached, and it took longer than usual for me to dress as my shoulders and neck were stiff. When I arrived downstairs in the kitchen, Mrs Stackpoole already had the kettle on the hob and sliced bread ready to toast.

"How are you this mornin'? Did you get any rest at all?" she enquired as I walked into the room.

"A little. The bath and brandy really helped. Thank you, Mrs Stackpoole."

"You are most welcome, poor dear," she said, spearing a slice of bread to hold over the flame of the stove. "You look much better than you did last night. Got some colour back in your cheeks." She turned the bread to toast the opposite side. "Your uncle has already breakfasted an' gone off on his ramble. He's that excited about his bloomin' lecture, he all but floated out of the door."

I smiled, then had a sobering thought. "Do you think it safe for him to be out alone after what happened yesterday?" I could not help but worry.

"Of course," she blustered. "That man can take care of himself." She placed the slab of toast onto a plate and gestured for me to come and take it. "The only danger he's in is breakin' his neck gallivantin' up and down those hills."

I spread butter on my toast. She was right. I pictured the old professor, surprisingly spry for a man in his late sixties. "'Tis a wonderful thing to have a passion in life, Mrs Stackpoole. I believe it keeps Uncle Jasper young."

"I don't know about that." She poured boiling water into a teapot and carried it to the table. Her vast grey curls spilled from underneath her white mob-cap, and her ample bosom jiggled as she took a seat.

The housekeeper poured our tea, and my mind reached back to the horror I had seen the day before. I quickly shook it away. Instead, I thought of the young woman I had met.

"Mrs Stackpoole, do you know much about the LaVelles?" Last night I had told her how their carriage had knocked me down, but not elaborated beyond that.

She took a sip of tea. "Well, as much as any of the village folk would 'bout a family like that, I s'pose. Why do you ask?"

"After the accident, I met Miss Evergreen LaVelle. She was most apologetic and concerned I was not badly hurt. She invited me to join her for luncheon tomorrow." I reached in my pocket and extracted her card. "She gave me this and said the carriage will collect me at noon." I leaned forward and passed it to the housekeeper.

Mrs Stackpoole studied it and returned it to me.

"How very nice," the housekeeper said with sarcasm. "It's the least she can do after practically runnin' you over. I imagine she'll have a nice spread put on for you, an' so she should. I think it's best you go. If nothin' else, you'll get a dandy look at the Lavelle's home. Hollyfield House is right on Lake Windemere, just past Wolfe Farm. Ooh, 'tis a lovely old place—well I always thought so." She raised an eyebrow. "Wait 'til your uncle hears about it. He'll be right pleased you've an invite there."

I wish I felt the same, for I was not particularly thrilled about the prospect of dining with a stranger. As it was, my mind was at sixes and sevens. I was jumpy and unsettled.

I put the card away. "I may send my regrets and not go."

Mrs Stackpoole put down her toast and glared at me. "Now, Jillian," she chastised. "It don't do no harm to be on good terms with the local gentry. The LaVelles have lived in Ambleside on an' off several years. I'll admit they're an odd family, what with that eastern fellow living under the same roof. But Mr Victor LaVelle, he's a good sort." She tapped one side of her nose. "An' there's plenty of money there I can tell you. If you don't go, they'll think you ungrateful, an' that would look bad for your uncle, now. Wouldn't it?"

I groaned. "But I have nothing appropriate to wear, Mrs Stackpoole. I am not in the habit of taking tea with high society folk." I owned a few dresses, but they had all seen better days. Seldom did I venture anywhere to warrant the purchase of new clothing. Now I was more than aware of my lack of finery, not to mention my inability to arrange my undisciplined plain brown hair. I considered Evergreen LaVelle with her beautiful blonde tresses and tailored clothing. How envious I was of someone pretty as she. Her skin was alabaster to my sun browned face, her lovely eyes so blue, and mine green as a cat's.

"Truly, I would rather stay here," I complained.

Mrs Stackpoole fixed me with a harsh stare. "That's as may be, Miss Jillian. But I'll remind you your behavior not only affects your reputation, but the professor's too. 'Tis a nice gesture Miss Evergreen has offered, an' you should mind your manners an' go along for luncheon." She smiled to soften her words. "What harm is there to be had? At the very least you'll get something fancy to eat."

AFTER BREAKFAST, I SET OFF on an errand to purchase stamps for Uncle Jasper. When I passed the butchers, I noticed people clustered in small groups talking. As I drew closer, one or two peered in my direction. I guessed why—and hurried along.

I reached Ambleside Post Office, and as I put my hand on the doorknob it suddenly swung open to reveal a man so intent on reading a letter, that he bumped right into me. With an earnest apology, he excused himself, smiled, and held open the door for me to step inside. I glanced at his face which studied my own intently, and I managed a quiet 'thank you'.

Mr Bonfield smiled a toothless grin from behind his counter. "Hello, again, Miss Jillian." His rheumy eyes squinted through thick spectacles. He had befriended me as I came regularly to post Uncle's work to several colleges across the country.

"Good day, Mr Bonfield. May I purchase three

first-class stamps please, and a bottle of your dark blue India ink, as well."

The old man opened a drawer and fished out the stamps which he slid into a piece of creased paper. Then he disappeared into the storeroom for a moment, returning with a small bottle of ink. He handed them both to me, and I placed them in my basket.

He tilted his head. "How are you feelin', Miss Jillian, if you don't mind me asking?"

"I am well, thank you."

"Terrible business if you ask me," he said soberly.

Comprehension dawned. I glanced out through the window to where the villagers still gathered. "Yes. It is dreadful. I am so terribly sorry for the man, and his relatives." His image came into my mind and I forced it away.

"Lucky really he had no family, just his old mother. An' she's beside herself with grief—poor dear."

"You knew him then?" My pulse picked up speed.

"Why yes, Miss Jillian. Everyone did. 'Twas Jareth Flynn, our village blacksmith, you found floatin' in yon lake."

I gasped. But then the door behind me opened, and another customer entered the shop. Stepping back quickly, I sought a moment to compose myself and suppress the nausea rising in my belly. Would it always be thus with the recollection of yesterday's tragic event? I turned my attention to a free-standing turnstile displaying varieties of postcards. I willed my mind away from the ghastly memory at Lake Windemere and forced my eyes upon the pretty cards instead.

They depicted tiny portraits of the area. I studied

them and found them lovely indeed. There were lake scenes with sailboats on the horizon, paintings of velvet green hills with rambling pathways, and fields dotted with sheep. My favourite was a beautiful depiction of a waterfall. Whoever created these was a talented artist.

I left the post office and turned in an alternate direction to avoid the ever-growing crowd of people gossiping on the corner. I took a detour to walk past the mill, for I loved the old building. Though still a newcomer to the village, this part of it was my best discovery so far. I loved to stand on the ancient stone bridge, watching the enormous wooden mill wheel turn in the narrow river. The constant movement churned rushing water into small foam-flecked waves. Having been born so close to the sea, I felt a tranquil calm descend whenever I was near a body of water. I stood transfixed in the moment and tried to unclutter my mind.

"'Tis a lovely place, is it not?" A smooth baritone voice pierced my meditation, and I started at the interruption and spun around. It was the young man from the post office. I swallowed the nervous breath caught in my throat.

"Forgive me," he said with a pleasant smile. "I did not mean to startle you."

I looked at him and instantly surveyed every detail of his face. His eyes were an extraordinary shade of amber bordering upon gold. Dark flecks around the iris rendered them striking. There was a suggestion of stubble on his face, a shade darker than his thick, wavy brown hair.

"Miss?" he said with an expression of concern.

I snapped out of my trance, irritated for being so

absorbed in my impertinent study. "Oh, excuse me," I croaked. "I was lost in thought."

He stepped beside me to look upriver, while my gaze lingered on his handsome profile. What classical features he possessed—one might see the likeness on any Greek statue. I checked myself and pulled my eyes away to fasten upon the view from the bridge. Though at that moment I knew which scenery I preferred.

"This is the best view in the village," he said, turning to face me. "By the by, I am Dominic Wolfe. I believe I literally bumped into you at the post office not ten minutes hence?"

I nodded, forcing my composure to return. Why was I so affected? "Yes, you did, sir. I am Jillian Farraday."

"Professor Alexander's niece?" And with my confirmation, he extended a hand to shake mine. I complied. His grip was firm, his hand warm and dry.

"Jasper is a fine fellow. A true academic if ever there was one, not to mention the foremost expert on local flora in the Lake District. You are new to the area, I understand?"

This man had obviously heard of me. "Yes," I concurred. "I am come to my uncle's house recently. Are you from these parts?"

He leaned an arm on the stone ledge of the bridge. "Born and bred in Ambleside. I live on Wolfe Farm, my family's property for the past two-hundred years." His feral eyes glinted with merriment. "I think that classifies me as a local, Miss Farraday."

It was my turn to smile. "Indeed, and a fine place to live, Mr Wolfe. Though I have seen little of it, Ambleside is a pleasant place to call home."

A breeze rustled in the warm air and teased the front of his hair. "Your uncle said you had joined him from Devon." He paused, "...and told me of your family's recent loss. Please accept my heartfelt condolences." His tone was sympathetic, and I appreciated his concern. I was still devastated from the death of my mother.

"It has been a difficult time," I said solemnly. "But being here with Uncle Jasper has made it far more bearable." My voice wobbled, and I quickly sought composure.

His brow furrowed. "Forgive me. I have distressed you."

"Do not apologize, sir. I am glad to speak to someone new, regardless of the subject. I have befriended few people since my move here."

His eyes twinkled with pleasure. "Then I consider myself absolved. Now, allow me to escort you home—if that is your destination? 'Tis seldom I meet new friends myself."

I accepted his kind offer, and we began walking back through the village, amiably chatting as though we had met several times before and not mere minutes earlier. As we walked, each person passing would greet Mr Wolfe, tipping their cap, or if perchance a woman, they giggled as young girls might do at the sight of a handsome beau. Their stares at me were of a different nature—that of curiosity. I cared not, for my spirits climbed, blossoming as a rosebud under a sunny sky from his delightful attentiveness. Mr Wolfe was refreshingly good company.

We spoke of my uncle and his upcoming lecture. I told him of Mrs Stackpoole's friendship to me, omitting that I suspected her romantic interest in Uncle Jasper. Mr Wolfe then regaled me with a brief history of Ambleside and its progress in the past decade. As we passed the Queen's Hotel, he slowed his step and nodded a greeting at a young couple who passed, arm in arm.

"Tell me, Miss Farraday," he enquired. "Have you ever ventured to London?"

I glanced at a liveried carriage pulled up outside the grand hotel door. "I have not, Mr Wolfe. My trip here to the Lake District marked my first venture away from Devon. I am sadly no traveller. But I imagine London to be a vast and wonderful city. Why do you ask? Are you familiar with our capital?"

He threw an easy grin in my direction, and again I was taken by his handsome features. I drew a breath and willed myself to stop this foolishness.

"I lived there not three years since, though in truth it seems a lifetime ago. London is a marvellous, vital place."

"Yet you returned to Ambleside?"

"I did indeed, but I still carry a fondness from my time there and enjoy speaking of it when I meet others who are familiar with the place."

At once, I felt uninteresting and overly aware of my lack of experience. I had been nowhere, done nothing, and at the matronly age of four and twenty, must be considered rather dull.

Mr Wolfe seemed to have read my thoughts. "Please do not misinterpret my meaning, Miss Farraday. I do not judge a person based upon their travels. I was simply curious." He finished speaking and I realised with some surprise we had already arrived at my gate. Before I could mutter a word of farewell, the front door opened, and Uncle Jasper stood on the step, his cravat askew.

"There you are, Jilly," he exclaimed in astonishment, as though discovering an errant coin in his pocket. His eyes lit upon my companion. "And Dominic, is that you, boy? Come in, come in."

Mr Wolfe gave a friendly hello and opened the gate for me, following me to the door where he paused as I brushed past Uncle Jasper, and entered into the hallway.

"I cannot stop, Professor," he commented. "I must get back to the farm and check on Billy. But I was pleased to introduce myself to your great-niece and accompany her back home." He turned his head to look at me. "It was a pleasure to make your acquaintance, Miss Farraday. I do hope we speak again soon."

"Likewise, Mr Wolfe," I said politely. My face felt flushed, and I was glad to be in the shadow of my uncle.

"Well, come back another time for tea, Dominic. I've a mind to discuss a new variety of lichen I spied just last week on Compton Hill."

Dominic thanked Uncle Jasper but looked directly at me. "You can count upon it, sir," he replied.

Chapter Three

I SPENT THE NEXT MORNING examining the last few pages of notes Uncle Jasper had given me the previous day, and soon became completely absorbed in my work. When the mantel clock chimed eleven, I put aside the papers and went upstairs to freshen my appearance. I looked frightful. My old dress had seen better days, the dark blue fabric almost grey from wear. But my hair was brushed and pinned into a chignon, and I was clean and tidy. It must suffice. Mrs Stackpoole pronounced me presentable, and when the LaVelle carriage arrived promptly at noon, I bade her farewell.

It was the same driver who had knocked me over. He opened the door and helped me into the vehicle and had the courtesy to look embarrassed. I gave him a friendly smile and hoped it would ease his mind.

The carriage went down the lane, turning onto Lake Road, the main thoroughfare which wound towards Lake Windemere. It was early May, and the tulips and daffodils were in riotous blooms of bright yellows, dazzling oranges and reds. We passed a small farm, and I admired the sumptuous green pastures full of lazy mother sheep with their frisky lambs. Nature astounded me with its palette—no wonder spring was my favourite season. The trees and bushes burst with colour, elegant red maples, vivid lemon forsythia, everywhere my eyes turned there was new life in abundance.

We rounded a bend with the calm, blue lake straight ahead and I kept my gaze averted from the direction I had been yesterday. I thought of the blacksmith's grief-stricken mother and quickly dismissed it. Having so recently known my own loss, it was unimaginable to comprehend a mother's pain.

Mrs Stackpoole had given a good account of my destination. Therefore, I easily identified the sizeable house situated on what looked like a small peninsula, where the land fingered into the lake. As the carriage turned into the driveway, I craned my head out of the window for a clearer view.

Hollyfield House was positioned so that both the front and rear of the building faced the water. It was not in the least ostentatious, being of modest size with a short driveway leading up to its entrance. Built from stone, the structure was accented with thick aged timber which framed many windows peppered along both storeys, along with tentacles of thick ropes of ivy. Though a dignified building, there was yet a wonderful rustic appeal. Tangled green vines clung fiercely to the walls, their tendrils snaking in all directions. High up on the pitched roof, I spotted a weathervane shaped in the fashion of a yacht.

The carriage deposited me at the front of the house, and I walked down the pathway admiring the well-kept beds, teeming with spring flowers.

A young girl in her early teens answered my knock on the door. She bobbed a deferential curtsey which I found extremely embarrassing as we were of similar social standing. I gave her a friendly nod, then stepped inside at her invitation and followed her through to the sitting room.

Evergreen LaVelle rose from a window seat, a vision in pale blue silk. She glided towards me like a swan, a broad smile spread across her lovely face.

"Miss Farraday, I am so pleased you are come." Her eyes sparkled, and she grasped my hand and led me to the window. "Let us sit here while we wait for luncheon to be served. Tell me, how do you feel? Improved I hope?"

"Yes, indeed," I assured her, for I was much better. "I beg you not to worry, Miss LaVelle. It was an accident and could have been far worse."

"Oh, do call me Evergreen, and I should also like to call you by your Christian name. After all, we shall be good friends. I am sure of it."

I know my expression registered surprise, yet she paid no notice and continued.

"I have learned only today that you were the unfortunate creature who discovered the dead man in the lake. No wonder you were in a state when first we met. My poor dear, you have had a rough go of it these few days. I cannot imagine what a terrible shock it must have been—"

"Please," I asked. "I appreciate your kind words, but I would rather not revisit the experience. In fact, I should prefer we not speak of it at all. I did not come here to discuss such upsetting things. Can we talk of other, more pleasant topics?"

She nodded in understanding, and the subject was dropped.

"Tell me, do you miss your friends in Devon?" Evergreen asked. But before I could formulate an answer, she continued. "I miss all of mine in London.

We always had such a jolly time of it. In truth, I am so very bored here at Hollyfield. 'Tis nothing like the city and I would leave in a moment if I could." She gave a mournful sigh.

I was somewhat bewildered at this sudden outburst. We were scarcely acquaintances, yet she spoke as though I was a trusted confidante. I did not respond.

"My father remains in the city but insists Perry and I spend several months here." She gestured with her hand. "In this awful place in the middle of nowhere."

"Perry?"

"My twin. He apprentices with Mr Nicholas Sneed, Father's accountant. Perry is to work with Father, and he insists my brother understand all facets of the company. Currently it is bookkeeping and accountancy he must study."

"What kind of business does your father have?" I asked, then instantly regretted my ignorance as she smiled at me as though I had been living on the moon and was the only person who did not know.

"Why, he is a shipbuilder. Tell me, have you never heard of LaVelle Shipping?"

I shook my head to the negative.

Evergreen giggled. "How amusing. My father is a self-made millionaire, Jillian, and I do believe you are the first person I have ever met who did not know of him. He is called the working-class man's hero," she exclaimed with a note of disdain. "Father has not a drop of blue blood in his veins, but he was clever enough to become filthy rich." She shrugged. "I am fortunate indeed to want for nothing, yet my father plans to marry me to a wretched title, probably one in need of a sound financial investment. I am a mere bargaining tool for him to auction off to the highest peerage."

I was lost for words. I had nothing to compare to Evergreen's statement, as my life seemed on an opposite hemisphere from her own. Did she want my sympathy? I cleared my throat.

"Miss LaVelle, I am unsure what you expect me to say? Am I supposed to empathise for one as fortunate as yourself?" I continued, oblivious of her reaction to my words. "I come from a social class whose main concern is whether they will afford one hot meal a day or lose their life from the black lung. Your concern of which wealthy husband you may have the misfortune to marry seems trivial in comparison. I am sorry, but if it is my pity you seek, I cannot give it honestly."

Much to my amazement, she burst into a peal of laughter. "Oh my—how refreshing you are, Jillian Farraday. I am constantly surrounded by people only too happy to agree with every word I say." Her face shone with pleasure. "Thank goodness you had the misfortune to be knocked over by my coach. To think," she grasped one of my hands. "I should never have met you otherwise."

"Evergreen?" A tall, dark-haired woman came into the room. Dressed in black bombazine, the style appeared harsh and too severe for one who appeared to be in her late twenties—not much older than myself.

"Marabelle." Evergreen rose, and I followed suit. "Jillian Farraday, this is my cousin, Marabelle Pike. She lives here at Hollyfield and is in charge of running the house. Cousin, meet my newest friend from Ambleside."

She assessed me with eyes black as pitch, and none too friendly.

I smiled and nodded a greeting. "Pleased to meet you, Miss Pike."

"Likewise." Her voice carried blatant disinterest. She turned her attention back to Evergreen. "Luncheon is served for you and your," she hesitated and glanced at me, "new friend."

The food looked delicious, but I derived no pleasure from the dainty sandwiches and fancy petit fours. I was entirely too uncomfortable being seated across from Miss Pike, who occasionally glanced up to look at me with a curious expression painted on her face. Evergreen monopolized the entire conversation, which suited me. I spent my time studying the two women at every opportunity.

Miss Pike resembled her name. Thin and serious, her face sullen, in direct contrast to her cousin Evergreen, who was all sunshine and brightness. We made decidedly odd companions.

I was relieved when the table was cleared, and Miss Pike rose first and excused herself. I was not sorry to see her depart. Evergreen invited me to take a turn around the gardens, and it was while doing this, I explained more about my uncle.

"How interesting to have a scientist in your family," she said. "I should like to meet the fellow. He sounds rather fun."

"Oh, he is that and more," I smiled. "I did not know him well as he was my mother's uncle. But when she died, Uncle Jasper invited me here to live with him as I have no other relatives. A kinder man I've yet to meet. I would be lost without him—in the poor house too."

We wandered down a narrow path away from the

house which led to a small copse of trees alongside a boathouse, and beyond it, the lake. I was quite taken by the beauty of the place. It was peaceful here and most serene. We neared the lake with its inky waters lapping gently at the sandy shoreline. Though not the repetitious sound of an ocean's tide, I was nevertheless still soothed by it. I was a coastal girl born and bred, and there was naught I loved more than the sound of the tide. A gentle breeze stirred, tickling the fresh new leaves on the trees, and in the distance, I made out the call of a swan.

"I find the water here revolting. It is so muddy and dirty. I much prefer Brighton, and the sea." Evergreen complained. "Salty air is so much fresher, don't you agree?"

"It is certainly different. I have never been to Brighton, though I have always lived near the ocean."

"Oh yes, I remember. Didn't you say your family was from Devonshire?"

"Yes. Except Uncle Jasper moved away for his studies long before I was born. My family remained in Devon as Father worked in the tin mines." We stared out at the water, at small yachts bobbing about in the lake. I thought of my father and imagined what he might have said were he stood beside me.

"When did your father die, Jillian?"

"He was killed in a mining accident when I was eight years old." His face flashed in my head, an image so beloved.

"I am sorry," Evergreen said. "I know what it is like to lose a parent when you are young." She paused. "Come. Enough of us being maudlin. Shall we walk a while longer?"

"I do not think so," I said, my mood darkened by memories. I was unused to such company and had stayed long enough to be polite. "I must return home, Miss LaVelle. I have multiple tasks to finish before my uncle returns."

Her face registered disappointment. "Oh, do call me Evergreen, please. I wish you might stay a while longer, Jillian. Still, you must come again." Her blue eyes implored. "I shall not take no for an answer."

I imagined Miss LaVelle often got her way, and in truth, it would be hard to turn down so friendly and engaging a person. "Perhaps." I would not commit to her enquiry, and I could see she had expected acquiescence.

"Please Jillian, I shall go barmy if you do not. Say you will visit another time, or I will return home along with you." She grinned, a sly look in her eye.

I relented. "All right, Evergreen, I will come again, but not for several days as I have my own work to do."

I took my leave of Evergreen LaVelle. Little did I realise my life would never be quite the same again.

Chapter Four

MRS STACKPOOLE WAS a matronly woman. Though she had only one child, she was nonetheless a kind lady with a propensity to cluck. Upon my return from Hollyfield, she declared me tired and pale. I had been plied with tea and fresh jam tarts until I felt more myself once again. The housekeeper told me it was natural to still be upset after what I had seen. "It will fade with time," were her sage words.

Uncle Jasper was in fine fettle when he appeared at sundown, his face smudged with dirt and carrying a bag full of mouldy samples. He entered through the back door, bringing the scent of the downs with him, earthy and damp. I encouraged him to pull off his socks as well as his muddy boots. While he went to change clothes, Mrs Stackpoole warmed up a pan of oxtail soup, and I cut the loaf of bread she had baked fresh that afternoon.

Uncle Jasper returned and we sat down to eat.

"The soup is delicious, Mrs S., I believe you are turning me into a fat old man with all this wonderful fare."

"'Tis no stargazy pie," she retorted, her eyes twinkling with pleasure at his compliment. "But it'll do."

I took a bite of bread. "How went the collecting today, Uncle? Did you find what you needed for the lecture?"

"Just about there, Jilly. Plenty to show those horticultural boffins."

I chuckled at his reference, for he was likely more of a boffin than all the others combined.

"I went to Hollyfield House today, for luncheon with Evergreen LaVelle."

"You don't say?" He glanced from me to the housekeeper. "And how did that come about?"

I had not explained the carriage accident the other night because our conversation centered on the murder of the blacksmith. I quickly recounted the events leading up to the invitation.

"My goodness, Jilly. You haven't been here five minutes and you are already rubbing shoulders with the gentry. And how was it, my dear? Did you eat caviar and drink champagne?"

"Of course not," I laughed. "Tiny sandwiches, fancy cakes and Oolong tea." I took a sip of my soup. "But I prefer our good soup and bread over that any day. Though I do envy them their home. It is quite lovely."

"Hmmm. The father does something with boats if I'm not mistaken?" Uncle Jasper said vaguely.

"Ships," I corrected him. "Shipbuilding. Oh, and he has rather a large fortune."

"That's right." He slurped another spoonful of soup and sat back in his chair. "Victor LaVelle. Nice chap. Donated a large cheque to the society last year. Has a son, tall lad if I remember rightly, though I never met the fellow."

"Victor LaVelle is a good an' generous man." Mrs Stackpoole contributed, not to be left out.

"That he is," agreed my uncle. "Spends most of his time in the city though. I haven't laid eyes on him in Ambleside for a long while. Don't think they've much interest in horticulture as their gardens are a bit mundane. But they are kept neat and tidy—I'll give them that." He returned to his meal, and I concluded that was the sum of my uncle's interest in the LaVelle family. Had they a root system and were they green, I am sure he would have known their entire life history.

"Did you meet the son?" Mrs Stackpoole asked.

"No." I said. "Though Miss LaVelle did say she had a twin. However, I did meet the cousin. A Miss Pike."

The housekeeper bristled. "Now there's a miserable woman if I do say so. She has a face on her t'would spoil milk. Too high an' mighty to speak to any of us in the village. I remember when the LaVelles first came to Ambleside an' bought the house from old Mr Morecombe." She paused to think. "Must be fifteen years since." Her hazel eyes looked directly at me. "The wife died in India if I'm not mistaken. Victor LaVelle brought the children here for a fresh start. They spend their time in London mostly. Come to think of it, they've been here for a longer spell than usual."

"Oh," I answered quickly. "The son is being mentored by the firm's accountant, a Mr Sneed. At least that is what Evergreen said."

"On first names, are we?" Mrs Stackpoole grinned. She turned to my uncle. "It might be time for missy here to get a new frock or two if she's going to be hobnobbin' with the gentry now."

SATURDAY DAWNED AND THE WEATHER was positively

glorious. Mrs Stackpoole opened all the windows and aired out the house while Uncle Jasper disappeared to capture his final samples for the upcoming lecture. Birds sung happily in the fresh breeze and the scent of spring was invigorating.

It was too nice to sit at the table working. So I took a leaf from Mrs Stackpoole's book and decided to clean out my own room. I stripped the bed, dusted the furniture, and swept my rug. My eyes turned to the wardrobe where I had placed my belongings when I first arrived at my uncle's. It was dusty and could use a liberal dose of oil to feed the wood.

I laid my meagre possessions on the bed, and with the bright sun beaming through the open window, I could see how grubby the old piece of furniture was. I set about cleaning with a rag soaked in lemon oil, and the wood soaked it up like a thirsty sponge. I finished the main area where my clothes usually hung and then turned my attention to the shelf above. I had trouble reaching it and dragged my small chair away from the vanity table and climbed upon it. I doused the shelf with oil, and as I wiped away years of dust, I knocked against something at the very back. I craned my neck inside the wardrobe and squinted. Practically invisible to the naked eye was a dark-coloured box, tucked right into the corner. I pressed closer and stretched my arm as far as I could. My fingers touched against it and, with some dexterity, I managed to move it.

It was grimy, thick with dust, and likely had not seen the light of day for many years. I stepped off the chair and took it over to the sunlit window while wiping off the lid. It was an old tobacco tin, the colours faded and the writing barely legible. Intrigued, I began to work on the lid and then hesitated. The tin did not belong to me. Should I show it first to my uncle? It was barely past midday, and he was still out on the hills. Curiosity burned. What could be inside? I made my decision, and pushed the lid from all sides, but it was on tight and would not come loose. I kept working at it until finally, it began to move, and then came away in my fingers.

The faint tang of sweet tobacco rose from the tin, still fragrant after many years. Inside lay a thick scrap of velvet, red as blood. I gently unfolded the fabric and then gasped. Wrapped inside the material lay a beautiful teardrop pendant the size of a penny piece. I lifted it out, holding it up to the light. It was beautiful. Cut prisms of the milky, glassy gem captured the sun's rays and projected shards of sparkling light around the room. Was it a diamond? I looked closely at the jewel. It seemed too white for a diamond, and too large. Then what could it be? I put it back in the tin and replaced the lid. Where had this come from and who did it belong to?

I thought long and hard. As far as I knew, Uncle Jasper had always lived here alone. Perhaps the tin had been in the furniture when he bought it? Puzzled, I slipped it into my nightstand drawer, determined to ask Uncle Jasper when he returned home.

THAT AFTERNOON, AN INVITATION arrived for us to dine at Hollyfield House for the upcoming Sunday evening. I instantly baulked at the notion, assuming Uncle Jasper would do the same, as Mrs Stackpoole told me he disliked formal engagements.

"He prefers a-talkin' to his blasted fungi," she had

commented when I read her the note.

But much to my disdain, when I spoke with him at supper, he appeared delighted by the missive, due to the existence of a particular moss growing in Hollyfield's grounds. A specimen would be worth any inconvenience he might have to suffer.

For myself, I did not understand the interest shown toward us. After all, Ambleside was a large enough village to boast of other families in the community more suited to the social class of the LaVelles. Perhaps Evergreen LaVelle saw us as entertainment? Our unimportant lives were far different than her own. She must be bored indeed.

After we ate, Mrs Stackpoole declared she had a headache and excused herself early for bed. I waited patiently until Uncle Jasper settled into his armchair for the evening, and then retrieved the gem from my room and joined him in the parlour.

"Uncle Jasper, I was cleaning out my wardrobe today, and I found this."

His thick eyebrows raised above his spectacles as I passed him the small container. "What of it? Looks like a tin of tobacco to me."

"Open it," I instructed, sitting down opposite him.

He pulled off the lid and frowned as he saw the velvet fabric. When he uncovered the pendant, his expression suddenly relaxed, and he leaned back in his chair with a great sigh. I noted the lack of surprise upon his face.

"Remind me where you found it?" Sadness laced his words.

"In the wardrobe, at the back of one of the shelves. Have you seen it before?"

He nodded slowly, lifted the pendant out of the tin, and held it in his large palm. He rubbed the stone with the pad of his thumb, and then looked up at me. To my shock, I saw his eyes fill with tears.

"Uncle Jasper, what is amiss? Are you unwell?"

This time he shook his head. "Calm yourself, Jilly, I am all right." He closed his fist over the gem. 'Tis just a moment of passing sorrow. This pendant brings old memories."

"Then you are familiar with the piece?"

"Indeed," he said solemnly. "Beautiful as it may be, it never brought any joy."

Puzzled, I began to ask a question, but he spoke before the words left my mouth.

"Some might not know this stone as 'tis uncommon in England. It can often be mistaken for an opal, even a diamond." He held it up where it caught the light from the gas lamp. "But this, my dear, is a moonstone. And this particular piece is probably from India, or Nepal."

"Like the stone in Wilkie Collins's novel," I said wistfully, the gem now more exotic because of its origin.

My uncle did not read fiction and therefore did not remark on my statement. He was focused upon the geologic explanation of the stone. "They are common enough, not as valuable as other gems, yet distinctive and lovely of their own accord." He pondered for a moment. "If my memory serves me right, the moonstone is a mineral from a group named feldspar. It is popular because of the alternating layers it possesses within, which makes the light diffract through the gem. Do you see?" He held it higher, and I saw exactly what he meant.

"The sheen on the stone gives the appearance of a crescent-shaped moon, hence the name." He placed it back inside the tin and closed the lid.

I was fascinated. My uncle's knowledge of the gem was far more interesting than his usual topic of ferns and flora.

"Where did you get it, Uncle?"

He cleared his throat. "Oh, Jilly, 'tis not mine. No, my dear. I was given the pendant by another many years ago and asked to keep it safe until the day when its owner would come to reclaim it."

"How mysterious," I exclaimed. "How long have you kept it?"

"Oh, long enough to have lost it until your discovery today." His pale eyes looked directly to my face. "Twenty-four years."

I smiled. "My goodness, that is as long as I have been alive."

"Indeed, it is, Jilly." Uncle Jasper's voice was almost a whisper.

"Why has the owner not reclaimed it, I wonder?"

"Because she is no longer living," he said softly. I looked at him then, saw the grief etched upon his face. Perhaps the woman who had owned the moonstone was someone he had romantic feelings for, an unrequited love? How tragic.

"Who was the woman, Uncle Jasper?" I asked boldly, not expecting him to admit her name.

Uncle Jasper extended his hand to me and placed the tin in my palm.

"It belonged to your mother. And now, Jilly, it is yours."

My face must have betrayed incredulity as I absorbed his meaning. I glanced at the tin in my hand and then back up at him.

"This was Mother's? I do not understand. Why would she own such a lovely piece and not keep it with her? She did not have much. I am certain this would have been a treasured possession. Uncle, I am confused."

He gave a compassionate smile. "Yes Jilly, it must seem odd, yet it is true. This pendant represented a time in my niece's history she held most dear. But when life brought a different chapter, she gave up the past, leaving its reminder with me."

"What?" I asked. "That makes no sense. What past. Which chapter?"

His gaze met mine. "Before your mother married, there was another man in her life. Someone unable to be with her—someone who broke her heart."

"That is ridiculous," I snapped with irritation. "My mother only ever loved my father, and he her. There was no one before him. She would have said something to me. We were always very close."

"My dear girl, of course, your parents were in love. What I speak of was before they met, when your mother was young and impressionable. I cannot tell you much for she never elaborated about what happened, but only gave me the pendant for safekeeping, lest she might have need of it one day. I was visiting your grandmother at the time, and your mother insisted I take it with me when I left. And Jilly, she obviously did not want it back, for she never reclaimed the gem."

"No, this makes no sense at all." I did not like his inference. My mother could not care for anyone other than my father, and that was an end to it.

"It is not for you to fret over dear girl. 'Tis a young woman's keepsake, not unlike a love letter, or a card from an admirer—something she would want you to have. Just put it away in a drawer and forget about it."

I opened the tin and looked at the moonstone. It was a beautiful stone, yet somehow tainted by what Uncle Jasper had shared. I was uncertain what I thought now.

"Do you think it valuable?" I asked.

"I am not sure," he said. "I imagine it would be worth something, yet moonstones are not rare, or as expensive as emeralds, sapphires or rubies. We might have it appraised and find out?"

I nodded and got to my feet. "I will put it away for now." I went to him and kissed the top of his head. "I am off to read before it gets too late. I shall see you in the morning, Uncle." With that, I left the room for the sanctuary of my bed.

BUT SLEEP EVADED ME, THAT night. I tossed in my bed, the pendant there whenever I closed my eyes, along with images of my father—his lovely smile and his happy face. That my mother could have cared for another was beyond distasteful, and I would not accept she had. Why was the pendant here? My parents had never been wealthy, and Mother could have sold the gem and used the money to ease their own plight. Yet she had not. I was uncertain if the thought of her selfishness irritated me more than the realisation she had loved my father second.

Chapter Five

ON THE NIGHT OF THE DINNER, when the door opened to admit my uncle and I to Hollyfield House, the lack of finery in our formal attire was shockingly apparent. Uncle Jasper's black suit reeked of mothballs, even though Mrs Stackpoole had it airing on the washing line all afternoon. My dress was one kept for Sundays and special occasions, a dark green cast-off from my mother's hope chest. I had wrapped a gold silk shawl about my shoulders, but it did little to improve my embarrassment.

We were shown into the parlour I had frequented earlier that week, and Evergreen instantly leapt to her feet, welcoming me with an unlady-like embrace, and a friendly nod to Uncle Jasper.

"Goodness, Evie, do let them come in before you devour them." A male voice chuckled from one of the armchairs, and as Evergreen led us over to the settle, a tall young man approached with one hand extended.

"Good evening, to you both." He smiled, and I noticed his obvious resemblance to Evergreen. This was the twin brother she had spoken of. Though not identical, their likeness was uncanny.

"Allow me to introduce myself," he added. "Peregrine LaVelle, Evergreen's long-suffering brother. Welcome to Hollyfield. We are pleased you could come at such short notice."

My uncle shook his hand vigorously. "Happy to accept, my boy. Pleasure is all ours." We took a seat upon a large satin sofa while the siblings sat facing us in two scarlet armchairs. I studied them. Both were blonde, yet Peregrine's eyes were lighter, unlike his sister's startling violet-blue. His face was the same pretty heart-shape, yet with harsher angles. They made a striking pair.

A man entered the room, a silver tray in his upturned palm. I almost gasped in surprise, for he looked as though he had stepped out of a page of the Arabian nights. His skin was the colour of strong coffee, with obsidian eyes beneath the deep scarlet of a turban. Garbed in a long white tunic over loose-fitting trousers, with sandals upon his feet, he was an exotic vision—flamboyant among the formal trappings of a stoic English parlour. This must be the 'easterner' Mrs Stackpoole had casually mentioned.

"Ah, Marik, there you are." Peregrine rose. "May I introduce our friend from India, Marik Singh. He is part of the family but insists upon acting thus when we have company—though he needn't." The Indian gentleman approached each person with the offer of a glass from the tray. He kept his handsome face expressionless, his back rigid. I could tell at once he was a man of great self-discipline.

"India," my uncle commented wistfully. "Now there's a place I'd like to explore." Uncle Jasper's face beamed like a young boy. "I'd enjoy a jolly good romp around the jungle. I daresay their flora would be a fascinating study."

"Not to mention the tigers," Evergreen added, and we all laughed.

"And cobras," said Peregrine, taking a glass of sherry from Marik Singh. "Were you ever in British East India, sir?"

My uncle shook his head. "Never was. Closest I got was Cairo, right after the Suez Canal opened. Caught a fever at Port Said and got sent right back to England. Good job too, or I'd probably have been a goner." His words stirred a vague childhood memory. A telegram to my grandmother, her worry at her brother's fate.

"India will always hold a special place in my heart," Peregrine said softly, and his eyes met those of his sister. "But our time here in Ambleside is—" He paused as the door opened to reveal the solemn figure of the woman I had met on my last visit. Marabelle Pike. Tonight, she appeared less formal. Her gown was russet brown, devoid of frills or lace, which did not serve to accentuate her looks, but rather make her seem even more sullen. I admonished myself for thinking such unflattering thoughts. Besides, who was I to criticize, wearing naught but a Sunday best dress, long past its prime.

"Dinner is served, Peregrine," she announced laconically.

I HAD NOT BEEN BROUGHT UP wealthy, yet I silently thanked the women in my family for teaching me social graces and polite table manners. My grandmother had come from a distinguished background but was cast out when she chose to marry my grandfather, a working fisherman. Her lifestyle had proved hard and difficult, though you would not have known it in her presence. Proper etiquette was second nature to my grandmother, and she took great pride in passing on what she knew to my mother and myself. Thank goodness. At least I knew the correct fork to use first, and could display what I hoped were decent table manners.

After the plain food at my uncle's table, dinner was simply mouth-watering. There was watercress soup and poached salmon, followed by carved roast beef and vegetables. Stimulating conversation had been ongoing, mainly between my uncle, and Peregrine LaVelle, their mutual interest of the Lake District an easy topic. When the raspberry cream tart was served, both men were engaged in their differing opinion of Darwin's controversial book, *On the Origin of Species*.

"But, Professor Alexander," Peregrine insisted. "How can you possibly believe the human race is descended from apes. It is an absurd notion."

My uncle was unfazed. "No more preposterous than a celestial being having the power to create life. And for what it is worth, my boy, human beings are not far removed from 'said apes'."

Miss Pike's voice suddenly perforated the atmosphere like a blade "That is easy to believe, Professor, when you consider the atrocities men do to one another. A perfect example is our propensity for violence. What say you of the murder of our blacksmith?" Everyone stopped talking and collectively we all stared at the woman. I felt the start of a blush creep across my face and dreaded what might come next.

"I understand you, Miss Farraday, were the unfortunate person who discovered Flynn's body?" Her beady dark eyes settled on me as the others turned my way.

"Good grief," said Peregrine. "Is this true?"

I nodded solemnly, reluctant to be drawn into the conversation.

"My dear Miss Farraday, that is absolutely shocking," Perry said, astonished. "You must have been terrified."

"I should hate to see something so abhorrent. Though I have heard an arrest was made," continued Marabelle. I looked at her and saw a malevolent gleam in her eye. She was enjoying my discomfort.

I lifted my chin. "That is a relief," I forced my voice to sound confident. "I should hate to think anyone could get away with murder."

"Marabelle, must you?" Evergreen glared angrily at her cousin who hastily averted her eyes. "I hardly think this appropriate conversation at dinner, in fact at any time. Our guests have come to dine and enjoy our company. It is in poor taste assaulting Jillian by asking unpleasant questions about an experience I am sure she would rather forget." She rose abruptly from her chair. "Come. We ladies shall excuse ourselves to the parlour for coffee." Marabelle and I instantly got to our feet and followed our hostess out of the room, leaving the men to their port and cigars.

The drawing room was a welcome reprieve from the topic of conversation at the table. I took a seat on the now familiar red sofa while the two ladies sat across from me. As before, Marik appeared like a genie and placed a small coffee tray on an ornate ivory inlaid table next to Marabelle.

With her face all seriousness, Marabelle poured the coffee. As we sipped the delectable brew, she spoke for the third time since we had sat down to dinner.

"Do you share your uncle's interest in plant life, Miss Farraday?" Her deep voice was not warm, and her expression devoid of character.

"Unfortunately, no." I smiled, though I still smarted from her earlier comments. "As much as I like flowers and vegetable gardens, his obsession with mosses and lichens is beyond my scope."

"I cannot think of anything more boring," Evergreen commented. "They all look much the same to me, except I rather like lavender. It is so fragrant and makes such a nice adornment for my hats." Her pretty blue eyes were guileless and naïve, yet I was not so foolish to believe the girl silly. She was toying with us.

"Marabelle thinks me frivolous with my propensity for gowns and trinkets," she continued. "It goes against her strict Catholic upbringing to wear gaudy costumes." She gave an unkind giggle, and I did not look at Miss Pike. Unlike her, I derived no pleasure from another's discomfort.

"Indeed," Evergreen continued. "My dear cousin believes my soul eternally damned for brushing a little rouge on my cheeks and lips, not to mention a dab of cologne."

Miss Pike set her demitasse in its saucer with a distinctive *chink*. She got to her feet. Ignoring her cousin, she looked at me directly. "Please excuse me. There is a matter I must attend to with Cook, lest I forget." With that, she hastened out of the parlour.

"Thank goodness," Evergreen sighed. "I am sorry she picked on you at dinner. Marabelle is such a misery-guts. Truly, I do not understand why Father allows her to stay. She is always so down in the mouth. Can you believe the woman is but twenty-eight, Jillian?

I think she was born forty years old." She laughed at that, and my fine opinion of her lost some of its shine at her capacity to be unkind.

She continued to chatter about inconsequential subjects until the adjoining door to the dining room opened and Peregrine entered the room with my uncle in tow.

"Ladies, I beseech you to dazzle me with vocal frippery, for I have spent enough time hearing about the complexities of horticulture. My brain is exhausted." He turned to my uncle, who took a seat next to me on the sofa. "Sir, I am drunk on knowledge."

Everyone laughed, and it did my heart good to see Uncle Jasper having such a pleasant time of it.

"Jilly," he beamed. "What do you think? Peregrine has agreed to my taking a specimen of his *Lycopodium annotinum*. It will be a wonderful addition to the collection."

I gave a grateful nod to my host even though I had no clue what Uncle Jasper was talking about. "Mr LaVelle, it is most kind of you. My uncle will be forever in your debt."

"Happy to help the cause." Peregrine grinned and sat in the chair vacated by Miss Pike. "Professor, feel free to wander and collect to your heart's content. I'll let Billy know so he won't run you off if he sees you in the gardens."

"Is that young Billy Wolfe you speak of?" My uncle asked, and I found myself suddenly most attentive at the mention of the familiar surname. Surely this must be the Billy related to Dominic Wolfe, the young man I had met at the post office.

"The same," Peregrine answered. "He took over

responsibility of the gardens when his father died. Very good with the plants I'm told—has a knack for making things grow. I'll have a word with him in the morning."

"Is Billy related to Dominic Wolfe?" I enquired, quelling the curiosity in my voice, and wondering why I felt such a sudden interest in the Wolfe family.

"Yes." This time it was Evergreen who answered. "Dominic is the older brother, a wonderful artist. Father commissioned him to paint his portrait years ago when Dom was a student at the London College of Art." Her eyes sparkled. "He's rather dashing. Artists are so romantic."

"Oh, please, must you?" Peregrine rolled his eyes at his sister. "Dominic Wolfe is a fine fellow, indeed. I have a great deal of respect for the man with the sacrifices he's had to make."

I was intrigued. And when my uncle agreed with the statement, I was eager to know of what they spoke. "What has Mr Wolfe sacrificed?"

"His potential career as an artist in London," Peregrine replied. "The man was under the tutelage of the great John Everett Millais himself. Gave it all up when his parents died of scarlet fever a few years ago, and he came back to Ambleside to run the family farm. Now all the man gets to paint are postcards which are sold to tourists."

I remembered the beautiful little paintings I had admired. A variety of thoughts crossed my mind at this information. Several questions presented themselves, and I asked the first which bubbled to the top.

"Could Billy Wolfe not take care of the farm without his brother?" This seemed logical to me, especially if he had a way with making things grow.

Evergreen laughed, and it sounded like a little bell. "Goodness no. Billy might be good with plants, but he can barely hold a conversation or do up his own buttons. The boy is disturbed, if you ask me."

I frowned, uncertain of her meaning.

Peregrine must have seen my confusion for he smiled kindly. "Billy Wolfe is not like a normal young man, Miss Farraday. He is struck with Mongolism."

I stared blankly at my host as I absorbed the term.

Evergreen interjected. "Surely you know what that means? The boy has the mind of an infant. He is an imbecile."

THE USE OF THE LAVELLE carriage was offered for our journey home, but Uncle Jasper politely declined. He announced, "The night is pleasant, the moon full, and a walk will help digest the gargantuan meal I have consumed." Though I was tired and the prospect of walking home was unappealing, I had to agree with his choice.

Uncle Jasper kept a steady pace. No doubt his legs were strong from all his rambling on the hills. As we went along, the conversation eventually turned to our evening of repartee. More than anything, I yearned to learn more about the Wolfe family. Though I could not define my reason, thoughts of Dominic Wolfe resided on the fringes of my mind. What was it about the man that held my interest?

"Uncle, how well are you acquainted with the Wolfe family?" I asked as we reached Lake Road, which was quiet at this time of night.

"I knew the parents before they died. They were good people. If I remember correctly, we first met when they gave me permission to examine a species of liverwort growing in one of their west fields. It was a wonderful specimen. Still have it in the study."

"What were they like?"

Uncle Jasper fell silent, gathering his thoughts. He cleared his throat. "Well, Arthur Wolfe kept a rather fine ale, and I seem to recall a delectable slice of Mrs Wolfe's plum cake which—"

"Uncle," I groaned. "I mean what kind of people were they?"

"Hmm." I realised the question was not an easy one for him to answer. My uncle could describe a mushroom in poetic detail, but human beings were of an alien species.

"I do not recall them being particularly spectacular, Jilly. Just hard-working farmers. But now I think on it they were a mismatched pair. Arthur was a respected village elder, a serious chap, never much to say. But his wife. Now there was a striking woman. Pretty eyes, I recall, and of elegant stature. Violet Wolfe was well versed in herbal remedies and such like. We had several interesting discussions on the healing components of lichens, especially when used as poultices on infected wounds. Although she was not a proponent of the use of leeches—"

"Uncle. I mean for you to tell me about *them*. What were their personalities like?"

He shrugged. "No better nor worse than most, Jilly. I did not know them well, you understand. As a matter of fact, I am on better terms with Dominic. His parents were good people who unfortunately succumbed to scarlet fever and left the care of a young boy to the more competent elder son. They have a small, working farm, and seem to rub along well—all things considered." He frowned and appeared to engage his thoughts elsewhere. I knew that was the total sum of his opinion of the Wolfes', and no more would be forthcoming.

As he prattled about his upcoming lecture, my mind drifted like a leaf upon the lake, and the rippling current of thought brought the image of a handsome dark-haired man—with eyes the colour of a tiger's.

Chapter Six

I AWOKE UNUSUALLY GRUMPY—the prospect of the day unappealing. I had slept fitfully, my dreams a cavalcade of strange events. I dreamt of the moonstone and my mother, of Marabelle and the blacksmith, though I could not remember anything more than feeling disturbed.

As the day progressed, Mother stayed on my mind. Her lovely smile, and her gentle touch. I would find myself pausing from transcribing Uncle Jasper's notes to stare off into space, my thoughts whirling with impotent understanding. Though I did not like it, I allowed myself to accept theoretically that Mother had been involved with someone other than my father. This unknown man surely gave her the moonstone, for she would not have had the coin to purchase the blasted thing. So, who was this mysterious person, and where had she met him? Why had their relationship ended?

I had too many questions and no answers. Those, Mother had taken to the grave. I would speak with Uncle Jasper once again. He must know more about what happened before I was born.

Mrs Stackpoole went off to the village to the butchers. Not long after her departure, I heard a rap upon the front door, followed by the sound of Uncle Jasper's feet going down the hall. I heard him speak and then the higher-pitched tone of a woman. Who on earth was here?

I put down my pen and went along to the study. There, among the cluttered room littered with piles of papers, sat Evergreen LaVelle. Why my uncle had not taken her into the parlour was beyond me. I was overwhelmed with shame at the poverty of our home, distressed she would find us in no fit state to receive company.

"—and here she is, Miss LaVelle." Uncle Jasper gestured in my direction as I stood speechless in the doorway.

"Come in, Jilly. Look, we have a visitor." His face beamed with pleasure and I knew he had no idea how out of place Evergreen LaVelle appeared sitting on our threadbare armchair by the hearth.

"Jillian," she exclaimed, a smile on her face. "I do hope you can forgive me for showing up unannounced, but I've come to ask a huge favour."

I stepped closer and took the opposing chair. Uncle Jasper mumbled something about going out to the vegetable garden and left the room.

"A favour?"

"Indeed." Evergreen sighed and leaned back in the chair. Her immaculate dove grey cloak accentuated how old and worn the furniture appeared. "I have commissioned Dominic Wolfe to paint my portrait as a birthday gift for my father."

"That is a lovely present," I said, "but what has it to do with me?"

She chuckled. "Jillian, you are so forthright with your manner of speech. 'Tis a little off-putting at times." She shook her head, "Still, I am sure you mean no harm. I have a request. Would you be willing to come out to the house while I sit for the painting? 'Tis improper for me to be alone with a young man—even an artist."

I shook my head at her ridiculous request. "I am sorry, but that is impossible. I have far too much work here to be spared. Can you not ask your cousin, Marabelle? She lives with you, after all."

"Absolutely not," Evergreen snapped, and all warmth flew from her pretty eyes. "I detest the woman. Besides, she thinks me vain to have the painting done at all."

Clutching my hands together on my lap I laced my fingers and struggled for a response. "Miss LaVelle—"

"Evergreen," she interrupted.

"Evergreen, surely you understand I am not in the same position as you to do as I please. My uncle depends upon my work, and I cannot ignore my responsibilities to spend time with you, especially when there is much expected of me here." My words sounded feeble even to my ears, for though I did have many duties, Mrs Stackpoole took care of cleaning the house and all the cooking.

"Jillian, please," she injected a pleading note to her voice. "I would be so grateful if you could find the time to help me in this matter. Hollyfield is such a dull and boring place. I shall go mad if left to my own resources."

"I am truly sorry for your unhappiness," I replied. "But I cannot leave my uncle—"

"What's that you say?" Uncle Jasper rejoined us. He held a small cabbage in his hand and granules of dirt fell to the floor.

"Professor Alexander," Evergreen rose to her feet,

her blue eyes shining in earnest. "I have asked Jillian to assist me in a small matter at Hollyfield while Dominic paints my likeness as a surprise for Father. Not only would it help me, but I should like to get to know her better. However, she insists she cannot leave her duties here with you."

Uncle Jasper set the cabbage down upon his desk. "What's this, Jilly? You shouldn't turn down a request for help, my girl. Wouldn't be polite. No, not one bit."

I stifled the groan trapped in my chest. "Uncle Jasper, 'tis not that I am unwilling to help, but my time is limited with all I need to do each day. What about your lecture notes?" I knew that would rally him to my way of thinking.

"Mrs Stackpoole can help," he suggested.

"What?" I was amazed. As intelligent as the housekeeper might be, she was not proficient in interpreting Uncle Jasper's technical work.

"Perhaps not." He had apparently come to the same conclusion. "But you should help Miss LaVelle, Jilly. 'Tis what a friend would do."

I looked at the wealthy woman who glanced from my uncle to me in anticipation of a final answer.

"It would only be every other weekday for three hours in the morning, for the next few weeks, Jillian. And I would be forever in your debt." Evergreen turned her beautiful smile upon Uncle Jasper. "Father will be so pleased with the portrait. And I shall tell him of your kindness, Professor. Of course, you could accompany your niece whenever you felt the inclination to spend time in our gardens and park. Not just for the specimens Perry granted you, but to procure anything which takes your fancy."

With that, my fate was sealed. Uncle Jasper was completely on the hook.

"What an excellent notion, Miss LaVelle, and a generous offer indeed. I should be delighted for Jilly to spend time with people of her own age. It will do her the world of good. Consider me in agreement. 'Tis all right with you, is it not?" he asked me as an afterthought.

I felt Evergreen's perusal. I had no choice but to comply, though I was not at all pleased with the outcome.

Uncle Jasper made small talk until Evergreen took leave of us, with my promise to attend her the next morning at ten o'clock. She would sit for her portrait for two hours, and then I would be given luncheon before returning home. I watched her step into her carriage and then I closed the front door. My new responsibility felt like a burden upon my shoulders. The only consolation was I would see Dominic Wolfe again.

THE NEXT MORNING, THE SULLEN grey sky reflected my mood. In the carriage, my mind knotted itself into a muddle of irritation. Though I had examined the reason for feeling so out of sorts, I determined it was from being at everyone else's beck and call. Seldom did my time belong to me, always to my family—and now, Miss Evergreen LaVelle, as well.

At Hollyfield, I rapped the knocker and was ushered inside by the same girl as before. But this time she led me through a library and out into an enormous glass conservatory. It was a veritable jungle, teeming with pots and baskets full of lush green plants, and all manner of flowers. Many were unfamiliar, but I recognised the pungent scent of honeysuckle blossom, which permeated each breath I took. The maid escorted me through a maze of gravel pathways, the plants brushing against me as we passed.

The far end of the conservatory opened into a broad area, filled with white wicker furniture, adorned with ornate pillows of bold green satin. Semi-reclined upon a chaise longue lay Evergreen, and my step faltered as I absorbed the picture she presented.

She could pass for a Roman empress in her gown of pure white silk. Several layers of sheer taffeta fell from underneath the bodice, and the square-cut neckline plunged to reveal Evergreen's creamy décolletage. I was so captivated by her appearance I failed to see she was not alone, so when Dominic Wolfe stepped out from behind a large easel, it startled me.

"Miss Farraday. It is a pleasure to see you again."

His greeting was friendly and my face warmed at his singular attentiveness. "Hello, Mr Wolfe."

"Oh, good grief." Evergreen swung her legs down, so her sandaled feet touched the floor. "You shall both need to dispense with formalities, after all, you two have already met."

Dominic inclined his dark head to acknowledge her command and then turned his amber eyes to fasten upon my own. I saw the question there and realised he awaited my consent.

"Yes. Do call me Jillian," I stuttered with embarrassment, though I knew not why. He smiled kindly, and I began to relax.

"Jillian, you are late. We have already begun the session." Evergreen remarked with a hint of petulance. She gestured to one of the chairs. "Do have a seat. Tell me, what do you think of my dress? I thought it whimsical and romantic for a portrait."

"It is beautiful." I heard the wistful note in my voice. "And you look lovely, Evergreen. Your father will assuredly adore the painting, once it is finished."

"Now, don't get ahead of yourself," Dominic chuckled. "I have just begun sketching. You will have to wait before passing judgement." He moved back behind the easel, and I took my seat.

We fell silent and I suddenly felt awkward. I sought to fill the quiet. "How long have you both known one another?"

Evergreen responded. "Since childhood, although I can't remember much of that. Father kept us in London mostly. Our time at Hollyfield was brief, but frequent."

"And I was more familiar with Perry, and Marik." Came Dominic's voice behind the easel. "We three played together when the family was in residence."

I glanced at Evergreen. "Marik has been with your family some time then?"

"Oh yes. He and Perry have grown up together. He is like another brother to me."

I recalled the dark face, the black eyes. What an interesting family the LaVelles were in comparison to mine.

"But thank goodness for Dom. If I am forced to stay this long at Hollyfield, at least I have one person of my age besides my brother and Marik. And now we have met, Jillian, I have two friends to amuse me while I die of boredom in this godforsaken village."

"Evergreen's behaviour has always bordered on the melodramatic," Dominic said dryly. "She forgets how fortunate she is and tends to complain about one thing or another."

I smiled while Evergreen pouted. "I do not. It is because I should be in London attending the theatre, going to balls, and—"

"—see what I mean." Dominic's head peered around the easel. He gave us both a devilish grin. Evergreen giggled and acquiesced the point.

How close were these friends? Was it a romantic alliance? The idea rubbed against me like an itchy wool vest. Why should it concern me one way or another? But I knew the answer. I was intrigued by Dominic Wolfe. From his tousled dark hair to those intelligent eyes and strong jaw. He was a good-natured fellow to be sure, yet I sensed something more mysterious lurking beneath his exterior. He was an artist. Therefore, I knew he would have a sensitive spirit and an open mind. If Dominic had studied with Millais, then he must be a member of that secret society of painters they called the pre-Raphaelite movement. I had read much about the men who embodied the ideals of reformists, daring to be unconventional.

As if knowing he filled my thoughts, Dominic stepped out from behind the easel and glanced at me before retrieving his bag. I watched him crouch to fumble through the leather satchel in search of an item. Though no giant in stature, he was still a well-built man with a healthy physique—no doubt from years of labouring on his family's farm. His back muscles rippled beneath the soft linen of his shirt, and my eyes followed the bulge of his thighs as he squatted down low.

I started as his eyes connected with mine, catching my intense study. Our gaze held a moment longer, and I was the first to look away. Had my face betrayed my reflections? My skin warmed with embarrassment. Then I saw the smirk spread across Evergreen's lips, and I felt ashamed of her observation. Her knowing eyes were full of comprehension and feline in expression.

Nervously I got to my feet. "Shall I get us some refreshment from the kitchen?" I offered.

"Don't be silly, Jillian. I'll ring for tea." Languidly Evergreen stretched out to the glass table next to her and rang a small silver bell.

Dominic resumed his sketching, but the atmosphere had shifted.

"What's all this then?" Perry LaVelle approached us, wearing a white linen suit and a friendly smile. He nodded at me. "Good day to you, Miss Farraday."

"Good morning."

"Wolfe, old chap. What on earth are you up to?" Perry shook hands firmly with Dominic, who pointed to the canvas before him.

"I have been commissioned to paint a portrait of your lovely sister."

Perry stepped behind the easel. After a moment he peeked around it and grinned at Evergreen.

"Damme, Dom, you've captured her perfectly. She's as broad as a house!"

Evergreen gasped, swung her feet to the ground and made her way to the easel. Her face flushed bright with indignance.

"Whoa." Perry laughed, signaling for her to stop. "I jest, dearest sister. Calm yourself. Dom has barely started sketching."

Evergreen wrinkled her nose in annoyance and

slapped her brother's outstretched hand. "You are a rotten swine, Peregrine LaVelle." But the grin on her face belied her beratement. Evergreen returned to her seat but did not resume the pose. "What are you doing here, anyway? I thought you were with Mr Sneed, studying father's boring accounts."

Perry sat on the end of the chaise longue. "I was. But poor old Nicholas has a chill. He was sneezing so violently, at one point, his spectacles popped off his nose."

We all laughed.

"So instead, I'm off for a ramble up Thatcher's Peak. Does anyone want to tag along?"

"I might." The Indian gentleman I had seen at dinner came towards us carrying a large silver tray. He placed it carefully on the table next to Evergreen.

"At least you shan't be in any danger now they have nabbed the murderer," Evergreen said drolly. I thought something passed between her and the foreigner, a slight change of expression. Or had I imagined it?

"Let us stop prattling about such a macabre subject." Dominic stated, looking directly at me. I understood he was aware of my involvement in the body's discovery, and I gave him a smile of thanks.

"Yes let's," commanded Evergreen. "I'd rather talk about something more exciting. Marik, do stay and join us. Miss Farraday has yet to be properly introduced to you."

The handsome man complied and pulled a chair closer so we could all sit together in a group. Our hostess poured tea and handed around the cups and saucers, and a plate of shortbread for those who were hungry.

"Miss Farraday." Marik sat to my immediate left, close enough for me to detect the musky scent of exotic perfume which I found very pleasing. "Evergreen tells me you are new to this part of the country. How do you find the Lake District?" His accent was crisp and British, as educated as any noble Englishman.

I smiled. "This is a beautiful part of England. Especially, I think, at this time of the year. I have yet to venture far, only the village and not much further. But I like it here very much." I took a sip of tea. "And you, do you like this part of the world? I imagine it completely different from your homeland?" In the background, I could hear the others having their own conversation regarding someone they knew from the village, but I was far more interested in speaking to this foreigner. Both his appearance and manner intrigued me. He was clean-shaven, his complexion smooth and even. His jet-black hair shone with lustre now there was no turban to conceal it as it had the evening of the dinner party. Strong brows were set above pitch eyes, and he had the thickest lashes I had ever seen.

"England and India are as similar to one another as the Sahara and Lake Windemere," Marik stated, his generous lips parted, revealing pearl white teeth. "There is much to appreciate about both countries, I believe. The opportunities available here to learn from fine universities are second to none. There is a wealth of history before our very eyes, and the beauty of the land is breathtaking. Yet in my country, there is the rawness of nature, untouched places and a wildness that renders England tame as a domesticated dog. Here you have your manners and polite society, in India lies the heart of the tiger, a call to prayer, the smell of spices in the wind and vivid colours only a fierce sun and heavy monsoons can paint upon the land."

I was mesmerized. As he spoke, my imagination saw the vibrant colours he spoke of, vast lands, wild beasts. "Your description fascinates, Mr—"

"Call me, Marik."

"Marik." I took a breath. "To have lived in a place so extraordinary is more than I can comprehend. In comparison, my life has been small, so uninteresting."

"Oh, please do not say so." He reached over to place his empty cup on the tray. "For there is no such thing as a small life, Miss Farraday. When you are the only player on your life's stage, it is an epic story you tell." He rose to his feet and bowed before me. "And now I must excuse myself and return this to the kitchen." Marik lifted the tea-tray and accepted the empty cups from the others.

"Can you be ready to leave in ten minutes?" Perry asked Marik.

"Naturally." Came the reply as he walked away from our little group. I watched him depart and then looked at Evergreen. Her face bore a curiously amused expression.

It was Perry's turn to get to his feet. "Well, Dom. I'm off. I'll leave you to put up with my sister. At least you have Miss Farraday to assist." He gave me a wink and then bade us all a friendly farewell.

I settled back in my chair, deep in thought. Evergreen resumed her pose and Dominic began working once again.

"I should like to paint that chap, one of these days," Dominic commented after a short while. "Marik has the most interesting bone structure. He would make a fine study."

"I have never met a person from his part of the world," I stated. "He is fascinating."

"Oh, Jillian. You are so impressionable," Evergreen laughed. "I do believe that is why I find you so wonderfully refreshing. You state your mind blatantly. One never has cause to wonder what you are thinking."

I did not look her way, instead preferring to allow her words to melt into the air and not touch me. Evergreen LaVelle, was an enigma. She was sugar and salt, sweetness and sting, and I was not yet certain which side of her personality was the most authentic. The more time I spent around the beautiful young heiress, I was reminded that sometimes the prettiest things in life can be the most precarious.

Chapter Seven

DOMINIC JOINED US FOR LUNCHEON, but Marabelle Pike did not. After we dined, I was more than ready to take my leave from Hollyfield, and accepted Dominic's kind offer to accompany me on my walk back to the village. If Evergreen objected to our leaving together, she did not show it. We parted with my promise to return in two days for the next session.

"Thank you for changing the subject, earlier." I said to Dominic once we set off down the lane leading to Lake Road. "I do not like to be reminded of that poor man in the lake."

"Think nothing of it," he replied. "Bad enough you had to experience something so horrific. It cannot help for others to keep bringing it up. Therefore, on a lighter note, tell me what do you think of Hollyfield House?"

"It is a fine residence." I said. "I know it is a stately home, yet I like that the place does not take itself too seriously. I mean, it is welcoming and comfortable."

"A fine analogy, Jillian." He grinned, and I noticed one of his front teeth was slightly crooked. This was no flaw. Indeed, it added to his character.

"I've always thought it a marvellous place," he continued. "And the grounds are wonderfully extensive." His voice held fond appreciation.

"You would be an authority on that subject I should think. If your family has worked here many years, I imagine you know it well." We turned onto Lake Road and hearing several geese squabbling overhead on their journey to the lake, I glanced up.

"I do. Father spent his life working Wolfe Farm, and taking care of Hollyfield also. Our family holding is not large, but enough to keep us in food. We have a wheat field which we harvest and take to the mill in Ambleside. A small flock of sheep, milk cows, pigs and chickens. My mother, and brother, helped out on the farm, which allowed father to earn extra money gardening for the LaVelles."

"Your father was a hard worker," I said respectfully. "Is it difficult now, managing the farm with only your brother's help?"

Dominic shrugged. "Honestly, it can be challenging at times. Billy has some problems, but he is a strong lad and not afraid of hard work."

Instantly Evergreen's unkind comments jumped into my thoughts. I pushed them away. "How old is your brother?"

"Fifteen last March, though you'd take him for grown if you saw him." Pride shone in his eyes as he spoke of his sibling, and I warmed to this man even more. Though masculine in each cut of his build, it was the sensitive side of Dominic Wolfe which I found so very endearing.

"Here is the farm," he announced as we rounded another bend on the road. "Why don't you come along and see the place, if you have time?"

"I would like that." I was, in truth, madly curious to see it. Wolfe Farm aroused an unsubstantiated interest in me.

The farmhouse was more impressive than I expected. It was built of brick and, like Hollyfield House, had thick ivy trailing up to the roof. To one side stood a barn in good repair, and next to that, a stable which might accommodate several horses. There was another building which I assumed must be the cowshed.

Dominic led me towards the house as a figure came out of the barn.

"Billy, come and meet Miss Farraday," Dominic shouted over to him, and the boy came towards us, wiping his hands on a piece of rag. As he approached, it became apparent that his features were unusual. His body was stocky and muscular, and though larger than his brother, he was not much taller than me. Billy's hair was thick and wavy, his eyes a similar colour to Dominic's, but there the similarities ended. It was as though a part of him did not belong to the other. His neck seemed too short, his head too small. The plane of his face and nose were flat. His lips were thick, and his eyes slanted upwards as though smiling.

"Billy, this is my friend, Jillian."

The lad grinned at me and held out a big hand. I took it. "Pleased to meet you, Billy." I smiled.

"You too, miss." He spoke with the pronunciation of a young child, though his voice was deep and his words quite clear. "Do you want to see the cows? There's babies."

"Spring is Billy's favourite time on the farm, Jillian. He has a soft spot for the calves and spends too much time with them. Don't you, brother?" Dominic ruffled Billy's hair.

"I like 'em," he said. "They be all soft an' new.

They smell good too."

"I would love to see them," I said enthusiastically, and he beamed and held out his hand. I took it and allowed him to lead me into the cowshed. Dominic stayed behind, but I felt comfortable enough with the lad.

The cowshed was darker than outdoors, but it smelled of sweet hay and livestock. Billy walked quickly towards the back of the shed. His face shone bright with pleasure and the excitement of showing me his pets. We reached the last few pens, and I saw three cows in their stalls with babies. One cow had twin calves, who were latched on to their mother, drinking hungrily.

"This one, she's named Sophie, that'n is Isabelle an' the brown one here is my favourite. Her name be Sally."

I peered over the metal gate at the sibling calves. "They are adorable, Billy. No wonder you are proud of them. They look so healthy. You must work hard taking such good care of them."

"I do," he said. "But we can't keep 'em—I wish we could, but Dom has to take 'em to market once they're weaned." He looked at me mournfully. "I cry when they go away."

His face was so sad, and his sentiment heartfelt. Billy was a contradiction in terms. His strong body, manly and mature, while his heart and mind were still that of an innocent, a child.

"It is always hard to say goodbye to the things we love, Billy. But you know they are going to new homes where they will be taken care of." I had no idea if that was even the case, but it seemed an appropriate response.

"That's what Dom says." He grinned. "Let's go an' find him."

Dominic was in the farmhouse, putting a kettle on the hob to boil. "I hope you enjoyed your tour?" He glanced up as Billy and I came into the kitchen.

"I did indeed." I scoured the room. It was a little untidy and devoid of female touch, but generally clean and welcoming.

"Would you have a cup of tea before you go, Jillian?"

"No, thank you, I had better not. There is a great deal of work waiting for me at home. Though Evergreen thinks me readily available I have much work to get done. Uncle Jasper is required to submit monthly papers to the university, and I have to transcribe his notes first."

He turned to look at me, his face troubled. "I am sorry Evergreen burdened you with this. I had no idea you'd get coerced into chaperoning when she asked me to paint her portrait. I was too busy thinking of what I might earn. In truth, I expected Marabelle to be there, or even one of the servants."

"Please do not apologise. I am sure Evergreen could have her choice of chaperone, but for some reason, she wanted my company. Though I do not know why."

His eyes were warm as he met mine. "Really? I do."

"Dom likes you," Billy giggled next to me. "He's gone all sappy."

Dominic stepped forward and good-naturedly put his arm around Billy's neck and rubbed his knuckles on the boy's head. "Less of the lip, little brother, or I'll have to give you a good walloping."

"Please." I stepped back out of their way, laughing. "I must be on my way before I change my mind."

The brothers ceased. "Will you be all right walking the rest of the way alone?" Dominic asked politely.

"Absolutely. I will be fine." After all, the murderer had been arrested. With that, I bid them both a good day and left the farm towards the village. As I made my way home, I contemplated my morning. It had undoubtedly been an interesting day. Speaking with Marik had been thrilling, meeting Billy, and then feeling Dominic's interest stir was exhilarating. I took a deep breath, looked up at the blue sky and felt my heart swell for the first time in weeks. Perhaps coming to Ambleside had been the right thing to do after all.

"IS THAT YOU, JILLY?" UNCLE Jasper called as I shut the door and hung up my coat. I followed his voice into the study. He sat at his desk peering into a microscope.

"Ah, you're back. How was the chaperone duty, were you terribly bored?"

"Surprisingly, no. Evergreen LaVelle is a nice girl, but so very spoiled. But I did enjoy chatting with her brother, and the Indian fellow, Marik. Then I walked back with Dominic as far as Wolfe Farm and he introduced me to his brother Billy."

"Did he now?" Uncle Jasper looked up. "He's a friendly young lad, isn't he?"

"Yes. He was knowledgeable about the livestock and so gentle with them."

"'Tis an unfair misconception held when it comes to those afflicted with mongolism, Jilly. The alteration of their looks can have a disarming effect on people who have regular features, yet it does not signify stupidity. There can be a negative impact on their capacity to learn as quickly or understand some things the way you and I might. They have more challenges to get by in this world than the rest of us, but given time, can learn and participate in life every bit as fully as we do."

"People are cruel, Uncle. I thought Evergreen a little harsh on him."

"I agree, my dear. But Billy is luckier than some. At least he has his brother looking out for him and a warm and comfortable home. Sounds as though you had an interesting day."

"Indeed, I have. Is Mrs Stackpoole about?"

"In the parlour, darning socks—last I checked."

"I think I'll pop the kettle on if you would like a cup of tea?"

Uncle Jasper grinned. "Only if there's a jam tart going."

THE NEXT MORNING MRS STACKPOOLE LEFT FOR Kendal to visit her daughter, Ruby. She would spend the night and return the following day. After a busy few hours, Uncle Jasper and I were in the kitchen finishing up our lunch when there came a knock on the front door. Dominic Wolfe stood on the step. My heart lifted. He was such an attractive man. I liked his tousled wavy hair, those interesting eyes. I might not be a great judge of character, but part of his appeal was the man seemed indifferent to his admirable qualities.

"Dominic. Come in." I stepped back.

"I hope this is a convenient time—"

"Yes, of course."

"Wolfe, what brings you here this fine day?" Uncle Jasper joined us, and we all went into the parlour.

"Why don't I make tea," I suggested as they both sat down. I returned promptly with the tea-tray and handed each man a cup.

Dominic and my uncle sat in the two armchairs, I settled on our rather threadbare sofa. They continued their conversation started while I was in the kitchen.

"There is much speculation about him," Dominic stated, and I quickly realised they were talking about the dead blacksmith. A wave of nausea hit me, but I took a sip of tea and willed it gone.

"Jareth had a reputation as a bit of a gambler," Dominic said. "There is talk of debt, and perhaps him being mixed up with the wrong people. The man they caught was a gambler as well. Apparently, there was bad blood between the two. But they have not yet found the murder weapon."

Uncle Jasper tutted and took a sip of tea. "Well, I am glad they have him locked up. I did like Flynn, but in truth, I cannot say I knew him that well. Always was a confident fellow, and a bit of a lady's man, according to Mrs Stackpoole."

"I am sure the police are working diligently to get the case before a judge and keep the fellow behind bars."

"Or hang him." The words blurted from my mouth. Both men looked at me with expressions of surprise.

"You did not see what had been done to the poor man," I said plainly.

Uncle Jasper awkwardly cleared his throat. "Dominic, will you attend the lectures at Mountjoy's?"

Uncle Jasper got back to his favourite subject, and I took the opportunity to slip out of the room. I returned to the kitchen and cleaned up from our earlier meal, but my mind kept straying to the man sitting with my uncle down the hall.

After some time, their voices grew louder as a door opened. I realised Dominic must be leaving, and hurried out of the kitchen only to find Dominic heading in my direction with my uncle nowhere in sight.

His smiled when he saw me. "Jillian. Might I speak with you before I leave?"

"Of course. What is it?" I drew closer.

"Let us step outside?" He led the way to the front door, opened it and the afternoon sunlight streamed in. He turned back to face me.

"Jillian."

He was close enough that I could see the thickness of his dark lashes, the golden flecks in his amber eyes. I took a breath to calm myself. Why did this man make my senses react this way? "Yes?"

He held my gaze. "I hope you do not think me improper, especially with all you have been going through. But I should like to ask you to accompany me on a walk tomorrow, after we leave Hollyfield. There are some places here in Ambleside I would love to show you."

His words were platonic, yet the look he bestowed upon me shone as richly as my moonstone.

"I should like that, indeed." I managed a quiet response, when in truth, I wished more than anything to smile broadly and sound a hurrah.

When he took his hand from the doorknob and reached across to take my own, I almost gasped with surprise. Carefully he held my fingers within the firmness of his grip.

"I want to get to know you better, Jillian Farraday. I find you not only lovely, but fascinating." He raised my hand to his mouth, and I felt the soft graze of his lips against my knuckles. My intake of breath was audible, but before I could breathe again, he had already gone.

WEDNESDAY DAWNED, AND THE sun shone as brightly as my heart. Though I was not looking forward to my time chaperoning at Hollyfield, I could barely contain my excitement at the prospect of my walk with Dominic afterwards.

"You seem in unusually good spirits this morning, Jilly," Uncle said, as he finished his breakfast. "Perhaps Dominic Wolfe should visit more often." He gave a cheeky wink, and I laughed.

"What nonsense." I picked up his empty plate and set it in the sink. "Now remember, I am away to Hollyfield this morning. There is cheese and ham in the cold pantry you can eat for lunch." I kissed the top of his balding head and bade him farewell.

As before, the carriage arrived promptly to collect me and whisk me away to Hollyfield House. I enjoyed the fresh morning air, the glisten of dew upon the damp green grass, and the playful young lambs already outside frolicking in the fields. By the time we arrived, my senses were almost vibrating with the anticipation of seeing Dominic again.

Marabelle Pike answered the door. I was taken aback, unprepared for the tall, dark figure and haughty face.

"Good morning, Miss Pike." I smiled.

"What are you doing here?" she said rudely. "You were not supposed to come, Miss Farraday. Your services are not required today."

I stood on the doorstep. "Oh. But the carriage called for me."

"That was a mistake, it should never have been sent."

I was stupefied. "Is something wrong? Is Miss Evergreen unwell?"

The cold black eyes assessed me. Her body tight and slender, she resembled a cobra preparing to strike. "Miss LaVelle has taken sick to her room, in light of the shocking discovery she made whilst out walking last evening." My expression must have implied confusion because she frowned. "You have not heard?"

"I do not know what you refer to, Miss Pike. Heard what?" My skin prickled with cold apprehension, and I was at once frightened.

"It is the Wolfe boy."

"Dominic?"

"No," she said in a monotone voice. "The idiot brother."

My heart sank. "What has happened?"

Marabelle Pike's face was unfathomable, still as stone. "He has been arrested. It was his knife that killed the blacksmith. Billy Wolfe has been taken to the gaol for the murder of Jareth Flynn."

Chapter Eight

I GASPED, AND MARABELLE'S dour countenance shifted to what I would swear was pleasure at my obvious discomfort. Was she so malevolent to the fate of young Billy, not to mention Mr Flynn?

"Will that be all?" she enquired; her disinterested mask slipped back into place.

I tilted my chin and straightened my spine as I replied, "Indeed. Good day." I turned my back on her before she had time to close the door in my face. As I reached the small lane, my anxiety grew. I pictured the young man I had met so recently, and I could not imagine the same gentle person being responsible for the ghastly scene I had stumbled upon in the lake shallows. What must Dominic be thinking? It was all too horrible to contemplate.

Without conscious thought, I left Lake Road and walked directly to Wolfe Farm. I had no idea if Dominic would even be there, but instinct drew me to him. As I entered the stable yard, all was quiet. The cows were in the pasture, as were the horses. Pigs grunted contently in their pen, and the chickens scratched the dirt, looking for tasty insects.

The farmhouse door was closed, and I knocked loudly. At first I thought no one would come, and then I heard footsteps approaching slowly. The door swung open to reveal Dominic, his face strained, dark circles underneath his eyes and lines furrowed across his brow. His clothes were disheveled as though he had slept in them, and his hair was wild and unkempt.

"Jillian." His tone was flat. "This is not a good time. I beg you leave. I have much to attend to."

"Please, Dominic," I implored. "Allow me to come inside. I have heard the terrible news and would help in some way if I could." Reluctantly he left the door standing open, turned and walked down the hall. I followed him inside.

In the kitchen he took a seat at the table, rested his elbows on its surface and buried his face into his hands. My heart grieved for him. I went to the hob and placed a kettle on to boil. My eyes scoured the area, and within a few minutes, I had cut a thick slice of bread and cheese and made a steaming mug of sweet tea, both of which I placed before him, though he paid no heed to my actions.

I sat in the chair beside him and gently pulled one hand away to grasp it in my own. He looked at me. The light in his eyes was gone, replaced by hollow anguish which pierced my soul. The poor man was wretched. Again, I felt such empathy, such sorrow for his plight.

"Dominic, I know you have no appetite," I said gesturing to the plate. "But you must stay strong for your brother. Starving will not help him one whit."

He nodded and pulled the food towards him, breaking pieces off and chewing them slowly.

"You are in shock, though I know little about it other than what Marabelle Pike shared when I was at Hollyfield, just now. What I do know is you cannot lose yourself in despair. It will serve Billy no aid whatsoever. You must take nourishment and remain clear-headed. 'Tis the only way to get to the bottom of this mess." I took a deep breath. "And I am here to help in any way I can assist you."

He swallowed and then took a sip of tea. "Thank you, Jillian. I am sorry for my manners and being so abrupt. They took Billy in the early hours of the morning, and I have been up since then, worried sick."

"Tell me what has happened," I urged. "Why do they accuse Billy?"

"It was his knife," Dominic said softly. "The blade which killed Flynn was my brother's."

"Are they sure?" To my mind, one knife looked much like another.

"Yes, they are certain. It is distinctive as it bears our family crest carved into the handle. The head of a wolf. It was my father's, and Billy always keeps it on him."

"What did Billy say when the constable came? Did he deny what had happened?"

"Not exactly." He drank more tea. "He became confused and started to cry. He was terrified."

I could only imagine. A level-headed person would find it distressing enough to be arrested, but a boy like Billy?

"They handcuffed him and took him away, and he just kept shouting out my name to help him. I followed them outside, and as they put him in the wagon, he said 'I lost my knife, Dom, I lost it', as they drove off." He pushed away his plate as though disgusted by food being close to him. "I will never forget the sheer terror on his face." He looked at me, and his eyes were dark as pitch. The chair scraped noisily as he rose to his feet. I stood quickly. Boldly I went to him and wrapped both of my arms around his shoulders. I could not bear to see him so distraught and broken. All I could offer was the comforting touch of another human being. We stood motionless for a time, and then he pulled away. He went to the kitchen window and stared out through the glass.

I remained where I was, allowing him some distance. When he turned to face me, his expression had changed completely. Gone was the drawn, beaten visage he had shown moments earlier. Instead, his jaw was firmer, his gaze hard and determined. He ran his fingers roughly through his tousled dark hair.

"I will clean up, and then I am going to the post office."

"Whatever for?"

He came towards me and stopped a hair's breadth from my face. "I must send a telegram to Victor LaVelle. I shall ask for his help."

I must have shown my surprise at his words.

He explained, "Victor has been good to my family for many years. I shall need sound legal advice to sort out this almighty mess. He is the only person I know with those resources."

I was both concerned and worried Dominic was on a fool's errand. His brother was charged with murder—surely no amount of legal help could change that? But I held my tongue, relieved to see the spark back in his eyes, hear the conviction in his voice.

"Go home to your uncle, Jillian. I must ready myself and take care of this business. I will stop by and see you and the professor, later today."

I did not want to go. In the course of one morning, it was as though an indescribable bond had taken root between us. I had seen him at his most vulnerable, and in that precise moment, something inside me had changed. For now, Dominic was no longer disparaged. He was devising a plan of action, and therefore his focus had returned. He needed no distraction.

"I shall go, Dominic. But please do come by later and let us know how you fare." I yearned to reach out and touch his arm but resisted the impulse. His mind was on far more critical issues than me.

I ARRIVED HOME TO FIND MRS Stackpoole ensconced in the study with Uncle Jasper.

"I thought you'd be back early," Uncle commented as I joined them.

"How did you know?"

"'Twas me," Mrs Stackpoole interjected. "For I'm not long back from Kendal and have told Jasper what happened during the wee hours." She shook her head in disgust. "What a to-do. How could that Billy Wolfe do something so wicked?"

Uncle Jasper sipped his tea. "'Tis a shocking turn of events, to say the least."

"You are both very quick to believe all you hear." I could not keep the irritation from my voice. Two grey heads snapped up and my uncle and our housekeeper looked at me with surprise. I cared not.

"Having known Billy Wolfe for many years, I am surprised you condemn him without questioning the findings?"

Uncle Jasper frowned. "'Tis hard not to, Jilly, when the boy owns the murder weapon."

"Yes, my dear," agreed Mrs Stackpoole. "Evidence is evidence. At least that's what my Ruby's husband says, an' he would know—he is a constable. Sidney had it straight from the Chief Inspector's mouth. 'Twas Billy's knife found in the bushes by Miss LaVelle an' one of the staff at Hollyfield, not ten yards from where the body was left."

"How strange it is only just now discovered, though a thorough search was made the day the body was found. Does it not occur to you that Billy would have removed the weapon, or at least hidden it, or thrown it into the lake to conceal his guilt?" I asked

"Fair points, Jilly." Uncle Jasper agreed. "Except when searching, it would be easy enough to miss the object with all the new growth of grasses and such. As for the disposal of the knife, your regular criminal type would have the wherewithal to be devious enough to do just that. But Billy, as you know, is not your typical young man. I doubt it would even occur to him to hide the knife."

"Yet you are ready to believe it *would* occur to him to stab a man to death in cold blood?" I was curt yet cared not. Why was I so quick to defend Billy Wolfe? Was I being fair giving him the benefit of the doubt, or was it because of my interest in his brother, Dominic? I pushed the notion away with distaste. I could not countenance the idea of the boy doing something so evil.

"You seem extremely sensitive to his situation, Jilly. May I ask why?" Uncle Jasper peered over his spectacles in inquiry.

I shrugged. "I stopped at Wolfe Farm on my way home. I was concerned for Dominic." I felt no shame in my actions, nor did I care if I breached proprietary.

"I see. How did you find him?"

"Overwrought, tired, scared at the prospect of what might happen to his brother. Dominic cannot believe Billy capable of killing anyone or anything, for that matter."

"Well now, he would think that being family," Mrs Stackpoole announced. "Only natural to defend your own. Why I remember—"

"He believes Billy to be innocent and intends to prove it." I snapped. "Dominic has not been able to speak with his brother yet, but he will, and then he can make some sense of it all."

Uncle Jasper nodded solemnly. "Jilly, you are right. Mrs Stackpoole and I should not jump to conclusions without knowing the entire story." He glanced at the older woman, who did not appear to echo his sentiments based upon the expression on her face. "You are correct in recognizing that a person is indeed innocent until proven guilty. Therefore," he rose from the chair. "I shall not discuss young Billy until I have more information. 'Tis for the law to determine the outcome."

Mrs Stackpoole placed her cup on the table and stood. "You think what you like, Professor. But mark my words. That boy lost his temper an' killed Jareth Flynn. Sidney says people afflicted like Billy Wolfe are touched in the head. They don't understand right from wrong, nor good from bad. Not out of wickedness, but because they are born idiots."

My sharp intake of breath stopped her before she went further. Uncle Jasper glowered at me not to speak, and I held my tongue until she had left the room. I let out a gasp of derision.

"Why are people so discriminating of others,

Uncle? Billy is no imbecile. He is stricken with a condition he was born with. Of course, he faces challenges we do not understand. But that does not make him an idiot, and I find it offensive when he is referred to as one."

Uncle Jasper came to stand by me and placed an arm about my shoulders. I sat where I was and leaned my head against his side. "I am sorry, Uncle. I do not mean to sound so angry."

"Don't apologise, Jilly. It is a terrible thing which has taken place in our little village. You have spent time with Dominic, who is understandably torn up with anxiety about his brother. 'Tis no wonder you feel strongly. You are upset, and justifiably I might add."

He moved away, and I got to my feet. As I went to the doorway Uncle Jasper took my place at his desk.

"Jilly, perhaps we should ask Dominic to join us for dinner today. He might need some company."

"He plans to come by later, Uncle. I am unsure of when, but it will be after he sends his telegram."

"Telegram?"

"Yes," I said. "He requests Victor LaVelle's help to prove his brother's innocence."

"Well now." Uncle Jasper was pensive. "That should put the cat among the pigeons."

TRUE TO HIS WORD, DOMINIC stopped by our house. He spent more than an hour behind closed doors with my uncle in the study. Mrs Stackpoole took them refreshment and a sandwich, but I abstained from joining them. I determined Uncle Jasper might offer better guidance without me in the way.

Later, I heard the study door open, and Dominic

came into the kitchen. His face was still drawn and worried, but his expression conveyed fortitude and purpose, not the defeatism and concern which I had witnessed earlier that day. I was relieved to see him thus. I understood it would take courage for him to engage in the legal battle that might ensue. He would need all his reserve of strength.

He stood close. "Jillian, thank you for coming to see me earlier. It was good of you." He reached for one of my hands and held it gently. "I was all at sea with what to do. Your visit anchored me so I could make a plan and go forward."

I smiled, and my heart swelled. My hand in his seemed to know it was in the right place. "Uncle Jasper and I are here to help in any way we can. You have only to speak, and we shall be there."

"Thank you," he said earnestly, and his eyes warmed. "A telegram is on its way to Victor LaVelle and I have high hopes he will be here by tomorrow evening. Then I shall consult with him and decide what road we must take." The muscle in his jaw worked. Even in his state of unrest and worry, I was again struck by how handsome Dominic was. I chased the thought from my head. It seemed wildly inappropriate to think so foolishly when his world was caving in.

"If I might offer some advice," I said. "You are powerless until Mr LaVelle arrives, and it would be prudent to get rest and nourishment for the long days ahead. You will benefit and be far better prepared. Go home, try to sleep, and come back here if you have need of company or food. You will be no help to your brother should you fall ill with exhaustion."

He nodded solemnly. "Are you always so wise?"

I smiled weakly. "Unfortunately, no. But I do understand hardships are impossible to overcome when your mind is weak from lack of rest."

"Then I shall take your advice." With that, he squeezed my hand and left. As soon as the front door closed, I went to my uncle's study.

"Has he gone, Jilly?"

"Yes."

Uncle Jasper shook his head, took off his spectacles and rubbed his eyes. "This is a terrible business indeed. Young Billy is in an atrocious mess. Lord knows it would be bad enough if he were like you or me, but in his condition—it is a nightmare. Dominic says the boy is frightened out of his wits and does not understand what is going on. The Wolfe brothers have a difficult road ahead of them."

I went to stand before the desk. "What about the man they first arrested? Has he been released?"

"Yes. According to Dominic, the fellow had a legitimate alibi. He was in Cartmel Village the night of the murder. There were many witnesses who saw him in a fist fight with another gambler. Apparently, it was that chap's blood, not Flynn's, all over his clothes. Anyway, they have let him go."

I considered this. What a terrible predicament Billy Wolfe was in. "Do you think Mr LaVelle will be able to assist the Wolfe brothers. Or even want to?"

Uncle replaced his glasses. "Hmm. I believe he will. The Wolfe family has strong ties to the LaVelles. According to Dominic, Victor has the reputation of a fair and just man. He was not always wealthy and is known for his benevolence to those in need. I'll warrant he'll help secure a solicitor and barrister to represent the boy, at the very least."

I pondered his words and then looked at my uncle. "Do you honestly think Billy capable of killing someone?"

"Jilly," Uncle Jasper said quietly. "If there is one thing I have learned about the human race, it is that when necessary, we are all capable of doing anything."

Chapter Nine

MRS STACKPOOLE FLEW INTO the kitchen after lunch the next day while I was working, and Uncle Jasper was reading and sipping a cup of tea. Her chubby face bore two distinct red spots on her cheeks, and her ample bosom heaved with excitement. I stopped reading to see what was amiss. Even my uncle put down his newspaper and looked up.

"Lord a'mercy the village is agog with gossip." She set her shopping basket on the kitchen table.

"Prunella, have a seat, you are quite breathless," Uncle Jasper said.

I turned my face to hide my astonishment, for when had my uncle become familiar enough to be on first name terms with our housekeeper?

Mrs Stackpoole sank onto a chair. I fetched her a glass of water which she gratefully accepted and took several unladylike gulps. Her hazel eyes glittered.

"What do you think? Mr Victor LaVelle has arrived this very day from London." She searched our faces for some recognition of shock or surprise. "It is said he's come to aid Billy Wolfe's plight, though why, no one knows. I had it from Mr Bonfield, the postmaster, that Dominic Wolfe sent a telegram askin' Mr LaVelle to come immediately. He's got some nerve; I'll give him that. How can a farmer, ask an important and rich man like Mr LaVelle, to drop everythin' and come to the rescue of his brother." She shook her head, and her chin wobbled.

I glanced at my uncle. His expression was unreadable. He did not seem to think it unusual at all. It gave me pause for thought. Why would he be in the minority when the residents of Ambleside found Dominic's actions audacious?

I shrugged. "Considering the Wolfe family have a long relationship with Hollyfield House, who are we to know the extent of their friendship?"

"Yes, Miss Jilly, but they are of different classes. 'Tis not as if the families ever meet socially. The Wolfes are employed by the LaVelles," she insisted.

"And there you have it." Uncle Jasper joined the conversation. "'Tis as his employer that Victor LaVelle graces us with his presence. And glad I am to hear it too. If you ask me, the boy will not have a fair trial without someone with power and money in his corner." He rose from the table, picked up his newspaper and tucked it under his arm. "And now I must away to my study. Mrs S., why don't you join me for a sip of sherry? Under the circumstances, I believe it might be medicinal."

Mrs Stackpoole was on her feet before he had completed his sentence. With newfound energy, she followed Uncle Jasper out of the kitchen, while I stood rooted to the floor with my mouth open. What on earth was going on between the two of them?

IT WAS A STRANGE DAY. I WORKED, but it took every ounce of my willpower to remain focused. How could I concentrate? The workings of a mushroom's gills were of no interest to me when a boy's life was at stake. Yet

I pushed myself along. These notes were important to my uncle, and at present there was naught I could do to help the Wolfe brothers.

I was relieved Dominic would now have the guidance of Mr LaVelle. Surely his influence would carry some weight in the matter. Time would tell.

I looked up as Uncle Jasper came in through the back door. He had been on an errand to the village. He took off his hat and placed it on a hook. His face was pale, his expression grim.

"What is it?" I asked, already getting to my feet. "Does something ail you?" I fought off the panic rising. I had lost my mother so recently and I could not bear to think of losing another. Uncle Jasper held out a hand.

"I am fine, Jilly. Do not concern yourself. I have just heard disturbing news, and that is what shocks me."

I went to him immediately and tugged his arm. "Then sit yourself down and let me make you a hot drink." I went to the stove.

"No, Jilly. 'Tis not necessary." But he sat at the table and gave a mighty sigh. "I have just seen Constable Bloom, not five minutes hence. He has been out at Wolfe Farm, searching through Billy's room."

My hand froze over the kettle. I turned around. "What has happened?"

Uncle Jasper shook his head. "They have found the blacksmith's wallet hidden amongst Billy's things."

"Oh, no." My heart sank. My first instinct was to rush to Wolfe Farm and speak with Dominic. Uncle Jasper must have read my mind.

"Do not think of going to see Dominic. He has enough on his plate to contend with, and does not need anyone bothering him, even someone with good intentions. Victor LaVelle will counsel him, and that is the only person he should talk to for the time being."

As much as I hated to agree, I knew Uncle Jasper had it right. But I felt useless. No matter how much I tried to push the thoughts from my mind, the dilemma of Billy Wolfe lingered.

I RECEIVED A NOTE EARLY THE next morning, requesting I come to Hollyfield House at my convenience. It was signed by Evergreen, and though I baulked at the notion of spending time with her, in truth, my curiosity got the better of me. I wanted to meet Victor LaVelle, the illustrious tycoon who was spoken of in such reverent tones.

I left as soon as I read the missive, looking forward to a walk. The day was pleasant, and I took my time, my steps slowing as I neared Wolfe Farm. But I remembered my uncle's advice and did not stop to intrude. Today, even the sweet lambs in the fields aroused no interest from me.

I arrived at Hollyfield before ten in the morning and was shown into the parlour where I sat alone, until Marabelle Pike entered the room.

"Oh." Marabelle stopped short upon seeing me settled in one of the armchairs. "What are you doing here?" Her tone was unpleasant, her question rude.

"I asked Miss Farraday to come." Evergreen's authoritative voice barked from behind her cousin, who bristled with indignation. She swept past the disagreeable woman and made a grand show of sitting down across from me. Her full dark blue skirts settled about her like a puff of cloud.

"Thank you for coming, Jillian." She smiled

prettily and then her gaze rose to give a hard glare at Miss Pike, who gave an angry huff, turned and left the room.

"That woman is insufferable," Evergreen commented disparagingly. "Now tell me, what do you think about all that has transpired since we last saw one another? Is it not exciting? Murder in Ambleside, and the village idiot to blame." She sounded almost amused by the prospect, and I could not stop my grain of resentment develop a little more towards this woman. How could she be so likeable, yet in an instant so incredibly cruel?

"I do not find it exciting at all, Evergreen. A man's life was taken, and another will hang for it. It is a tragic state of affairs, and I cannot fathom how you find it anything else." My words sounded harsh, but I cared not.

"Well said, young lady," a male voice interrupted, and my eyes darted upwards. Coming through the doorway was a tall, well-built man. His black hair peppered with white, his skin dark from the sun, his eyes a piercing green. He wore no facial hair, and though older, he was one of the most handsome men I had ever laid eyes upon.

My daughter," he continued, "can be quite insensitive to the trials and tribulations of others." He strode in on long legs and went to stand next to where Evergreen sat, dwarfing her. He patted her shoulder. "Yet we love her regardless of her imperfections." He smiled, and I could see that Victor LaVelle was larger than life, and assuredly a force to be reckoned with. No wonder Dominic wanted him to help Billy. I judged him to be in his late fifties, yet he carried himself with the confidence of a young man in his prime.

He stared at me, and something shifted in his expression. Then he seemed to brush it away and turned to his daughter. "Evie, please introduce me to this plain-speaking friend of yours, I do not believe we have met?"

"Oh Papa, this is Jillian Farraday, Professor Alexander's niece."

I watched him closely, and he paused momentarily before walking over to where I sat. He extended a hand, which shook mine firmly.

"Victor LaVelle. Pleased to make your acquaintance. You are new to Ambleside?" He released his grip.

"Yes," I replied. "I have been here but a few weeks."

"We met when our carriage knocked her down, Papa. Honestly, I feared the worst."

"Goodness. You were not badly hurt, I hope?"

"No, just a little rattled." I smiled. "Your daughter plied me with tea and crumpets, and I made a miraculous recovery."

"That sounds just like her," Victor grinned. "God forbid Evie should ever take up nursing. All her patients would stay sick, yet simultaneously become obese."

"Papa," Evergreen protested.

"I jest dearest. Now—" his face became serious. "I am away to visit Dominic Wolfe. I shall be gone all morning." He nodded his head towards me, an odd expression in his eyes. "A pleasure to meet you, Miss Farraday. I hope to see you again soon."

We both fell quiet as he left. I considered the man I had just met. Victor LaVelle appeared used to hard work yet had the refinery of a gentleman. It was an odd combination, though it served him well. His bearing gave him an air of authority, which increased my relief that he had come to aid Dominic and his brother. All at once, Billy's dire circumstances did not seem as insurmountable.

"I cannot believe my father is helping Billy Wolfe." Evergreen's petulant voice sounded immature. "What can he do anyway? The boy killed a man—even Father cannot change that." She rose and went over to the window.

"You are right. He cannot alter what has already happened. But your father has the power to influence the outcome by ensuring Billy gets a fair trial." I joined her at the window, and we stood side by side. "Who knows what may have happened, Evergreen. Perhaps Flynn tried to harm Billy. He could have stabbed him in self-defence?"

She looked at me and there was no warmth in those beautiful blue eyes. "Billy still left Flynn's body in the lake and threw away the knife. Not the actions of an innocent, wouldn't you say?" I met her gaze. For a moment, I believe we both tried to read each other's real thoughts.

"Why, Miss Farraday." Perry LaVelle entered the room. "I did not know you were coming this morning." He smiled and went to his sister, kissing her lightly upon the cheek. "I'm off to see boring old Sneed."

"Poor you." Evergreen laughed, all animosity gone from her face. "I'd rather have a tooth pulled than spend the day studying figures and sums. You have my deepest sympathies, dear brother."

"Oh, Sneed's not such a bad fellow," Perry said

amiably. "A bit eccentric, but a bloody mastermind with numbers."

As I watched their exchange, I had the sudden urge to leave Hollyfield and go home. I did not want to be rude, so I told a white lie. "Evergreen, I feel the start of a headache. Would you mind very much if I went home? I am sorry."

"No, of course." She was at once all kindness. "I understand. You must come back another day when you feel better. Let Perry walk with you some of the way. He is headed in the same direction. Are you not, Perry?"

"Yes, indeed. Come along, Jillian. I'll be pleased to escort you."

After saying our goodbyes, Perry LaVelle, and I set off down Lake Road. He chattered about inconsequential matters and was friendly. His personality was far different than his sister's. They were both outgoing and amicable, yet Evergreen appeared to have a sharp sting always at the ready. In contrast, Perry, or what I knew of him anyway, had a more jovial disposition.

"I met your father this morning," I commented. "He was charming."

"Pa's a good chap. Though he can be a bit of a tyrant at times, his heart is in the right place."

"He would make a formidable opponent. He has quite a presence." I hoped I did not sound rude.

"Indeed," agreed his son. "Father built his business from the ground up, you know. My mother's family helped him get a start, as Grandfather was with the British East India Company. Father got into the shipping business right as the cotton trade took off. He made a fortune, paid my grandfather back every penny, and then went on to form one of the largest independent shipping lines in Europe. He has earned the right to be a tough businessman. He's a lot for me to try and live up to—I can tell you."

He continued to speak of their time in India, but I was not giving him my full attention. My mind wandered back to his father, and what he might be able to accomplish with Billy's awful situation.

"…and then Marik came with us."

I snapped my focus back to our conversation. "How did that come about?" I hoped I was not too inquisitive.

Perry did not appear to mind the question. "Marik's father was my tutor, and we studied together as children. When Ashok died, Marik became part of our family."

"It must have been quite a change for him, living in England."

He chuckled. "Oh, yes. I think he almost froze to death the first six months we lived here. But after fifteen years, I believe he has finally acclimated." Perry spoke of Marik with the affection of a brother. I warmed to him even more.

"Well, here we are. This is where I must leave you, Jillian. I hope your headache doesn't tarry and that you'll be back at Hollyfield soon. Do tell the professor to come with you next time and have a forage." He bowed his head politely and turned to go.

"Perry?"

He paused.

"We did not speak about the murder of Jareth Flynn. Can I ask you, do you think Billy Wolfe capable of such a heinous deed?"

"I am unsure what to think," he said finally. "What I *do* know of Flynn was not entirely favourable. Yet I would not have thought it in Billy's nature to harm another."

"Do you think now your father is here, Billy will at least have a fair trial?"

Perry smiled. "Miss Farraday. With Victor LaVelle on his side, anything can happen."

Chapter Ten

AFTER LUNCH, I EXCUSED MYSELF and spent a few languid hours reading up in my room. But by four o'clock I became restless and went downstairs to see where everyone else was. I was in the mood for company, but as I neared the parlour, I heard the distinctive sound of a feminine giggle. I put my ear against the closed door. There it was again. Good lord, it was Mrs Stackpoole! There was a rustling noise, and then the low chuckle of my uncle. I quickly backed away and hastened through the kitchen and out of the door.

Whatever Mrs Stackpoole and my uncle were doing together suggested more than just chatting. The thought was disconcerting, yet the reality was the two of them had likely been friendly long before my arrival in Ambleside. Had I inadvertently spoiled their situation? Though it was uncomfortable visualizing the two of them in any kind of romantic situation, I held no poor opinion if they were involved. Good for them. Life was too short to spend unhappy and alone.

Alone—which is what I was. My mind travelled to the Wolfe brothers. I longed to know what was happening with Billy now Mr LaVelle had arrived. And where was Dominic at this very moment? Perhaps at Hollyfield House with Victor LaVelle? Or on the farm? I wanted nothing more than to go to him and find out if there was any news. Apart from the impropriety of my visiting alone, it was too late in the day. Dominic would be busy tending to the livestock.

I found myself strolling along the road towards the village. Plenty of people were out and about—some were familiar faces who acknowledged me. I walked along with no particular destination past the old mill. I paused on the bridge, remembering it was where I had first met Dominic.

The afternoon was drawing to a close and I turned back to go home. But as I neared the bakery, a delectable fragrance of hot pies wafted in my face. They smelled so delicious, that on a whim of indulgence, I popped inside and purchased one.

The hot pastry was so flaky, it melted in my mouth and the beef was rich and tender. I walked along the road trying to eat the blasted thing without making a mess but was having little success. I spied a bench outside the village church. I had plenty of time before it would grow dark, so I sat down to finish my pie.

Ambleside Village was not so different from my home in Devon. The people here were friendly enough, the lake and surrounding area scenic and interesting. I did miss the sea, but then I considered it natural. 'When you are born with salt air in your lungs, you'll always pine for the water,' my mother had often said. I missed her so much. Each day there would be a moment when her face would float into my thoughts, and my heart would ache.

"You goin' to eat all o' that?"

I started at the unfamiliar voice. A woman stood not a few yards away in a ragged dress and a man's scruffy overcoat. Her hair was wild. Long, tangled, and so filthy I could not determine its colour. She looked older than Uncle Jasper, though it would be difficult to guess her actual age.

"Who are you?" It was all I could say. She stepped a little closer, and my nostrils involuntarily tried to staunch the fetid odour emanating from her unwashed body.

She gave a semblance of a smile, which twisted her face, as though one side of it would not work or move. "Peggy Nash, though I've not clapped eyes on you afore, missy, an' I know all the folk 'ere in Ambleside." Her eyes darted to the pie in my hands. I held it out to her, and she moved quickly to snatch it from me and stepped back again. I watched as the woman thrust the food into her mouth as though starved. Guiltily I looked away, embarrassed by my good fortune while she must not have eaten for a while. She wiped the back of her hand against her mouth when she was finished.

"Will you tell me yer name then?" she asked, her voice thin and sharp.

I glanced at her, unsure if I should, then shrugged off my misgivings. "I am Jillian Farraday. I live with my uncle, Jasper Alexander."

Her eyes brightened. "The professor?"

"Yes."

She grinned again, and I realised she must have had a stroke or some such ailment as the right side of her face was practically frozen in place.

"'E's nice, the professor," she said. "'E gives me 'alf 'is sandwich when I see 'im on a ramble." That made me smile. I could imagine Uncle Jasper doing just that. His kindness was one of his most endearing qualities.

I rose from the bench, ready to go home. "Yes, my uncle is a good man. Now I must be on my way, Miss Nash. It was nice to make your acquaintance." The comment sounded ostentatious even to my ears, I was not leaving a soiree, but walking away from an unwashed woman in beggar's clothing, who had just eaten my leftover pie. It was a bizarre encounter. Peggy Nash did not utter a goodbye, but I could feel her eyes on my back as I headed down the street.

UNCLE JASPER AND MRS STACKPOOLE were eating at the kitchen table when I arrived home.

"Why, there you are, Miss Jillian," the housekeeper announced. "We would have waited, but the professor was hungry."

I went to the sink and poured myself a mug of water. "That is all right, Mrs Stackpoole. I went out for a walk and then treated myself to a nice steak pie." I caught her look of disappointment. "I happened to walk by the bakers when they had just come out of the oven. They smelled so good I could not resist."

"Well," she said mollified. "As long as you've had somethin'."

Uncle Jasper took his last bite and beckoned me to join them at the table. "Mrs S. has made a rhubarb crumble. I am sure you have room for some?"

"Absolutely." I took a seat and was pleased to see the housekeeper happy with my enthusiasm. She set three bowls in front of us and began spooning out the hot dessert.

"'Tis unlike you to be out in the evening, Jilly. Where did you go?" said Uncle Jasper.

"Nowhere special. I walked into the village over to

the mill. On the way home I stopped and bought the pie, then sat on the church bench and ate it there and then."

"Did you indeed?" He laughed. "How cavalier of you, my girl. You are becoming entirely too modern for your own good."

"I met someone while I was out. A very strange woman who looked a little wild and was dressed like a beggar."

"Ah," he smiled. "Peggy Nash. Our local soothsayer, or witch as some call her."

"What?"

"Peggy has lived here all her life and was brought up in the forest by her father. He called himself a wizard, and claimed to be a Druid. Anyway, when he died, Peggy stayed on in the woods. She's harmless but very odd."

"I'll say. She asked if I would give her the rest of my pie when I was only halfway done with it. I felt sorry for her, so I obliged. And then she said how much she likes you, Uncle, because you share your sandwiches with her."

"Does he now?" Mrs Stackpoole exclaimed, her eyes round with surprise.

Uncle Jasper chuckled. "Now I'm for it, Jilly." He smiled at the housekeeper. "Don't take on, Mrs S. Peggy can smell one of my sandwiches miles away. She's got a nose like a bloodhound. It doesn't matter where I am, she'll find me."

"Well, I never," Mrs Stackpoole muttered as she got up and carried her empty bowl to the sink. "You've kept quiet about it all this time."

Uncle Jasper glanced at me, his expression that of a

boy caught stealing apples from an orchard. Then he shrugged and tucked into his pudding.

AFTER DINNER, I WENT UP TO my room and while looking in the bedside table drawer, remembered the moonstone. I had not given it a thought since all that had happened with Billy Wolfe. On an impulse, I put it into my pocket and went back downstairs to the parlour.

Uncle Jasper was sipping on a small glass of sherry and reading a book. I waited a moment and then withdrew the tin.

"Uncle, can I ask you a few more questions regarding this?"

He glanced at my hand. "Again, Jilly? I don't believe I can enlighten you anymore on the subject. I did tell you I was away working at the university when this came about. All I know is what your mother shared with me—and that was not much."

"Are you certain she never gave the man's name?"

"Positive. All Gwen said was he had to go abroad and could not take her with him. There was a job waiting for him in India, one he hoped would make his fortune."

"But why didn't he simply send for my mother later on? Would that not have solved it all?"

Uncle Jasper pondered this for a moment. He set down his glass. "You know I believe I asked her the same question all those years ago, and I think your mother knew in her heart there was another agenda."

"I don't understand."

With a sigh he closed his book and set it on the table next to him. "Back then, many young men sought fame and fortune in India. The British East India

Company was very powerful, which drew those looking to make their fortunes. The British population in India was decidedly short of young men with good prospects, while there were a number of wealthy young women in search of husbands. My guess is whoever this chap was, he was already promised to another. Oh, he might have fallen for a young Devon girl, but he would marry where the money was." He gave a shrug. "Of course, I do not know if my theory is true, but I believe it the best explanation. There is also the possibility the poor man might have succumbed to a nasty foreign disease. No matter, dear girl. There is nothing more I can tell you." He smiled kindly. "The pendant is symbolic of something which lasts forever, and it is the only relic dear Gwen had after the young man went away. Fortunately, she met your father, and marrying Thom Farraday was the best thing that could have happened to her."

I was disappointed. Part of me had hoped for a tidbit of information which might explain away my questions. I popped the tin back into my pocket and changed the subject.

I told Uncle Jasper of my meeting that morning with Evergreen's father, the wealthy businessman. "I hope Mr LaVelle has been able to help Dominic. I have not seen or heard anything else since yesterday. Has Mrs Stackpoole any news from Ruby's husband in Kendal?"

Uncle Jasper looked at me thoughtfully. Surely, he realised I knew something of their relationship, yet I knew he would not speak of it.

"There is talk of Victor engaging a London solicitor. That is all though. But 'tis early days, Jilly, early days." With that, he picked up his book, adjusted his wiry spectacles and began to read.

I returned to my room and placed the tin back in the drawer. My mind had moved from my mother's past, back to Dominic. I was so pleased he finally had someone on his side. Surely a person with Victor LaVelle's means could impact Billy's fate. I sat down on my bed and closed my eyes, my heart heavy with the thought of the Wolfe brothers' awful predicament.

Tomorrow I would try and see Dominic. Perhaps he would have better news or at least more information. Yet as I contemplated my visit, I realised it was not merely to find out more about Billy's situation. I would use any excuse to be able to see Dominic Wolfe again.

Chapter Eleven

FOUR DAYS REMAINED BEFORE UNCLE Jasper's lecture at Mountjoy Manor. He was up early. I looked in on him as he worked in the study. He glanced up, and I could see from his expression that his anxiety had peaked once again.

"I'll be in the kitchen if you need anything," I said quietly and went to leave.

"Wait, Jilly." He stopped me. "Are you all right? You look a little tired. I believe all this melodrama is taking its toll upon you."

"I am fine," I assured him. "But perhaps I could work this morning and then take the afternoon to do something more relaxing."

"Excellent notion. I won't have anything new for you to do until tomorrow at the earliest. You go off later and get some fresh air."

I left him to his work. He had been right about me. I was tired. But then so much had happened since my arrival in Ambleside. I had barely become used to living with Uncle Jasper, when I had made the shocking discovery of a body, closely followed by the accident with the LaVelle's carriage. Since meeting Evergreen, my life felt changed, chaotic. I chided myself to stop thinking about everything. Instead, I made a strong cup of tea, which I took over to the kitchen table and settled down to business.

The morning passed quickly. After luncheon with my uncle, I collected my things and set off outdoors. I had no specific plans, but it was a sunny afternoon, the temperature clement and I yearned for some good wholesome spring air. My feet automatically led me willingly to Wolfe Farm. I did not consider it improper for me to stop by in the middle of the day, although I was not certain Dominic would be there.

I arrived at the farmhouse and heard the low rumble of male voices talking inside. I lifted my hand to rap upon the door and then hesitated. Should I go away and not intrude? My curiosity was piqued. I knocked.

"Jilly?" The door opened revealing Dominic's surprise at my being there. But he smiled and invited me in.

"If you have company," I stated. "I do not want to interrupt. Would you prefer I come back later?"

"No, you are most welcome," he said, and our eyes met briefly. In that moment I knew a sense of relief, for Dominic looked much improved since our last meeting. It must be due to the arrival of Mr LaVelle.

"Come into the kitchen, Jilly." Dominic led the way. "Victor is here, and I would like him to meet you."

I followed. "Actually Dominic, I have met—"

"Miss Farraday." Mr LaVelle rose from the kitchen table and gave a curt nod. He appeared conspicuous within the unadorned room—by contrast, he was polished and sophisticated.

"Dominic, I had the pleasure of meeting this young lady yesterday. It seems Miss Farraday is quite popular with my family, and apparently yours as well." He gave a dashing grin and I warmed to him immediately.

"Jilly and I are new friends," Dominic stated. "But I feel as though I have known her a long while. She and Jasper have been most kind and supportive." I liked that he used the affectionate abbreviation of my name.

"Good to know, Dom." His green eyes drew level with mine. "I've long held a high regard for the professor. Miss Farraday, won't you take a seat?"

"Please call me Jillian, Mr LaVelle."

"I shall, and likewise, you must call me Victor. Now, Dominic, shall we continue with this later?"

I had disturbed them. I rose to leave.

"Jillian," Dominic said quickly. "I want you to stay." He looked over at Victor. "Jillian has offered to help with Billy's case in any way she can. I should like her to remain, if you are in agreement, Victor?"

The older man nodded. "Whatever you decide is acceptable with me." He threw a friendly smile in my direction. "Now. Dominic and I were discussing the evidence brought forth against Billy. All quite damning, unfortunately."

"What evidence do the authorities have?" I asked.

"The murder weapon, of course. And a wallet belonging to Flynn, found in Billy's room. Other than that, there is nothing else. But those two items are enough to convict him."

"But there must also be a motive." I rebutted. "What was the relationship between Billy and the blacksmith?"

"There wasn't one, as far as I know," said Dominic. "Flynn was a show-off; he liked the sound of his own voice. He'd teased my brother on several occasions, usually if he had an audience. But it seldom angered Billy. If anything, it would make him cry. I was the one who would get angry about it. I had more motive to hurt the man than my brother."

"What of Billy's whereabouts the evening of the murder? Does he have an alibi?" I asked.

"He was in the woods looking at the baby bunnies." This time it was Victor who spoke. "Billy has no real concept of time, but he insists that is where he was. Unfortunately, it would not be difficult for any solicitor to question him upon that point and confuse him. The problem with a lad like Billy is he is guileless. He does not understand his tenuous position and cannot in truth defend himself."

No one spoke as we absorbed Victor's words. He was right. This was a horrific situation for any person, but for a boy like Billy, it was a nightmare.

I chewed my bottom lip. "If Billy did not kill Jareth Flynn, then who do you think did? After all, initially they must have had cause to arrest the other person. A gambler I believe someone said?"

"He was," answered Dominic. "And it seems more likely that would be a far stronger motive. Perhaps not the fellow they held, but what about another? Flynn was a gambling man and money is often the cause of heinous crime. As for Billy's motive, although he didn't take kindly to being ridiculed by Jareth, he is easily intimidated by people. It would be one thing for him to hit the blacksmith or knock him down in a fit of temper, but quite another to stick a knife into a man's heart. Jillian, you've seen him with the calves and the livestock. My brother doesn't have that kind of rage in him."

"But the knife—" I began.

"Ah, the knife." Victor nodded. "The murder weapon is such damning evidence for the boy, and there's no doubt it was his knife which was used. But Billy says he'd lost his knife, and we believe him."

"So, do you think someone found the knife by chance and killed Flynn? Or is it more likely they stole it intentionally, to blame Billy?" I asked them both.

They looked at one another, smiled and then looked back at me.

"Well done, Jilly." Dominic sounded pleased. "You've a quick mind and have arrived at the same conclusion we did."

"Indeed," Victor frowned. "We doubt this was a random killing. We believe Flynn must have had many enemies, including one with a strong enough motive to kill the man. We must prove the theory as quickly as possible, or Billy will assuredly be sentenced for a crime he did not commit. Therefore, our first task is to discover who had something against Jareth Flynn? Enough to want him dead."

WE TALKED FOR ANOTHER HALF an hour, until Victor got to his feet.

"Dom, I must get back to the House, I've pressing business to attend to. Come by and join us for dinner later. All right?" He squeezed Dominic's shoulder and then stopped to extend a hand to me. "A pleasure to see you again, Jillian. I am grateful for your help with this." He gave me a wink and then Dominic walked him to the door.

I remained where I sat, my mind a whirl with their conversation.

"What did you think of Victor?" Dominic asked as

he rejoined me at the table.

"I like him. He seems intelligent and a fair man."

"Yes, he is. I think that is why he has been so successful in business. Victor's employees are loyal to a fault. He commands that trait from every one of them, and he compensates them well. Have I told you he has engaged a solicitor? A Mr Roger Kemp. He comes with a solid reputation and hopefully will be able to get to the bottom of this mess."

"It is very decent of Victor to come to your aid. That he would travel from London is especially considerate. He must think very well of your family." I meant it kindly but then saw the serious expression upon Dominic's face.

"I am sorry. Have I said something to offend you?" It had not been my intention.

Dominic gave a heavy sigh and then looked right at me, holding my gaze. "Jillian, I may as well tell you, though 'tis not common knowledge among the village, and I would ask you keep it to yourself."

"Of course." I held my breath. What was he about?

"Victor LaVelle is helping us, because he is Billy's father."

Chapter Twelve

MY MOUTH DROPPED OPEN IN surprise. "What? Billy's father? I do not understand."

"My mother strayed from her marriage," Dominic said softly. "And Billy was the result of that indiscretion." He rose from the table, pushed the chair back in, and leaned his elbows on the frame. "Mother was forty-nine years old, too old to carry a healthy babe, but carry she did. When Billy was born, the doctor explained there was a high incidence of Mongol children born to women in their later years. But my mother loved Billy regardless, as did Victor."

"And your father?"

Dominic shrugged. "My father was a difficult man of little words. He loved my mother and ultimately forgave her. He even continued working at Hollyfield. Fortunately, the family were in London most of the time, so Father and Victor seldom encountered one another, which probably helped alleviate the tension. Victor provided a monthly stipend for Billy's care and needs. Though my father was a proud man, he was also sensible. There was not much money to go around, and he needed whatever he could get."

"Does Billy know?"

"Yes. I told him after our parents died because he was grieving badly. I decided he would cope better if he knew he still had a living parent. That was when Victor told his family the truth of Billy's parentage. It did not sit well, especially with Evergreen. Perry is for the most part indifferent, but they both avoid the boy. Victor does what he can, but he will not allow Billy to live at Hollyfield. His only demand was that I come back home to care for my brother."

It was much to take in. My mind could not decide which fact to run with first and explore. I looked up at Dominic, and my heart softened. He had sacrificed his future as a result of other people's actions. It was so unfair.

"You gave up your own dreams to raise your brother?"

"I don't like to look it that way—but I suppose I did."

"I think it wrong for a man like Victor to place his responsibility upon your shoulders. Why should he pursue his career, while you cannot?" My good opinion of the wealthy shipbuilder was tarnished. "It seems particularly selfish for him to have those expectations."

"Perhaps," he agreed. "But what are my options? Force Billy to live at Hollyfield with people who do not love him? Move him to their London residence where he would be ostracized more than he already is? Or send him to an institution, so none of us have to look at his face each day?" He raised an eyebrow. "Which of those choices do you consider better than him growing up in his family home, a place he feels safe and loved?"

Of course, he was right. Had I been in Dominic's situation, I would have done exactly the same. A sudden rush of admiration for this man filled me. He truly was a good person to put his welfare after that of his half-brother's. I was also glad Victor had good reason to help Billy. This brought another thought. "Is Victor concerned the truth of Billy's parentage could come out in court?"

"No," he answered easily. "Though it is not yet broadly known hereabouts, Victor does not need the public's approval. He is successful enough to weather any gossip or bad press should the newspapers pick up on the story. Obviously, he would prefer the matter be kept private, but he is far more concerned with Billy's future than his own reputation."

"Well, that is a relief." I glanced at the clock on the mantel. I had tarried too long and should get home. I stood up. "I really must go, Dominic. But tell me, what else can I do?"

He came around to my side of the table and stood facing me. Again, I marvelled at the handsome angles of his face, his soulful eyes, his full mouth. There was an earthy masculinity about him which affected me whenever he was close.

Suddenly dry, I wet my lips. "I just want to help," I whispered.

He took a step towards me, and I sighed as his fingers brushed back a tendril of my hair which had come loose. He tucked it behind my ear and then traced a path down my cheek to my lips where he stopped. Gently, the pad of his thumb stroked my mouth while his amber eyes fastened upon my own. There was no kind emotion in his expression now, but a smoulder which connected to what must be radiating from my own. My breathing came a little faster. My heart accelerated as he moved closer still, until I could feel the stir of his breath upon my mouth.

His head tilted, and warmth engulfed my lips as he

claimed the kiss. His arms wrapped around my waist as mine reached up around his strong shoulders. I was lost in the sensation, feeling the roughness of his skin graze against mine. I forgot who I was, where I was, and became an instrument under his instruction. As his tongue gently teased mine, I abandoned all thought, except the feel of his mouth upon my own.

A new awareness seeped into my being, a pleasure at once strange and delightful. It coiled in my stomach, ached in my breasts, and I felt an urgency at the very heart of my womanhood which took my breath away. Though I did not know it, I somehow recognised this as desire. Unsure what exactly I craved, I knew only he could satiate it.

Dominic pulled out of the kiss and we stared at one another, our breathing laboured. Warmth flooded my cheeks as I battled with my feelings of embarrassment, but at his broad smile, my worry disappeared.

"I've wanted to do that since I first met you," he said, his voice deep and sultry.

I smiled, self-conscious in a role I had never played before. "I am glad you decided not to wait any longer." Heat burned beneath my skin.

He took my hands in his. "Jillian, I care for you, but my mind fights it. Guilt ravages me because I desire you while my brother sits in a gaol. Yet how can I ignore what is happening between us? Damn, but the timing is all wrong! 'Tis an injustice for us to begin something that deserves our full attention. Yet it cannot be a priority…"

"I understand," I interrupted. "Billy's predicament must be your focus. Nothing else can distract you until this is resolved. I can wait, Dominic. It does me good knowing you care, as I feel the same about you. That is enough, for now."

He picked up my hands and pressed them to his lips. "Dearest Jillian. I am drowning in despair and worry, and you are a lighthouse in my storm. Thank you for your understanding and compassion. It means more than I can say."

MONDAY MORNING, EVERGREEN LAVELLE arrived unannounced. She was pretty as a picture in a pale lemon gown which complemented her striking blonde hair. She carelessly waved away my offer of refreshment. "No thank you, Jillian. I have come to collect you."

"I beg your pardon?"

"My carriage awaits outside. I would like you to accompany me on an errand."

Her casual request irritated me. Unlike her, I was not at liberty to do as I pleased every day. I wasted no time telling her. "Evergreen, I cannot go anywhere. I have a great deal of work to get finished today. You forget, I have an obligation. Though you may discount it, my uncle depends upon my administrative support for our livelihood." I glowered at her, and much to my amazement, she burst into tears.

I was at a complete loss. I expected her irritation, not sorrow. She stood by the hearth, and I quickly went to her and touched her arm. "Forgive me if I was harsh, Evergreen. I did not mean to upset you."

She sniffed and pulled a handkerchief from her reticule, simultaneously waving me away. "'Tis not you who upsets me." She smiled through tear-filled eyes. "But this whole mess. Father is home and has the countenance of a bear with a toothache, Marabelle mopes after him like a love-sick limpet, and Perry and Marik have gone off to spend a jolly weekend at a spa in Bath." She gave her nose an unladylike blow. "I am bored and lonely, and there is absolutely nothing to do. I think I shall go mad."

"Where is your father?"

She plopped down into the armchair and sniffed. "With Kemp, the damned solicitor. Discussing Billy—again."

I took a seat in the opposing chair. "You cannot hold that against him, Evergreen. He is trying to make sure justice is done. If Billy is convicted, he will hang."

"Then he shouldn't have killed the bloody blacksmith, should he?"

I was shocked at her outburst and language. Was she so unfeeling then of her half-brother? I resisted the impulse to remark upon it and held my tongue, as I had promised Dominic.

"Why is Marabelle love-sick?" I remembered her comment.

Evergreen gave an unkind laugh. "'Tis my father. She is in love with him, and he notices her as frequently as he does our cook. Father thinks of Marabelle as family. She's part of the furnishings at Hollyfield, yet she is besotted, and ridiculously annoying to boot."

For a moment, my heart went out to the dour, sour-faced cousin. But then I looked at Evergreen LaVelle and her tear-streaked face. Compassion got the better of me. "Where is it you are going, and why on earth must I go along?"

Victorious, she grinned; all tears forgotten.

THE TOWN OF KENDAL HAD BEEN my first introduction to the Lake District. It was to this railway station I had come on my way to Ambleside. I had not returned to Kendal in the few short weeks since moving in with Uncle Jasper.

As we left Evergreen's carriage, I felt a rush of excitement joining the hustle and bustle of a busy, well-populated place. The air was charged with an energy absent in Ambleside Village. We alighted onto the main street, which was bordered with shops of many types.

"There now, are you not pleased you came along?" Evergreen smirked as she saw me smiling. I was rather pleased. In the weeks since I had lived in Ambleside, I had forgotten how exciting it felt to be among so many people. The sights, smells and sounds of a hamlet were a welcome change from the quiet of my new home—at least for a short while.

Our first stop was a Milliners, where Evergreen tried on several garish hats which I thought looked ridiculous. She bought three, much to my horror and the shopkeeper's delight. From there we went into a shoe shop. The lady who assisted us gave a brief history of the shoe industry and how important it was to the area.

"Kendal manufactures shoes which are exported all over England," she bragged. "You won't find a better-quality shoe made anywhere." Evergreen agreed and promptly purchased several pairs. After another hour, this time in a dressmaker's, I begged for a reprieve.

"You aren't used to all this shopping, are you?" Evergreen said, handing her parcels to the coachman as we made our way to a nearby tearoom.

"No, I am not. It is more exhausting than washing laundry or tending the vegetable garden. I do not know how you manage to decide what to buy and what not to?"

"Hah," she giggled. "'Tis such a heavy burden for me to bear—but I manage." We both laughed out loud.

"Here we are," Evergreen announced and opened the door to a small tearoom. We were seated near a window. There, we could watch the shoppers going by. Sandwiches and cakes were ordered, and by the time our pot of tea arrived, I was both thirsty and hungry. Our conversation lagged while we ate and sipped our drinks to revive ourselves.

"Jillian, have you always been poor?" My companion asked as she took a bite of a delicious custard tart. I almost choked on my mouthful of Victoria Sponge.

"That is rather a blunt way to ask." I dabbed at my mouth with a serviette. "For all your wealth and education, Miss LaVelle, your manners are somewhat lacking." I said sternly. I glared at her and then noticed a large dollop of custard hanging from her top lip. She looked ridiculous, and I burst out laughing.

"What?" she asked, brows drawn. I gestured to her face, and she wiped it away. "I didn't mean anything bad, Jillian. I am simply curious. You are such an odd duck. You don't come from a wealthy family, yet you are educated and intelligent."

"And you are typical of the upper-class, Evergreen, who must equate intelligence with financial status." I took another sip of tea. "It may shock you to learn that money does not necessarily relate to being clever. You of all people should know that. Look at what your father has accomplished."

"Oh, you mean his rags to riches story?" She put

down her fork. "There is some truth to that, but if he had not married Mother, he would never have been so successful." She sat back in her chair. "Father is an adept businessman, but it was my mother's fortune which founded his company. So, you see—" she arched one brow. "There is a correlation between money and brains, after all."

"Perhaps," I replied. "Yet your father's acumen was there long before his fortune. I do not equate wealth with intelligence whatsoever. I argue intellect is either there to be nurtured through education, or absent. I have met many rich people who are as ignorant as a tree stump."

"Do you count me as one?" she said quickly.

I shrugged. "Only when it comes to your taste in hats."

UNCLE JASPER AND MRS STACKPOOLE had already supped when the carriage dropped me home. I made myself a sandwich, and once I had finished eating, joined my uncle. He was alone in the parlour with his snifter of whisky. Mrs Stackpoole had popped next door to have a word with our neighbour, Mrs Parker. I sat down on the sofa and loosened my shoelaces.

"Well, how was it?" he asked as I removed my shoes and sat back with a sigh.

"My feet ache as though I have been dancing a jig all afternoon. Goodness, Uncle, Evergreen LaVelle shops like a starved dog in a butcher shop. I should not care if I saw one more milliner in this lifetime."

Uncle Jasper laughed as he lit his pipe, then relaxed back in his chair as aromatic smoke spun into the air. "I am sorry you had no coin to purchase anything pretty for yourself, Jilly dear." His wrinkled face was apologetic, and I felt a twinge of guilt.

"I did not have need of anything, Uncle," I soothed. "Truly, there was nothing I saw I could not live without. Though I did enjoy the tea and cakes more than I ought." As he smiled, I pulled out a small box from my pocket. It was true I had little money to buy a fancy hat or fashionable dress, but I had enough to purchase a small gift for him. I passed it over, and he looked up in question.

"What is this?"

"A present for you." He began to speak, but I held up my hand to silence him. "Please, do not say anything, just open it. 'Tis only a little thing, but it is a large thank you for all you have done to make me feel I have a home once more."

His chubby fingers clumsily opened the box, and then he glanced up at me in utter delight. My heart swelled with happiness. I had been thrilled to discover my find in the back of a cluttered shop selling trinkets and odds and ends. When I spied the dusty, fossilized toadstool, I knew my uncle must have it. Fortunately, it was cheap.

He held the piece of limestone and smiled at me. "Well, I'm blowed! What a wonderful gift. I've not got one of these in my collection. 'Tis marvellous, Jilly. You are too kind to think of me." His pale eyes shone. "I shall treasure it always." He looked at me fondly, and then the moment passed, and he set the gift down upon a side table and drew again on his pipe.

"Though I am not overly fond of shopping, Uncle, it was a pleasant change going somewhere different. Were you able to spend time preparing for the lecture?"

The long-awaited meeting at Mountjoy Manor was but three days away, and Uncle was submerged in all things fungal.

"Indeed, I was. Though I am content with my progress, there still remains much to do. There are new notes on my desk, ready to transcribe as soon as you are able. 'Tis the last of it. Once you have finished my report, I have only to organize which samples I need to take along with me and pack them accordingly." He gave me a sheepish grin. "Mrs Stackpoole has offered to help in that department. She plans to attend the lecture and assist me with my lichens." Uncle Jasper's cheeks turned a shade of pink, and he was at once bashful.

"Uncle." I smiled. "I think it singular you have a special friendship with her. I wish you would not feel uncomfortable speaking of it. I do not judge. I am pleased for you both."

"We are merely friends, Jilly. Pray do not read more into it than that." He attempted to sound convincing, but I was not fooled.

Uncle Jasper leaned over and tapped the ash from the bell of his pipe into the fireplace. "I forgot to mention to you about tomorrow."

"What about tomorrow?"

"We are invited to Hollyfield for dinner. It came this afternoon from Victor LaVelle."

"Did you reply?" I had mixed feelings about spending even more time at the House, though I could not explain why precisely.

"I accepted, of course. It will still be daylight when we arrive, and I've a mind to take a stroll through their gardens and see what I can spy." As he beamed at the prospect, I could almost envision the child's face which had been there long before the wrinkles and whiskers.

"I haven't spoken to Victor in an age. It will be good to see the man and hear his news."

I nodded in agreement. But then a thought came to me. What did my uncle know of the true relationship between Victor LaVelle and Billy Wolfe?

Chapter Thirteen

IT WAS A DIVERSE GROUP THAT assembled at Hollyfield House for dinner. Marabelle and Evergreen were there, but instead of Perry and Marik, as on the first occasion, it was Victor at the head of the table, with Lord Montague Mountjoy next to him, and across from Uncle Jasper. I sat beside Lord Mountjoy, with his wife directly opposite.

Lady Louisa Mountjoy was several years her husband's junior, at a guess at least two decades. His lordship was of an age with Uncle Jasper. Though where my uncle was short, stout and bald, 'Monty' Mountjoy was tall and regal, with a full head of white hair. He and my uncle were delighted to be in one another's company, and in the full regales of a discussion on the upcoming lectures which Lord Mountjoy would host.

Consequently, Lady Louisa, was only too happy to chat with me. I was glad of her attention yet felt extremely self-conscious in my dowdy dress.

"Well, Miss Farraday," she said through rouged lips. "I daresay you have found Ambleside to be rather more entertaining than you might have originally expected?" She smiled, and her dark brown eyes sparkled. She was a striking woman, with the enviable complexion of a Mediterranean or some other exotic nationality in her blood. Her jet-black hair shimmered in the lamplight, her olive skin smooth.

"You could say that, Lady Mountjoy. Though I am saddened by what has transpired since I arrived here. It is a tragic set of circumstances for everyone involved."

"Do you know the Wolfe boys?" she asked and placed a spoonful of syllabub into her mouth.

"I do, though not well. Billy, I have met once, but Dominic and I are friends."

One thick black brow arched. "I see. Then I am sure you are relieved by Victor's involvement assisting the boy and his upcoming trial?"

"I am." I looked at her without being able to read her expression. Did she pity Billy, or perhaps she believed him guilty? Was Louisa Mountjoy privy to Victor's genuine relationship to him?

"For someone like Billy, it would prove difficult for him to articulate his innocence when in a strange place, and so terribly frightened." I added.

"Then you think him innocent?"

"I do."

"Yet you stated only meeting him one time. How are you convinced when you do not know the boy well?"

Did Louisa Mountjoy intend to bait me? "Well, I am no authority on the matter, Lady Mountjoy, but you asked a question, and I answered honestly. In my short time speaking with Billy Wolfe, I found him to be a kind young man, gentle and unassuming. To view him as a cold-blooded murderer is beyond my capacity."

"Well said," Victor spoke loudly from the table's head and I was shocked to realise the others had been listening. My face warmed.

"I disagree." Evergreen sat at the foot of the table

facing her father. Her face contorted into an unbecoming scowl. "That boy has always been strange. I mean look at him, he's unnaturally strong for a lad of fifteen. He would be a force to be reckoned with, were someone foolhardy enough to cross him."

Victor LaVelle glowered at his daughter. "What a spiteful thing to say." An undertone of anger laced his words. "For a gentle-born woman who has had the benefit of an education, and is considered to own some intelligence, you speak like an ignorant plebeian."

Evergreen glared at her father, unfazed by his stern comments. She nonchalantly picked up her glass of wine and sipped.

He continued. "I thought better of you than to stoop so low, Evergreen. That was badly done."

Much to my surprise, she shrugged her shoulders and brushed off her father's reprimand.

Marabelle joined the discussion. "Billy has never misbehaved to my knowledge." Her eyes gazed at Victor, and even I could see how hard she wanted to please the man. "In all the years he's worked at Hollyfield, his manners have been exemplary. Why, the boy is usually off in his own world, that of the gardens and tending livestock." Marabelle's expression was soft and sanguine, almost unrecognizable from her usual sharpness.

"Oh, for goodness sake, stop sucking up to Father," Evergreen snapped with irritation. "You dislike Billy every bit as I, so don't be disingenuous, Cousin."

"Enough." Victor banged his fist upon the table and the room fell silent. The moment grew awkward.

I quickly turned to the man beside me. "Tell me, Lord Mountjoy, how do your preparations for the

Pharmaceutical Society's meeting fare? Are you ready for the grand event?"

"Indeed I am." The older man fixed his gaze upon me. "And I do hope you will be in attendance, Miss Farraday, as it promises to be a most delightful evening. Several prominent members of the society will be present, and there is much excitement about your uncle's speech."

Monty Mountjoy had once been a handsome man. His eyes were still a piercing blue, his profile aquiline and haughty. Yet he had a pleasant way about him, and I did not feel uncomfortable conversing, even with the vast gap between our class.

"Do you have any interest in flora, Miss Farraday?" Louisa Mountjoy asked as the hint of a smirk played at the corner of her mouth. Did she mock me? Perhaps.

"Not in the slightest," I stated, and Victor burst out laughing.

"My but you are such a blunt young lady," he said, dabbing his serviette against his mouth as he set down his glass. "Jasper, is your niece always so—forthcoming?"

Uncle Jasper nodded. "I am afraid so. Indeed, I can assure you sir, Jilly is on her best behaviour this evening. Usually, she would be far less polite, especially about flora and the like."

"I have to agree with her, for I find the subject rather tedious," Lady Louisa said huskily. "Dear Monty can expound upon the topic of a leaf until I am almost in a coma."

"Like Father and his blasted steamships," Evergreen added. "He can go on all day about engine pressures. Men are easily amused by simple subjects."

"I find the shipping industry interesting." Marabelle countered with a glance at her host.

"Of course, you do dear." Evergreen threw her cousin a wilting look.

Victor rose. "Well, if we are finished at table, let us adjourn to the parlour for coffee," he suggested. He glanced at the men. "Unless Monty, Jasper, you prefer to remain in here for cigars?"

Lord Mountjoy smiled benevolently. "No, Victor. I'm happy to accompany the ladies. I'd rather look at them, than you and the professor."

We settled in the parlour. I found myself seated next to Lady Mountjoy while Marabelle hovered close to Victor as he conversed with the two other men. Evergreen sat in her chair observing the guests, her expression that of a hungry cat determining which bird to pounce upon.

"Are you originally from this area, Lady Mountjoy?" I struggled to make polite conversation.

Her mahogany eyes contemplated me. "Good lord, no. I hail from Taunton, in Somerset. I am a long way from home—much like yourself." Our eyes met and locked, and I realised Louisa Mountjoy was not exactly a mean-spirited woman, for I detected a little glint of amusement there. In a moment of sudden comprehension, I recognized what it was. She was bored. And not just with the evening's entertainment, but with everything. At once, I became far less intimidated by her demeanour.

"What activities do you partake of, I mean, to keep yourself occupied while Lord Mountjoy attends his hobbies?"

A brow lifted, and she studied me. Then she gave me a conceding nod as though I had passed some type of test. "Why, dear girl, I am a writer."

I leaned forward—interest piqued. "How fascinating. Do tell me, what do you write?"

She shrugged. "I write a weekly column for our local paper, and short stories which have been in various publications, both local and also in London." She took a sip of her coffee.

"How marvellous." My interest was sincere. "It is time women were able to contribute to the news of the day. Bad enough 'tis a man's world we share, and tragic we have no voice nor vote."

"You speak as though you are part of the suffrage movement."

"Oh, if only I was," I exclaimed. "I do take *The Woman's Suffrage Journal* when I am fortunate to find it. Uncle Jasper has great respect for Miss Lydia Becker because she is a friend of Charles Darwin, *and* a biologist. So, he takes no issue with me following their beliefs."

"Then Professor Alexander is quite a progressive thinker." Lady Louisa gave an approving glance to my uncle, and then she turned to her husband standing close to him and frowned. "Unlike some others I might mention." She arched a brow. "Miss Farraday, I am impressed you have a good head on your shoulders. I take a regular subscription to *The Woman's Suffrage Journal*. I shall forward my copies to you after I have read them. Would you like that?"

I was momentarily at a loss for words at her unexpected kindness. "Thank you, that is a generous offer, Lady Mountjoy."

"'Tis nothing," she said. Her eyes travelled to Evergreen. "Are you and Miss LaVelle becoming good friends?"

I shrugged. "Unlikely acquaintances would be a better term." I chuckled. "We met accidentally, and she has seen fit to require my companionship on several occasions."

"Ah, I see." Lady Mountjoy commented. "Evergreen has always been quite a demanding young lady. Before you, it was Dominic Wolfe she pestered. He is probably enjoying the break." She gave a little laugh.

Her words stung, though I did not think it her intention. Yet the thought of Dominic and Evergreen spending time together bothered me. I was jealous.

"I believe the LaVelles and Wolfes are friends of old," I replied.

"That is one way of saying it," she said sardonically and then got to her feet. "Miss Farraday, I have enjoyed our chat this evening. I hope to see you again soon." She nodded towards me and walked in the direction of her husband. "Come, Monty. 'Tis time for us to take our leave."

There followed polite goodbyes, and then the Mountjoy's were gone, leaving Uncle and I to make our own farewells. I rose to go over to where my uncle stood, but was stopped as Marabelle Pike drew near.

"You seem keen to gain Lady Louisa's good favour." At first, I did not realise she was addressing me. The woman had made it her practice to ignore me at every other encounter.

"Not at all," I replied, irked at her tone. "We found something of common interest to discuss."

Evergreen arrived to stand with us. She shot her cousin a withering look. "For goodness sake, Marabelle. Stop being so annoying. Are you so aggravated at anyone enjoying their evening that you must spoil it?"

Marabelle stiffened, and walked out of the parlour. Evergreen chuckled, and though I was still annoyed with her dour cousin, I found her delight in Marabelle's discomfiture unsettling.

Uncle Jasper came over with Victor behind him. "Jilly, Victor has offered us the use of his carriage home. I have accepted as the hour grows late and I am tired."

"Thank you, Mr LaVelle." I smiled politely at our host. He waved a hand.

"Say nothing of it. I am pleased you were able to join us this evening. I hope my family's outbursts did not offend?" His green eyes slanted over to Evergreen, who held her head high and met his disapproval without flinching.

"Not at all," I said, looking between the two LaVelles. "Better to be forthright and honest than not." I extended my hand to shake his. "Thank you for a nice evening. It was kind of you to include my uncle and I."

"Indeed," he said pleasantly. He escorted me out to the hall with Uncle Jasper and Evergreen close behind still in conversation.

"Miss Farraday. I wonder if you would be available to meet at Wolfe Farm tomorrow. Shall we say at one in the afternoon?" My heart leapt at the mention of Dominic's farm. I would welcome any opportunity to see him.

"Of course. I would be happy to come."

"Where are you going?" Evergreen asked as she had overheard her father. "And why am I not invited?" Victor stopped at the front door. He turned towards his daughter.

"It is none of your concern." His voice was flat and cold.

Evergreen bristled, spun on her heel, and trounced away. My level of discomfort grew. Was this family constantly at odds with one another?

Uncle Jasper came to the rescue. "Come along, Jilly, dear. The carriage awaits. Thank you, Victor, I will see you at the lecture Thursday evening." He shook our host's hand, then led me through the door and out into the evening.

I was not talkative on the journey home, though Uncle Jasper did not remark upon it. I was busy recounting Lady Mountjoy's comments regarding Evergreen and Dominic Wolfe. Was there more than a childhood friendship between them? It was entirely possible. After all, they were both attractive, interesting people. It would be natural for them to form an amorous alliance over time. Yet surely it could not be, for had not Dominic kissed me? Had he not declared the desire to get to know me better once Billy's situation was resolved?

I hated my naiveté, that I had no experience with romance. For though my heart ached to strengthen my feelings for the handsome artist, my common sense reminded me that to entangle myself with Evergreen LaVelle's dislike, was tantamount to treason.

Chapter Fourteen

I BARELY CONCENTRATED ON MY work the next morning. I was obsessed with thoughts of seeing Dominic later in the day. For every speculation of what might have transpired between us had Jareth Flynn not been murdered, there was another where I pictured Evergreen LaVelle wrapped in Dominic's embrace.

The irony was that after months of solitude, my move to Ambleside had unexpectedly brought someone into my life. A man who I not only had a physical attraction to, but also a profound interest in learning about as an individual. I liked Dominic Wolfe. I respected his kindness, his sense of duty to family, and the quiet strength I sensed lay within. Did I have the nerve to ask him about his feelings for Evergreen?

After luncheon with Uncle Jasper and Mrs Stackpoole, I excused myself to go to Wolfe Farm. The day was sunny and warm enough to leave my shawl at home. I wore an old cotton dress of my mother's, and though the fabric was now a faded periwinkle blue, I still loved it as it reminded me so much of her.

I walked briskly down Lake Road, nodding occasionally as I passed by other pedestrians, some whose faces were growing more familiar. The sky was a brilliant blue and completely cloudless. I marvelled at the beauty of nature's palette as I surveyed the bright green grass fields that contrasted so magnificently with the faultless sky.

Dominic opened the farmhouse door to me with a welcoming smile, and I felt a spread of warmth fill my heart. As I stepped inside, he pulled me into a warm embrace.

"I am so glad to see you, Jilly," he spoke softly into my ear. "You are a wonderful tonic when the rest of my world seems so upside down." His eyes searched my face and settled upon my lips. He touched his mouth to mine and kissed me deeply, only stopping at the sound of carriage wheels out in the yard. He drew back and gave me a lingering look. "Come through to the kitchen. I have made tea. Victor will let himself in."

I followed Dominic down the hall, my mind conflicted by his attentions.

When Victor LaVelle joined us in the kitchen, I was again struck how much more significant he appeared than most men of his years. He was immaculately turned out, sporting a brown tweed jacket which suited him immensely.

"Good day to you, Jillian." He sat down at the table and Dominic served the tea and then took a seat. Victor retrieved a small notebook from his pocket and laid it on the table.

"Roger Kemp has arrived in the village. He wishes to call upon you later this afternoon, Jillian. Although it will be distressing, he will ask you about finding Flynn's body." He glanced at Dominic. "I collected him from the Kendal train and took him directly to meet Billy. They spoke at length, and though the boy remains distraught, he responded to Roger surprisingly well. Even in his confused state of mind, Billy remains adamant about losing his knife."

"He has no reason to lie about it, Victor," Dominic said vehemently. "The knife was Father's, and he treasured it."

"Yet he did not mention the loss to you at the time?" Victor stated.

Dominic thought for a moment and then shook his head.

"Damn," said Victor. He wrote a note on the page. "It would have been better if he had. To establish the knife's value to the boy, it would have helped if Billy had bemoaned the fact to you back when he initially lost it. From a jury's point of view, they would expect the boy to be upset and remark upon it being mislaid."

"Not necessarily," I interjected. They turned to look at me.

"Many years ago, I lost a beloved brooch given to me by my grandmother. I did not tell my mother for days because I feared she would be disappointed, or even angry with me. It occurs to me that Billy was probably worried what Dominic's reaction might be."

Dominic nodded. "Now you say it, Jillian, it makes sense. I do scold Billy for losing things because it happens so frequently. Usually, it's a tool from the shed or something of that nature. But he hates it when I am cross with him. No wonder he kept it a secret."

Victor pursed his lips for a moment and then smiled at me. "Jillian, you raise a good point. I'll pass it onto Kemp. If it goes to trial, he will need to know how to coax the boy into explaining his not wanting to let Dominic down by the loss of a family heirloom."

Dominic's face fell. "Dear God, I can't imagine my brother on the witness stand. He will be petrified. His testimony might even make the situation worse than it already is."

"Then you must prepare him," I said enthusiastically. "Billy will be the better for it if you can get him used to the idea. Repetition will ease his fears."

Victor nodded. "She is right. 'Tis an excellent suggestion. You should see the boy as often as they will allow." He finished off his tea. "Now, the next question I have, Dominic. Did you search through Billy's things as I asked?"

"Yes. After Constable Bloom was finished in his room, I looked at everything." He frowned. "What I don't understand is why Billy had Flynn's wallet. He is no thief, but a scavenger. Billy collects things he finds in the woods, broken things or colourful objects, items you or I would easily disregard. But he has no material interest in anything, except animals. He gets his pocket money each week, and unless he buys buns or something sweet, he saves it up in a jar on the shelf to buy plants or treats for the livestock. This entire situation is too hard to absorb. Everything Billy is accused of is completely out of character." Dominic rose and retrieved a box sitting next to the stove. "This is Billy's box of special things he's found. I might add, the wallet was not discovered here, but tucked underneath his mattress, which is odd. There isn't much to speak of in the box, but there is one item I found curious."

Dominic placed a small wooden crate on the table. It was full of bric-a-brac which he began to remove. A ball of string, bird feathers tied together, a small leather pouch of stones and what looked like an old doll. There was also a sheaf of papers. They were of different sizes and shapes, bound together with a thin string of ribbon. Dominic took these and placed them next to the box. He untied the bow and then picked up the top page to show to Victor and sat back down.

It was a small scrap, torn at the edges and dirty. But the writing was still distinct. Victor took the paper and brought it close to read.

"Hmm," he said after a moment with a glance at us both. "It appears to be part of a letter from someone." He squinted, and then passed it to me. "Here Jillian. Your eyes are far younger than mine."

I studied the writing. It was poor, but legible. "Have you read this yet, Dominic?"

"Yes, but you look at it and see if we draw the same conclusion."

I read aloud that which I could decipher. "*'I saw you in'*—the rest of that sentence is missing. The next line says—*'against nature'*—and then—*'on Tuesday at four, by the boathouse or else'*." I glanced up at Dominic. "What do you make of it?"

"Well," he said. "We agree on what was written, though it's anyone's guess what it actually means."

"Against nature conjures up several possibilities," Victor spoke as though still in deep thought. His hand rubbed his chin. "It depends on what the definition is referring to. An action? A behaviour? Cruelty? It could be anything."

"Yes, but whoever wrote this must have witnessed something," I said. "And whatever it was, they believed it to be wrong, at least in their eyes."

"The *'or else'* sounds ominous," added Dominic. "And stating a place and time would indicate a meeting wouldn't it?"

"It would appear so," Victor agreed. He leaned back in his chair and picked up the scrap of paper. "I think Billy may have stumbled upon something here. But we do not know when or where he found it. So, it may have no bearing on the murder."

"Then I'll ask him," Dominic said, getting abruptly to his feet. "You never know. It might be of significance, don't you think?" He looked at me and then Victor.

"It is worth you finding out," I said. And then another idea took hold. "Billy is no killer, but perhaps he saw something he should not have, and maybe he doesn't even realize it himself. What better way to confuse him than to get him arrested?"

AS I SET OFF BACK HOME, Billy being framed preoccupied my thoughts. To me it seemed a logical explanation, far more plausible than the boy being capable of murder or theft. After all, to commit such a violent act would take a person pushed beyond reason, especially if it was reactionary, or self-defence. But to hide a weapon, and a wallet? That took planning and deviousness. Billy might not be perfect, but the limitations of his condition seemed contrary to someone being premeditative. Yet who would want to frame Billy Wolfe, knowing he might swing for it? The answer was simple—the real villain.

"Dearie me, missy. You're away with the fairies." Peggy Nash stood on the pathway, dressed in the same dirty outfit I had seen her wearing previously. I stopped short, and then took an involuntary step back, for fear of the woman's 'unique' odour.

"Hello, Miss Nash."

"You been at the Wolfe's then?"

"I have," I answered, though what business it was of hers I did not know.

"I like 'em boys, 'specially little Billy." Her comment softened me, for it took a gentle soul to understand someone like Billy Wolfe.

"Billy never stabbed that Flynn. Not Billy. I watched 'im takin' 'is last breath. An' I saw with my own eyes that knife sticking through 'is ribs. But it weren't Billy who stuck it there."

"What do you mean, Peggy?" My pulse picked up speed. What did this strange woman know?

Her tongue moistened her lower lip, and she gave her sly lopsided grin. "Billy weren't near the boathouse on yon lake." She pointed in the general direction of Lake Road. "'Ee were off in the woods lookin' at the new bunnies. I saw 'im talkin' to 'em. Then I walked down to the shore an' there came a mighty splash in t'other direction, over near the boathouse. But it weren't no fish." She chuckled.

My mind registered her meaning. She was confirming Billy was not at the murder site, but far away enough to establish his innocence. I stepped towards the woman.

"Peggy. Would you be willing to tell this story to Billy's solicitor? It would help the boy, for he is in dire trouble."

Her dirty brow wrinkled. "Dunno 'bout that. I'll think on it," she said quietly and turned to leave the way she had come.

My step was quicker as I hastened home. Victor had told me to expect Mr Kemp that afternoon to go over my account of the day I discovered the blacksmith's body. But now I would be able to tell him so much more. A lightness of spirit surged in my breast, and it took all my willpower not to run all the way back to Wolfe Farm and tell Dominic my news.

"NO. I'M AFRAID HER TESTIMONY will not be enough for them to drop the charges against Billy, Miss Farraday."

My heart sank. I had eagerly shared Peggy Nash's conversation with the middle-aged man sitting across from me at the kitchen table. Roger Kemp wore the comfort of his fortune in the cut of a fine tailored suit, crisp white shirt and neat cravat. With the tidy appearance of a military man, he sat with perfect posture, as though he was *at attention* in our small kitchen.

"But surely she is a prime witness? She can place Billy away from the scene of the murder."

The older man stroked his neat moustache with a forefinger. "Miss Farraday, I do not doubt the woman believes everything she says. But by your description, if she is thought of as a touch light in the head, her testimony would not be credible. Someone with her reputation would be laughed out of the courtroom. I doubt she would even show up to the trial, let alone be able to cope with being cross-examined."

I was completely deflated—my excitement at the possibility to prove Billy's innocence splintered. I allowed my shoulders to sag and I stared glumly at a small mark upon the table.

"Please do not be disheartened, miss," he said kindly.

I looked up and met his brown eyes. "I cannot help it, Mr Kemp. I feel so badly for the Wolfe family."

"We have yet to exhaust all our avenues of detection, Miss Farraday. Bear in mind if this Nash person saw Billy, it stands to reason others may have witnessed him in the woods as well. That should be our focus. If we can corroborate her statement with other testimony, we might really be able to get the charges dropped against Billy Wolfe." Roger Kemp gathered his papers from the table and placed them inside his briefcase. He got to his feet, a tall, solidly built man with the look of a sportsman about him.

He placed his hat atop greying hair and then reached out a hand which I accepted and shook.

"Please, let me know if there is anything I can do to help, Mr Kemp."

"I will. Thank you. It would be beneficial if you could ask around the village, see if anyone else saw Billy that day? Sometimes information can come from the least expected source."

"Like Peggy Nash?" I said flatly.

He had the grace to smile. "Touché, Miss Farraday."

Mrs Stackpoole had fried thick slices of bacon and made us all sandwiches. But I barely tasted the food, so preoccupied was I with the events of the day.

The knock on the door was unexpected, for it was almost dark. Uncle Jasper went to answer it, returning with Dominic at his side. My heart gladdened with the sight of him.

I rose. "Is everything all right, Dominic?"

"Yes, Jillian. Please finish your supper. I was making my way home and thought to stop in and see everyone." I sat back down and gestured for him to join us.

Mrs Stackpoole sliced two thick pieces of bread, buttered them and made Dominic a sandwich. He accepted the proffered plate gratefully, and she rose to fetch another mug so he could have tea.

After swallowing a mouthful, Dominic took a sip of his drink. "I have been with Billy this afternoon. They allowed me to stay for several hours to talk to him."

"Decent of them to bend the rules," Uncle Jasper said generously.

"Oh, they didn't really want me there," Dominic replied disdainfully. "But Billy had a bit of a tantrum this morning, and they couldn't stand to listen to him shouting and crying. He only stopped when he saw me."

"The poor boy," I said quietly, instantly feeling empathy for the man sitting across from me. "How was he when you left?"

"Much better, thank you. He has these episodes periodically. They used to be triggered when our parents were angry with him. He would become belligerent and have a fit, only to crumple and cry afterwards."

"The lad must feel frightened in such a different environment than he's used to," Uncle Jasper commented.

Mrs Stackpoole said nothing, and I was glad of it. Her feelings about Billy's guilt were still a sore point between us. I only forgave her because she did not believe it out of spite.

Dominic turned to face my uncle. "He is so scared. He's locked in a small room with no windows and nothing to occupy him. Billy is used to being outside in the fresh air, so naturally, he feels trapped."

"Do they allow him to do anything?" My knowledge of gaols was minimal.

"I took some of his books, and they let me leave them for him. That will help immensely. He's also got some paper and pencils as he likes to draw pictures of animals." Dominic finished his sandwich and tea. "Thank you for the meal, Mrs Stackpoole. I had no idea how hungry I was."

He looked at me searchingly, and I realised he wished to speak with me alone.

"Uncle Jasper, would you mind if I spoke with Dominic for a moment?"

"Not at all," he replied good-naturedly. We both made our excuses, and I led the way down the hall and into the parlour.

As soon as the door was closed behind us, Dominic spoke. "Did you meet with the solicitor, Jillian?"

I nodded. Dominic had been in Kendal with Billy all afternoon, so would not have heard any news. "Mr Kemp spent the better part of two hours here, Dominic."

"And?" I could see the eagerness upon his face.

I recounted my discussion with the solicitor, and then told him of my encounter with Peggy Nash. Dominic's face brightened. I hated to continue with what the solicitor had said, but I did, and watched sadly as the flame of hope faded and was snuffed out.

"You must not despair," I said with more enthusiasm than I felt. "It only substantiates what we already believe about his innocence. Kemp suggests we enquire around the village because if Peggy saw Billy, perhaps someone else did too."

Dominic seemed to draw strength from that, which pleased me.

"Did you ask your brother about the piece of note you found in his box?"

"Yes. It took a while, but he said he found it in the woods by Hollyfield House. He spends a lot of time in the grounds when he's up at the house gardening, as there are some pretty spots close to the lake."

"Did he recollect when he found it?" I was unsure if it had any bearing on the matter.

Dominic nodded. "He thought it was before the bunnies were born."

"Do you know when that was?"

"Unfortunately, no. But if Peggy is right about Billy being with the rabbits on the day Flynn died, he must have found the note prior to the murder. So, we cannot dismiss its significance yet. However, Billy finding it in the proximity of Hollyfield House, interests me a great deal."

"You think there is a connection?"

He sighed, and I saw shadows underneath his golden eyes. He had to be exhausted. My heart went out to him, and I fervently wished I could be of more help.

"Well, the reference to the boathouse and the location of the note certainly points to Hollyfield, doesn't it? After all, it is the only home in that area. Though what relevance it has puzzles me. I have read the blasted thing several times, and I do believe the *'or else'* is a threat. Wouldn't you agree?"

"Yes. Therefore, the writer of the note saw something they considered wrong and then referred to the boathouse, which would imply a meeting of some sort. Yet why would they want to speak to a person who had disgusted them?" My question hung in the air.

Our eyes met across the space between us, and then in perfect unison we both spoke at the same time.

"Blackmail."

Chapter Fifteen

WHEN DOMINIC LEFT FOR HOME, it was late in the evening. Though I believe we both felt a thrum of anticipation at our potential discovery. I was to meet him at the farm the next morning, and we planned to take a look around the boathouse at Hollyfield House.

Before taking his leave, Dominic collected me into his strong arms and pulled me close. The lingering kiss he pressed against my mouth had caused a spread of warmth and pleasure, yet the question of his relationship with Evergreen burned on my lips. Why could I not ask him? Nevertheless, I slept like a baby, cocooned in a swathe of new love, the taste of Dominic's kiss still on my mouth.

I awoke to a miserable and rainy morning. After breakfast, I excused myself and got ready for the walk to Wolfe Farm. When I left, Uncle Jasper was already ensconced with Mrs Stackpoole in his study. They were deep into the preparation of his lecture which would be that night, and I do not think they even heard my farewell.

It was pouring outside, hardly an ideal day to be out and about. By the time I reached Wolfe Farm, my coat was soaked, and my umbrella sodden and blown inside out. The wind from the lake had played havoc with my hair, and when I stepped inside Dominic's cottage, I knew I must look like a wild banshee.

He laughed when I told him as much. Then he pulled off my coat and hung it on a peg to dry in the hallway, then guided me to the fireplace where I took a seat. I was grateful for the hot drink he pressed into my hands while I basked in front of the fire.

"I cannot believe it is so cold out there. It is May for goodness sake." I complained.

"Ah, but you are not in Devon now, Jilly. Here in the hills the weather is changeable. When the wind and rain comes off the lake, the damp burrows into your bones."

I shuddered and drank more of the brew, which chased away my chills. "Will we wait for the weather to pass before going to the boathouse?" I had no desire to get soaked once again.

"I fear the rain is here for the day, but hopefully it will lighten some, and then we can venture out. For now, you'll have to stay here with me, and I shall make the most of having you as my captive." He gave a rascally grin, and I smiled back, rather pleased with the intent lacing his words.

Dominic came over to where I sat and knelt before my chair. He took the mug from my hands and set it down upon the floor. We stared at one another intently. When he reached up and tugged at the pins which held my hair in the remnants of a bun, I sighed. As he removed each one, the weight lessened from my head and my tresses fell down past my shoulders.

"Oh, Jillian," he sighed. "Would that I could paint you. You are so beautiful."

His eyes were like liquid amber. I wetted my lips.

"You are like Athena," he said softly, "with your velvet brown hair cascading down your back." He threaded his fingers through the mass at my shoulders. "I want to capture you in oil, Jillian. Then you will become immortal." His face came closer to my own, and I could see the flecks of bronze in his irises, the thick fringe of dark lashes, the hint of whiskers darkening his complexion. Drawing nearer, he released my hair from his hands and slid them down to rest on my shoulders. Gently he pulled me towards him.

I watched his lips part, and I was in a trance as we came together, our mouths meeting in sweet expectation. It was a tender kiss, slow and purposeful. But it grew in intensity, and as his warm tongue entered my mouth, I knew the moment my needs became urgent. The kiss grew wilder, and my senses abandoned everything, all so I might languish in this time—this moment.

And then suddenly he stopped. As Dominic drew away from me, I knew he could see the naked hunger on my face. My breath came in gasps from my lips, still swollen from his kiss.

"Dominic?" Some primal urge had taken hold of me. "Dominic," I whispered, "I want you."

I saw the play of emotion ripple across his face—a mixture of desire and responsibility. As I watched him give into the latter, the heat began waning from my veins, and I was sorry for it to leave.

"Dearest Jilly." Dominic lifted his hand and traced the line of my jaw with a finger. "You have the passion of a temptress." He smiled, and the breath caught in my throat, this feeling he stirred within me was so powerful.

"Though it becomes more difficult each time we meet, I will not take advantage of you,"

The surge of disappointment which engulfed me took me by surprise. I almost did not recognise my wanton self as I sat before this sensual man who radiated masculinity. The thought sobered me. I must stop my licentious behaviour before I went too far. Heat rose in my cheeks along with a sense of irritation that I could be such a hypocrite.

Dominic rose to his feet and gave me an encouraging look. "I believe you and I have much-unfinished business, Jilly." His expression gladdened me; it showed the promise of things to come.

"But for now," he continued. "I must concentrate on Billy and this horrible situation. What I feel for you should be addressed another time, and not tainted with worry and concern which are my constant companions of late." He went to the hob and stoked the coals.

I reached down to the ground and collected the pins Dominic had taken from my hair and then went over to a small mirror hanging in the kitchen. With practised hands, I gathered my tresses and secured them neatly into a bun.

"I prefer it down," he said softly.

I had no reply. This role was new to me, and the level of intimacy something I had not known before. Beyond a flirty glance or lewd whistle, I had never been the object of anyone's desire. Now that role was like a dress I had yet to grow into. Perhaps in time, I would metamorphose from the ingenue I believed myself to be.

I walked over to the window by the kitchen sink. "How fares our weather?"

"Wet," Dominic said drily, coming to stand beside me. The sky was grey, the clouds morose as rainfall pelted against the building. "If we are to go, we might as well get on with it. I think the rain has settled in for the rest of the day." He walked out into the hall and then returned carrying two coats. He handed one to me.

"Here, you can wear Billy's. These are waterproof and will keep us drier than your umbrella." We slipped on the coats, and Dominic handed me a pair of Wellington boots.

"These were my mother's boots, try them on and see if you can wear them. They will keep your feet nice and dry."

The boots were a little large, so Dominic found a pair of thick socks which enabled my feet to stay comfortable. We were ready to go.

WE REACHED THE BOATHOUSE WITH little conversation as it took concentration to navigate the sodden ground as we traversed through the woods. Dominic thought it better to approach the boathouse from the lakeshore, rather than from Hollyfield House itself. He did not want to draw attention to what we were about.

As we reached our destination, I recognised the boathouse from my first visit to Hollyfield. The base was built of sturdy bricks around a small dock, with windowed rooms up above. Inside, a small boat was anchored, the front of the building wide open to face the body of Lake Windemere, which was choppy due to the weather. The upper level, Dominic had said, was accessible by a staircase inside the boat dock.

We entered the building, and I glanced at the sailboat bobbing restlessly in its mooring. I kept close to Dominic as he navigated around the perimeter of the damp, quiet place. Here I could still feel the blustering wind, but at least we were sheltered from the cold rain.

"What is up there?" I wondered aloud.

"It is where they keep all the sailing equipment," Dominic answered. Down here remains open to the elements, so the sailboat is chained and padlocked. The storeroom upstairs is for everything else that should be kept dry. It is kept under lock and key."

"Have you ever been up there?"

"Yes, a long time ago. I got permission from the family to use it as a studio. Back then, the LaVelles seldom came to the lake."

"Why do you think they are come to stay now?"

Dominic stopped at the base of the stairs. "According to Perry, Evergreen was indiscreet and exhibited some unladylike behaviour in London. Victor thought it best to bring her here to avoid a scandal." His face registered distaste.

That surprised me. Both Evergreen's actions and Dominic's expression.

"Are you shocked that your friend is no paragon of virtue?" Dominic frowned.

"Not terribly. Though Evergreen told me they were here for Perry to study with an elderly accountant."

"Oh, you refer to Nicholas Sneed. Well, that part is true. Victor wants Perry to learn the financial side of the business for when he takes the helm. Come on, let us go up. The door will probably be locked, but I'll check it anyway." He turned and mounted the wooden stairs with me close on his heels. When Dominic reached the door at the top, he frowned—it was ajar.

"Not too secure, then?" I stated.

"Hmm. The boat is used once the weather is warm enough. I'll warrant Perry or Marik have been out sailing recently and forgot to lock it back up."

I followed him inside.

It was a large, square room, with a musty scent lingering in the air. The light was dim due to the cloudy day outside, despite a considerable number of windows which lined the length of the space. From the back, the blurry silhouette of Hollyfield House was visible, standing sentry in the distance.

Ropes, oars and paddles were hung on stout wooden pegs, dotted across the walls. I saw other objects, but they were utterly foreign to me. I assumed they would be articles used on sailboats. Piles of netting lay in heaps across the floor, and I recognised some type of material possibly used for sails. There were two pieces of furniture in one corner, an old sofa and a small table. But the place felt as though it had long been abandoned.

"Someone's definitely been here recently," Dominic said, in direct contrast to my thoughts.

"Why do you say that?" I asked.

He pointed to the faded patterned couch where a blanket had been tossed—the table before it bore an empty bottle with two dirty glasses. I glanced at Dominic and he appeared troubled.

"Is something wrong?"

He cleared his throat. "Not at all. Come, we should leave." He turned and abruptly left the room.

"Wait." I hurried after him. "I thought we were going to look around and see if we could find anything? Perhaps whoever wrote the note was here and met with someone? After all, there are two glasses in there."

But Dominic acted as though he had not heard me and kept going. He went down the stairs, not stopping until he reached the bottom.

"Dominic, whatever is the matter?"

He did not answer. I tried again. "Has something upset you?"

He walked over to where the boat rocked. "I think the boathouse is being used for an assignation."

I blinked. "I don't understand."

His mouth slanted. "Jillian, there have been people meeting secretly up there, the blanket on the sofa—"

I finally understood. "Oh." I felt so foolish and naive. "Who do you think it is?" And then I remembered his comments about Evergreen. "Do you think Evergreen has met someone in Ambleside? Surely there are no potential suitors tucked away here in the country?"

"Why do you presume it is Evergreen?" His tone was sharp, and it took me off guard.

"After what you just told me about her behaviour in London, I surmised you thought it likely to be her." I did not care for the way he had responded. The tiny nagging doubt that he and Evergreen had more than a platonic friendship between them resurfaced. "What do you suggest we do, Dominic? Ask her if she has been coming here?"

He whirled to face me. "No. We had better stay out of it. At least for now, until I have had more time to think." He reached for my hand. "Come along. Let us get away from here before we are seen. I am sorry I brought you out in the rain for no purpose."

"No need to apologise. I have had quite the adventure."

Without a word, he pulled me into his arms, and pressed the warm caress of his mouth against mine.

Thoughts of Evergreen tumbled from my mind as I became supple as a wet leaf and leaned against his strong body. The kiss was long and lazy. My senses supine, as sheer pleasure rippled through me as the rain poured outside the boathouse.

Dominic ended the kiss but kept his forehead pressed to mine. "It seems when I am with you, Jillian Farraday, I cannot keep from touching you." His golden eyes shone with desire, and I knew mine mirrored his.

"And I am glad of it," I said softly, while our fingers wove together.

"We should go," he said reluctantly.

But as we moved away, my foot caught on a coiled piece of thick rope, discarded on the wooden planks of the dock. Dominic tried to catch me, but it was too late. I tripped and fell, my hands taking the brunt of my weight as I landed.

"Jillian, are you all right?" His voice was weighed with concern, and I quickly responded, feeling somewhat absurd at my lack of balance. He made to scoop me up to my feet, but I stopped him.

"Give me a moment to catch my breath," I asked, dusting away granules of dirt embedded in my sore hands. It was then it caught my eye. Lying by the rope which had caused my fall, I saw something shiny which looked out of place. Slowly I rose to my feet and took a step closer.

"What is it?" asked Dominic with a frown.

"There is an object stuck underneath the rope." I bent down and reached for the article. My fingers tugged it from its hiding place, and I straightened back up, simultaneously opening my palm to show my find. It was a small watch fob. Not ornamental, but sturdy and well worn. The clock face was scratched but framed by an engraved horseshoe. I turned it over to study the back. Here was another engraving, this time it was initialed, faded but still legible.

"Look at this, Dominic." I held out my hand so he might see what I had read. The letters 'J.F.' were clearly marked. Dominic turned it over and looked at the front of the fob and then his eyes swung up to meet mine.

"Jareth Flynn?" I said quietly.

"Yes," he agreed. "'Tis the blacksmith's watch."

Chapter Sixteen

WE HURRIED BACK TO WOLFE Farm. The trek was wet and muddy, and the wind howled. After hurriedly shedding our raincoats and boots, we hastened into the kitchen where Dominic quickly put a kettle of water on the hob and stoked the fire. Before long, we sat in front of a roaring blaze sipping our tea, while our limbs thawed from the damp.

"Jareth must have been at the boathouse before he was murdered." My mind had been spinning theories since finding the timepiece.

"It certainly appears that way. Because if he didn't leave his watch there, who did?" Dominic's frown deepened between his brows.

"It could have slipped out of a pocket onto the floor of the dock. But it was underneath the rope, so it must have been dropped and then slid under there."

Dominic stared at me. "What is your theory?"

I shrugged. "Flynn's watch could have come off if the chain broke. Or, if the blacksmith was there, he could have been in a tussle which would have snapped it." It was a guess, but to my mind it made sense. "He was murdered, and his body found quite close to the boathouse, Dominic. It is quite possible he was in a struggle, perhaps he was even stabbed there? The killer could have moved his body into the lake. Peggy said she saw him take his last breath."

Dominic nodded. "Plausible—but still guesswork. Someone has definitely been using the place, judging by what we saw. I just wish I knew who."

"Perhaps Jareth was meeting someone there? Could he have had a rendezvous with Evergreen?" I did not know anything about the man, but Mrs Stackpoole had told me he was a handsome fellow. Was Evergreen LaVelle involved in a relationship with him? It seemed far-fetched to me.

"Unless he was here to spy on someone else," Dominic commented, in between sipping his tea.

"But who else is there?"

"Well, the fact there was a wine bottle leads me to believe it was none of the village folk." Dominic rose to pour himself another mug of tea before sitting back down. "They are far more likely to drink ale. So, it would be someone with easy access to a wine cellar, and who isn't overly concerned about using a place owned by the LaVelles."

"Then it has to be someone from Hollyfield House, be it one of the family, or a servant," I stated.

"Seems logical to me." Dominic retrieved the watch from his pocket and studied it.

I watched his expression. "What shall you do with it? Take it to Constable Bloom?" I did not think for one minute he would. My guess was he would pass it on to Victor.

"No, Jillian. I'd rather show it to Victor first and get his opinion."

I agreed it was the wisest choice to make based on the little we knew.

Suddenly, there was loud pounding on the door of the cottage. Dominic leapt to his feet and went to answer it. He shouted my name, and I ran into the hallway. In the doorway stood a child of about seven, his large brown eyes wild with fear and his conversation punctuated by sobs.

"What is it?" I cried in alarm as Dominic threw on his coat and boots.

"Jem cannot find his sister—says she's run off and he's scared she's gone down to the lake. I'm going to try and find her." With that, he was gone—out into the pouring rain.

Quickly I threw on my wet coat and muddy boots. I slammed the door closed as I ran to catch up with them. I followed Dominic and the lad, who were quite far ahead of me. Where were the parents of this waif-like child? The boy was too young to be out alone in such bad weather, and not dressed warm enough either.

It did not take long to reach the banks of Lake Windemere. The usually calm waters slapped against the shore, whipped up by the wind and rain. Dominic began calling out the girl's name, which sounded like Jenny. He walked along the shoreline, looking for a sign of the child. I finally caught up with them, and he gestured for me to go in the opposite direction so we could cover more ground. I did, and began shouting her name as loud as I could.

We appeared to be the only people about, and no wonder. The weather had turned nasty, and I heard thunder rumbling overhead. I scanned the land and water before me, but all I could see were rolling grey waves. But then, something bright caught my eye. It was a speck of red in the distance, easy to see against the backdrop of the gloomy day. I turned and shouted to Dominic but did not wait for him to get to me. I ran towards a small outcrop of trees whose branches reached out quite a way over the water. Perched near the end of a large branch, hanging on for dear life was a tiny slip of a girl.

"It's all right, Jenny," I called as I drew closer. "Hold on. We're coming to get you!"

Dominic passed me at a full run with Jem close on his heels. By the time I reached the trees, Dominic had already discarded his boots and coat and was climbing the trunk of the enormous willow.

The little girl had somehow crawled practically to the end of a branch which would not support the weight of an adult. I watched in utter dismay as Dominic tried to find a parallel branch that could support him, so he might be able to pluck her to safety. He finally selected one, and I covered my mouth to stop the cry of anguish which threatened. Beside me, a small hand crept its way into mine, and I squeezed Jem's cold fingers in reassurance.

Gingerly, Dominic dragged his body carefully along the branch, edging slowly down its length as he neared the child. Below the tree, the lake swelled, and I could not tell how deep it might be.

"Can Jenny swim?" I asked Jem, who leaned against me, tears streaming down his face.

"No, she can't, miss," he cried. "She be only four." He began to sob. I could not comfort the lad because I had my eyes fixed upon Dominic. He was almost close enough to reach Jenny. I watched as he held tightly to the tree limb and then reached down his arm to the girl. I could not hear him, but saw his mouth moving, trying to encourage her to take hold of him. But Jenny was too scared, and she shook her little head. The seconds stretched into minutes, or so it seemed, as Dominic begged her to grab onto his outstretched hand.

And then she reluctantly let go of her grip to reach out to him, just as a mighty crack sounded and Jenny's branch tumbled into the water, taking her with it.

"No!" screamed Jem, running full speed to the water. I chased him, grabbing his clothes before he could rush in, as from the corner of my eye I saw Dominic drop into the lake from the safety of the tree.

I put my arms around the writhing boy, and he calmed when he realised what was happening. I scoured the water for a sign of Dominic, or the girl. I saw Dominic's head break the surface and the breath caught in my throat. But just as quickly he disappeared again beneath the roiling waves. My heart hammered, not in fear for this man I cared so deeply for because I knew he could swim. But I was terrified for the poor little mite he sought to save.

All at once, his head reappeared. Both Jem and I were transfixed as we saw first his head and neck clear the water, then his shoulders, and finally his arms, wrapped tightly around a small figure clinging to him like a barnacle.

As Dominic made it to shore, I took off my coat and wrapped it around the shivering little body he placed into my arms. She weighed almost nothing, and her skin was blue with cold and fright.

"Hush," I soothed. "You are safe now, little one. No need to be scared now, hush." I pulled her to my breast and held her tight, willing any warmth from my body into hers. Dominic collected his coat and boots, and we quickly left the lake for home. We dispatched Jem to the mill to fetch his mother, with orders to bring her to Wolfe Farm straight away.

The next hour passed quickly. I removed Jenny's wet clothing and wrapped her in a blanket before the fire. Dominic changed into dry clothes and then warmed a mug of fresh milk for the child. As she sipped the drink, I saw the grey fade from her skin as her pallor slowly returned to normal. By the time Jem arrived with his frantic mother in tow, Jenny was sitting on Dominic's lap while he read her a story from one of Billy's old books.

"Oh Dom, how can I thank you for savin' my Jenny?" The slightly built woman had tears in her eyes as she collected her daughter from Dominic's lap.

"No need for thanks, Maggie," he said, getting to his feet. "I'm just glad we got her. Her big brother is the real hero. He was clever enough to find help." He reached down and tousled the boy's hair. Jem gave a broad grin, devoid of front teeth.

I felt strangely left out as I watched the scene before me. Not being a local, I knew so few people. I turned my head to stare into the fire.

"Jillian, come and meet Maggie Riley." Dominic said. I rose and joined them. The young woman reached a hand to grasp mine.

"Thank you, miss, for comin' to their rescue. 'Tis so naughty of Jenny to slip out. She do like that water, and we can't seem to keep her away from it. As soon as yer back is turned, she's away!"

"Is there no one else to watch her while you are working?" I asked, although I did not want to sound judgmental.

"Usually, it's my oldest boy we leave in charge of the young'uns. But he went to Kendal to get our horse shod—with Jareth gone we've no blacksmith in Ambleside. Jem here had to watch over 'em instead—" She fixed the lad with a harsh glare and his face reddened as he stared to the floor.

"Still," she continued. "As long as no one comes down with a chill, they'll be no real harm done." She smiled at me and I saw the etching of fatigue around her dark eyes. At once, I felt fortunate indeed with my situation. Maggie could not have been much older than me, yet already her hard life took its toll.

The young mother declined the offer of a hot drink and instead wanted to get home and settle her children. She bade us farewell, and I waited while Dominic saw them out of the farmhouse.

When he returned to the kitchen, he pulled his chair closer to mine so that he faced me and then reached out to grasp my hands in his. "My goodness, Jillian Farraday. You must wonder what kind of wild place you have landed in since you came to Ambleside. It has been one adventure after another, has it not?"

I smiled. "I would hardly call it that, Dominic. But you are right. It has certainly not been dull." I squeezed his fingers. "You did a fine thing today, saving little Jenny. You are a courageous man. 'Tis no wonder I find you so dashing."

He gave a low chuckle, "Then you are easily impressed, madam." His eyes shone with the glow of the fire, and he leaned forward. Our lips met gently, and the slow ripple of pleasure trickled through my senses as it always did whenever he touched me. It was a lingering, tender kiss, no urgency or passion, simply a joining together and a comforting acknowledgement. I drew away after a time and stared at his face.

"Are you all right?" I said softly, for he looked spent—and no wonder.

"I am fine. Cold, tired and worried. But at least I have you to bring a little sunshine to my night. You have been invaluable as my dearest of friends. Thank you for helping me." He reached for my chin and lifted it, so that our eyes met. "I mean it sincerely, Jilly. You are more than a tonic to me at this terrible time."

Abruptly he got to his feet and pushed the chair back to its usual place. "But now, I must get ready. I am to see Billy later this afternoon. It looks as though the rain is beginning to abate. Will you excuse me while I go and dress for the journey?"

"Of course," I too stood up. "I had better make my way home and see to Uncle Jasper. There is bound to be something I can help him with in readiness for this evening. Will you attend the lectures tonight?"

"Yes, I would not miss it." He paused thoughtfully. "About Jared's watch, can you keep the discovery between us for now?"

"Why?" I frowned—it was an important find, after all.

Dominic looked at me, earnestly. "Because of its implication. If indeed it was Evergreen meeting Flynn at the boathouse for a tryst, I would rather keep our suspicions from Victor, until we have substantial proof. The man has enough on his plate as it is."

Dominic was right. I agreed and slipped on my sodden coat. I gathered my umbrella. "I shall see you tonight then." We embraced, and our lips met briefly, but I could see his thoughts had already travelled to his next concern, and I could not fault him for it.

JUDGING BY THE MESS IN MY uncle's study, an observer would have thought the world was coming to an end. Uncle Jasper was in a dither, his wispy hair stuck straight up, his spectacles were askew, and papers lay scattered upon every surface. Mrs Stackpoole stood by his desk, her hands placed on her hips. Several strands of white hair had escaped her mob-cap, and she appeared quite vexed.

"Is something amiss?" I enquired having just arrived home.

"'Tis page eighteen," Uncle Jasper gasped. "I cannot find it." His eyes were wide, and his worry evident.

I went to him and took his shaking hands. "Do not panic, Uncle. It will be here somewhere." Behind him, Mrs Stackpoole rolled her eyes. I glanced at her. "Would you pop the kettle on while I help Uncle Jasper?"

She raised an eyebrow and then shrugged. "Of course." She left the room.

I helped my uncle to the fireside, and he sat down. Whenever he was upset, I had noticed he would suddenly appear very frail and old. I did not like to see him in such a state.

"Uncle, you need to have a nice cup of tea while we think about where you last had your papers." A long conversation ensued. By the time Mrs Stackpoole appeared with a tray of refreshments, page eighteen was nestled between seventeen and nineteen once more. All was right with the world.

I SPENT THE REMAINDER OF THE afternoon preparing for the evening at Lord Mountjoy's home. I took great pains to iron Uncle Jasper's shirt, cravat and suit. I fervently hoped he would take a stiff brush to his hair and trim his beard.

I was aware how plain I looked in my dress. It was the same one I had worn for both dinner engagements at Hollyfield, and I sorely wished I might have something more fetching tonight. I smoothed down my skirts and patted the back of my hair. I had fashioned it into a chignon but placed a few tiny silk flowers tucked in here, and there, with the hope it might make me appear less dull. I thought about what Evergreen might be wearing tonight. No doubt something exquisite and fashionable. She was far bolder than I, especially with the revealing necklines of which she was so fond.

I never wore low-cut gowns, and not just because of modesty. I was born with a dark brown birthmark, an oblong shape roughly the size of a strawberry. It had never bothered me as a child because it was seldom visible. Now a woman, I felt far more self-conscious of the blasted thing. Though no eyes but my own ever saw it.

IT HAD STOPPED RAINING IN THE middle of the afternoon, and when Lord Mountjoy's carriage arrived promptly at six o'clock, it was pleasantly warm once again. A footman assisted Uncle Jasper with the boxes containing specimens and items for his talk, while Mrs Stackpoole and I got into the cab. We were both excited and nervous at the prospect of an evening at Mountjoy House. I had never seen the grand estate, and Mrs Stackpoole, though local, had never been inside. I also anticipated speaking with Lady Louisa. I thought it fascinating she was an actual writer. How I yearned to be as independent and intellectual as she.

Mountjoy House was situated on the other side of the lake to Hollyfield. It was further away than I expected, but as we turned into its long drive, I caught my breath in wonder. It was a magnificent stately building. Regal and imperial, bold with its black and white Tudor design. Even from our distance at the entrance of ornate gilded gates, Mountjoy House was a jewel in the heart of the district.

Our driver took his place behind a long chain of carriages which snaked along, eventually slowing as they neared the front steps, stopping briefly to allow each passenger to alight.

The excitement was palpable. I followed my uncle and Mrs Stackpoole up broad steps and through wide-open doors where several footmen stood awaiting the guests. Uncle Jasper and Mrs Stackpoole, were escorted to the great hall to prepare for his lecture. I was shown into a large reception room, where many tables were laden with drinks and sweetmeats.

I glanced around to see if Dominic had arrived but could not see him. I did spy Evergreen, however. She was listening to a handsome young man, an expression of boredom spread across her lovely face. She caught my eye and without a word, simply walked away from the man while he was in mid-sentence.

"Thank God, you are come, Jillian." She rolled her blue eyes dramatically. "I have been here not twenty minutes, and already I am bored beyond comprehension."

I shook my head. "Evergreen, you are so very difficult to please. The young man you were just speaking with was quite comely—"

"Your eyes must be failing, Jillian. He is some scientific boffin from Oxford. I'd rather talk to a sofa." She flicked her eyes over my attire. "Goodness, my dear, we really must purchase a new gown for you. I cannot bear to see you wear the same droll dress for every occasion."

Her sting found its mark. "Be that as it may," I snapped, "I would rather be unnoticed in my dowdy clothes than a strutting peacock with everyone witnessing both my triumphs and disappointments."

She gave a little laugh. "Bravo, Jillian. That's the spirit." Evergreen was incorrigible. But there was no denying how stunning she looked tonight. The Wedgewood blue of her silk gown complemented her eyes, so that one could hardly believe their colour was natural. Her hair was up in an intricate arrangement of curls, with one blonde ringlet framing each side of her face.

"Father is with Mountjoy, in the hall, and Marabelle is here somewhere." Her voice held disdain at the mere mention of her cousin's name. I was surprised at the vehemence of dislike in her tone.

"And there is Perry, and Marik. They just arrived back from Bath this afternoon and have had a wonderful time there."

The two men crossed the room to join us. Though they were so different in appearance, they cut a fine pair, and several feminine eyes studied their handsome features as they approached.

"Miss Farraday," Marik held out his hand to shake mine. Perry did the same.

"Welcome back, gentlemen. How was Bath?"

"Wet," Marik said with a laugh. "Which sounds

appropriate for a place with such a name. Does it not?"

"It does. I hope the weather did not spoil your time there?"

"On the contrary," interjected Perry. "There are such interesting places to explore in Bath. Many of them indoors, thankfully."

"The ingenuity of Roman architecture and engineering is impressive." Marik continued. "For an early civilization, their ideas were far beyond their time."

"They were barbarians," Evergreen said drily. "They fed people to lions for goodness sake. How 'modern' a notion is that Marik?"

The Indian slid her a stare, and his mouth turned up slightly on one side. "In my experience, most barbaric people are usually cleverly disguised as persons more palatable to our society." He gave a sarcastic smile, and I could not help but notice a spark of irritation in Evergreen's eyes as she glared back at him.

Perry seemed oblivious to their fencing words. "We found a wonderful tailor there and made arrangements for him to make me several suits. I truly liked Bath. If it were not so far inland, I would persuade Father to open an office there and I'd volunteer to run it—" he trailed off as Lord Mountjoy entered the room where he stood for a moment and waited for the general hubbub to quell.

"Ladies and gentlemen," he announced loudly. "Please join us for tonight's featured lectures, from The Royal Pharmaceutical Society of Great Britain."

The hum of conversation arose once more as the throng slowly wound their way into the great hall for the evening's presentation.

I FOUND THE LECTURES INTERESTING. I gained newfound respect for Uncle Jasper, as he spoke about his lichens and fungi. A topic I found mundane at home came alive when he spoke so passionately in front of a crowd. The audience rewarded him with hearty applause when he was finished.

After the program, the speakers remained in the hall to mingle, answer questions and encourage those who wished to sponsor the society. I noticed Mrs Stackpoole remained close to Uncle Jasper, and I opted to stay away and allow them their moment together. Prunella Stackpoole looked quite fetching this evening in her black gown. Gone was the mob-cap she usually sported. Tonight, her hair was artfully arranged, and she was radiantly happy.

During the lectures, I had sat with the LaVelle siblings. At one point turning to see Victor sitting a few rows away, with Marabelle at his side in a bright pink dress. I was rather surprised to see her in such a vibrant colour when normally she wore understated tones. I also kept looking over my shoulder to find Dominic. But he was absent. I was disappointed he had not come, yet guessed there would be a valid reason. Dominic was not the type to make false promises.

In the reception room, the discarded plates and glasses from earlier had been cleared away, and fresh platters of food were laid out for all. There were many in attendance enjoying the fine wine and cuisine, most of them strangers to me. I assumed this event would have attracted prominent families from many miles outside of Ambleside, perhaps even as far away as Workington. Perry and Marik were off in the distance, speaking to another young, well-dressed man, but I had lost sight of Evergreen among the swell. That was fine with me, for tonight she was petulant. Her personality was always at odds with itself. She was either kind or mean spirited, and never anything in between.

I sipped on my wine and wandered over to the glass panelled doors overlooking the gardens. They had been left wide open to allow fresh air into the room and provided an extensive view of the estate. Though little light was left in the sky, I could still see the stretch of lawn, a fountain, and flower gardens which culminated at the shore of the lake. Now the rain had long moved away, the massive body of water was calm.

I gazed at the horizon. The sky was pink and grey, with remnants of clouds skittering across the water. Lost in thought, I almost dropped my wine glass when a large object suddenly dropped in front of the window before me, landing with a resounding thud. It was so unexpected, I gasped out loud, taken entirely by surprise. I stepped out onto the flagstones to see what it was.

A mass of pink silk lay in a crumpled heap upon the ground. It took a moment for my mind to register what was right before my eyes… "Dear God!" I shouted. "Someone fetch a doctor!" For there, lying broken and twisted upon the sodden grass, was Marabelle Pike.

Chapter Seventeen

MY BODY STILL SHOOK. I SAT in a warm study with a glass of brandy clutched between my trembling hands. Next to me on the sofa, Lady Mountjoy looked intently at my face, her brown eyes soft with compassion.

"How are you feeling, dear?" she said gently.

I let out a breath. "I am unsure. It does not seem real, Lady Mountjoy."

"Louisa, please." She touched my arm in reassurance.

"How can Marabelle have fallen from up there?" My mind whirled. What possible reason could the woman have to be upstairs in the family's private quarters?

"I do not know, Jillian," Louisa replied. "That is for the constable to discover. Victor and Perry are up there with him as we speak.

I finished the brandy and placed the empty glass upon a side table. "I am better now, I think. I would like to see my uncle if it suits you." I rose to my feet, and she followed. "Thank you so much for taking care of me, Louisa. I believe I should go home now."

We left the study and found the reception room empty. As we approached the great hall, Uncle Jasper met me and took me into his arms. Tears pricked my eyes, and I willed them gone. This was neither the time nor place to allow my emotions to run riot.

"May we go?" I asked.

Uncle Jasper nodded gravely.

When the Mountjoy carriage arrived at our house, I was never so happy to be home. I was exhausted. Uncle Jasper insisted Mrs Stackpoole take me straight inside while he helped the footman unload the items from his lecture.

I was already in my bed when Uncle Jasper came upstairs. He knocked on my bedroom door, and I bade him come in. My gaslight still burned, and I was sitting up with my book laying untouched on my lap.

"Are you all right, Jilly dear? Is there anything you need?"

I shook my head. "I will be fine, Uncle. It was the shock of seeing her." I heard my voice wobble and swallowed hard. "In truth, there was no friendship between us, but she did not deserve to die in such a terrible manner."

"You are right, my dear. But you must not dwell upon it for it will only cause you grief. As a member of the LaVelle family you can rest assured that Victor will get to the bottom of it. 'Tis their worry, Jilly, not yours. Try to push it from your mind this evening, for rest is important after a nasty shock. You will be able to think clearer come morning. I'll bid you a goodnight." He gave me a thin smile, kissed the top of my head, and left the room.

I did not move but willed my mind to stop thinking. I could feel the tug of brandy in my system lulling my nerves to settle down, so I turned out my lamp and sank underneath my quilt. I closed my eyes and reflected upon the irony that I had left Devon to escape the grief my mother's dying had brought. Now, after a few weeks of living in Ambleside, death had found me yet again.

WAS IT A NIGHTMARE? UPON WAKING, it took a moment for my thoughts to tumble into order. I staunched a cry of anguish remembering Marabelle Pike was dead and had died right before my eyes. I blinked back tears. I must pull myself together. Why was I so emotional? It had to be shock, I deduced. But that was not acceptable. I was a strong woman, was I not? I swallowed the lump in my throat and forced myself out of bed.

By the time I joined Uncle Jasper and Mrs Stackpoole in the kitchen, I had composed myself. There were eggs warming in a pan, and the teapot was on the table.

"Morning, Jilly. I hope you got some sleep?" Uncle asked kindly. He was tucking into scrambled eggs.

I pulled out a chair and sat down. Mrs Stackpoole brought me a plate and ladled a spoonful of eggs onto a slice of toast.

"I did sleep. Thank you. I am better for the rest." I glanced at the housekeeper whose face was drawn. She looked tired. "Mrs Stackpoole. How do you fare?"

She joined us at the table. "I'm a right bundle of nerves, my dear. In all the years I've lived in this village, never has there been so many tragedies. It's distressin' to say the least."

"Indeed," agreed Uncle Jasper. "Mrs S. has the run of it. I don't know what things are coming to. A shame, if you ask me. It had been a glorious evening, up until the accident." He took a sip of his tea. "By the by, I would anticipate a visit from the constable, my dear. He said as much last night. He wants to speak with you as well, Prunella, so you ladies should remain at home today. Best place for you both, all things considered."

"Yes, Uncle. I had decided as much myself." I took a bite of scrambled eggs but could not taste them. I put down my fork. "I cannot stop thinking about why Marabelle was upstairs in the Mountjoy's family apartments? What was she doing there? And how did she fall from that balcony?"

Uncle Jasper munched on his toast, in deep reflection. "She could have taken a dizzy spell, or became light-headed from a glass of sherry?" He took another bite.

I was unconvinced. "I cannot agree with you." I rose from the table and cleared away the remains of my uneaten breakfast, my appetite gone. "I think something else happened to her. Though I harboured no fondness for Marabelle, she did not deserve such a fate."

Uncle Jasper took a sip of tea and looked at me. "What are you suggesting? Do you suspect someone had a hand in her death, Jilly? Surely not. Why the woman was naught but Victor's housekeeper."

I fixed him with a hard glare. "And that might be the very reason she is dead."

IT TOOK ALL MY SELF-DISCIPLINE TO concentrate on my work that morning. But once I became deep into the translation of Uncle's watery shorthand, there was not much room to think about anything else.

Before lunch, Constable Bloom paid us a call. He sat in the parlour with a cup of tea and a jam tart, taking notes as I related my version of the previous evening's events.

"Miss Jillian, 'tis sorry I am that your time in

Ambleside has been wrought with such goin's on," he stated. "This is usually such a sleepy village, an' not only is it shockin' these terrible things have occurred, but horrific for a young lady like yourself bein' a witness to 'em all."

I thanked him for his thoughtfulness while my stomach became queasy. I did not want to think about either ghastly event, truth be known.

Mrs Stackpoole kept him plied with refills of tea and tarts while he asked more questions. After he finished with me, he spoke with both my uncle and Mrs Stackpoole. At length he departed, along with the housekeeper and Uncle Jasper, who walked into the village to purchase something for the evening's meal.

Alone in the house, I struggled to keep my ever-threatening tears at bay. I forced myself to return to work—anything to keep my mind off what I had seen last night—when a knock came at the door. I thought it might be the constable once again, but it was Dominic. Without a word, he stepped inside the hallway and took me in his arms and held me tight. My body collapsed against him as though my bones had turned to gelatine, and tears spilled down my face.

How long we stood this way, I do not know. But eventually, I stopped crying, and my strength returned. Reluctantly I loosened my grip and stepped back. "I am sorry, Dominic. I do not know what has come over me," I led him into the parlour.

He took my hand as we stood before the hearth. "Good God, Jilly, of course you are upset, you've had a terrible shock. Any other person might have taken to their bed today. Don't be so hard on yourself. Come, let us sit."

"Constable Bloom has only just left."

"I passed him on the street. How did it go with him?"

"He asked questions about what I saw last night, but there was not much to tell. I do not know what they think about how Marabelle came to fall from the balcony, but it was no accident."

Dominic's eyes widened in surprise, and he leaned forward with a frown. "What? I heard she took a fainting spell and lost her balance."

"I cannot believe that for a moment. Marabelle was a strong woman. It does not seem likely to me. Besides, she should not have been up there in the first place. The guests were on the ground floor only. For some reason Marabelle was in the Mountjoy's private rooms."

"That is odd," he agreed. "What would have induced her to go up there?"

"I cannot say." I lifted my eyes to settle upon his. "Dominic, why did you not come last night?"

His face fell. "I am sorry, Jillian. But by the time I returned from Kendal after seeing Billy, and tended the animals, I was done in. The prospect of spending the evening with you was more than tempting, but I had no desire to be among the community, especially with things the way they are. If I had been less selfish, you would not have endured this alone. I am truly sorry." He reached across and took my hands, a gesture I was becoming familiar with.

"There is no need for you to apologise. I completely understand. It is far better you spend time with your brother. I would wish nothing else." I thought of Hollyfield. "I wonder how the LaVelles fare this morning. They must be devastated."

He nodded. "There was no love lost between Evergreen and Marabelle, but the woman was cousin to her mother. It will be a shock, I've no doubt. I plan to call on Victor this afternoon for I have other matters to discuss with him. I'll let you know how the family are coping once we have talked. That is if I may call again?"

"I would like that."

MY UNCLE RETURNED JUST after Dominic had left. He was not alone, for I heard him talking to someone as he came down the hall. I thought it was Mrs Stackpoole, but when the parlour door opened, it revealed both Uncle Jasper, and of all people, Lady Mountjoy.

"Jilly, my dear. Look who has come to call." He offered Louisa Mountjoy a seat and then left us alone while he went to make us tea.

Louisa Mountjoy sat down and glanced over at me. "How are you faring?" she said, with genuine concern. She looked tired herself. Her face was pale and drawn, lacking the vitality I had seen in her before.

"I hardly slept a wink," I answered honestly. "You?"

"The same. Exhausted. Monty and I are devastated that something so tragic happened on a night which was supposed to be pleasant. Why Marabelle was upstairs in our private apartments defies explanation. 'Tis beyond my comprehension and that somehow makes everything seem so much worse."

"I wonder the very same thing," I said quietly.

Louisa's dark eyes were compassionate. "And for you to be so close when she fell. I am so sorry."

"Lady Mountjoy—"

"Louisa."

"Louisa, May I be frank with you?"

"Of course."

"I am uncertain about what happened."

"What do you mean?"

"Jareth Flynn was murdered recently, and now this bizarre accident with Marabelle. Do you not find it coincidental that a village this size has two tragedies occur within weeks of one another?"

She gave a sharp intake of breath. "What are you suggesting? You think them connected?"

I shrugged. "I do not know. I am no sleuth, but I cannot help but think it strange."

Her expression changed, she looked frightened.

"What is it? Are you troubled?" I asked, and much to my surprise, she looked as though she was about to cry.

Louisa rummaged in her reticule and pulled out a small, lace handkerchief and dabbed at her eyes. I remained quiet while she composed herself.

"I wish to tell you something of a sensitive nature. But it must remain confidential," she said with a muted tone. "I do not know you well, Jillian, but I think you a sensible girl. As a matter of fact, you remind me of myself many years ago, before I was a member of society.

"Back then I was a shopgirl, working at a famous department store in London called Liberty. It was there I met Monty, who was a widower. He was childless and lonely, and it was not long before we became dear friends. Much against his family's wishes, he proposed to me and I accepted. After we married, Monty brought me to Ambleside. Ours was not a romantic relationship, more companionable, you understand."

I was both surprised by the tale, and ill at ease being told such personal details by a woman of her standing. But out of respect, I remained quiet. She continued.

"A few years ago, I met Jareth Flynn and was instantly smitten. You may not have known the man, but he was a handsome devil who knew the powerful effect he had upon women. We were close in age, and similar in upbringing, if the truth was known. Before I could stop myself, I had quite fallen for him." She paused as the clinking of teacups rattling on a tray became audible.

"Here we are," Uncle Jasper exclaimed as he entered the study and set the tea things on the table. He looked at us and with unusual tact, sensed he had interrupted something private. He blinked several times. "I shall be in my study ladies. If you will excuse me." He backed out of the room.

I rose to pour our tea.

"You are shocked by my confession, Jillian?"

"I am."

Louisa smiled weakly. "I do admire your frankness, my dear. I have never confided this to a living soul."

"I am flattered by your trust in me, Louisa. Truly."

"I would continue with my tale if I might?"

"Indeed. Please do."

"Jareth ardently returned my feelings, or at least, so I thought. We had three wonderful years together. My marriage with Monty was comfortable. My husband seemed happy with his choice of wife. I placed his wants and desires before my own and tried to be an exemplary Lady of Mountjoy House. But Jareth was the only person I had in my life who accepted me for myself. An ordinary woman—with desires and needs. I believed he cared for me as much as I did him. Until this spring."

"What happened?"

"Something changed. He became distant. It began with him not showing up at our arranged meetings, a place we frequented for more than two years." Her eyes watered once again. She set down the cup and saucer to retrieve her handkerchief.

I had little experience being on the receiving end of such a confidence. Especially to a person with Lady Mountjoy's standing within society. I could offer no counsel to this woman. What did she expect me to say?

"Jillian, I know you wonder at my telling you." She sniffed and took a sip of tea. "I speak of my secret because of what has happened recently. When I learned of Jareth's death, I was utterly devastated."

"I can imagine." And I could after what she had just told me.

She held up a gloved hand. "No, please let me finish. I was devastated but also immensely relieved."

I almost dropped my cup. "I beg your pardon?"

"You heard me correctly. Though I loved him, Jareth Flynn was a scoundrel. For the past two months, he had been blackmailing me."

Chapter Eighteen

I WAS INCREDULOUS. HER COMMENT was the last thing I expected to hear. "Blackmailing you—why?"

She set down her cup. "Because of our affair, of course. Jareth threatened to tell Monty everything, unless I paid him a weekly stipend." She looked at me sternly. "Please do not tell me I was foolish to pay him. I had no choice. I was guilty and consequently paid the price for that indulgence."

"Does anyone else know?"

"Of course not," she gasped. "And if you speak a word of it to anyone, I shall deny it all! Look," her tone softened. "I did not plan to ever speak of it, Jillian. But with what happened to Marabelle, I am unnerved, though I cannot tell you why. You are a bright young woman, and Victor remarked that you and Dominic are making enquiries about Jareth's death—which is understandable with Billy in such awful trouble. I wanted you to have my side of the story in case you discover anything that links him to me." Her pretty face looked drawn. Sharing such a dark secret had taken its toll upon her.

"How did you pay Jareth?"

"In coin, for I could not risk anyone connecting us." She got to her feet, and I did the same. "Jillian, I do not know if the two deaths are even connected. Yet, like you, my instinct tells me different." She held out a gloved hand and took mine. "Remember, I have put my trust in you and hope you will keep my confidence."

"Of course, Louisa," I said gravely. Though in my heart, I wondered what she expected me to do with her information.

I closed the front door behind Lady Mountjoy and contemplated all she had said. Though I was more than a little surprised at her affair with Flynn, it was hardly implausible. I could well imagine a beautiful young bride brought to Mountjoy House and ultimately meeting the handsome blacksmith. They were both young, attractive, and she, bored with life far away from London. But in a small hamlet such as Ambleside, it must have been challenging to keep their love affair secret.

Then a thought occurred as I remembered the scraps of paper Billy had hidden in his box. Had they come from a letter of blackmail as we suspected? More importantly, could they have been written by Jareth?

IT WAS ALL I COULD DO NOT TO run to Wolfe Farm. I needed to speak to Dominic and share my suspicions. This would be difficult without betraying Louisa Mountjoy's secret, but I intended to try anyway.

I arrived at the farm, and after knocking several times at the front door, I realised Dominic was not at home. I searched the barn and cowshed. He was likely gone to see his brother again. Yet he had mentioned talking to Victor. Perhaps he was at Hollyfield House?

I made up my mind, left the farm and headed towards the LaVelles. If I passed anyone along the way, I did not notice, so intent was I on my mission. But as I neared the turn-off for the lane, I changed direction and instead walked toward the boathouse and not the house itself. I do not know what compelled me, but I allowed my feet to take me there.

The boathouse looked far more welcoming than it had been yesterday during the terrible rainstorm. Had it only been a day earlier I had been here with Dominic? It was difficult to come to terms with the fact Marabelle Pike had still been alive then. I chased the thought from my head. The time to mourn would come later. There was much to be done first.

As I neared the building, I caught the murmur of voices and I stopped in my tracks. Where were they coming from? Quietly I stepped closer to the boathouse and leaned back against the brickwork. I closed my eyes to focus. There it was again—the hum of conversation. A wooded area divided the main house from the boathouse. I deduced whoever was speaking had to be somewhere in there.

Slowly I inched my way towards the sound of conversation, glad the sodden ground muffled my footsteps. I moved with the stealth of a cat, reluctant to have my presence known. As I drew closer, the voices grew clearer. Then all at once, I could make out two figures ahead of me. I stopped and aligned myself with the thick bark of an oak tree to hide. I peered around and looked again.

Evergreen and Marik were in the midst of a heated discussion. I strained to listen.

"Dear God, it is tragic. And I feel all the more wretched because there is also a feeling of relief," Marik said solemnly.

"Don't be so weak, Marik. Though we wish she had not had the accident, do not feel guilty that her passing eases the situation. We just have to hope she kept quiet as promised," Evergreen spoke with disdain.

Who were they talking about? It had to be Marabelle.

"If she told anybody, I will be suspected." His voice sounded worried.

"Oh, honestly, Marik. Why must you always be so eaten up with fright? The woman had no friends and seldom spoke to anyone other than the servants. If she had said anything to Father, we would know by now. And you have done nothing. Indeed, the only person responsible for Marabelle's death is Marabelle herself. So please, pull yourself together. No more of this drama. It gives me the headache."

"I am sorry, Evie." Marik went to her and gave her a brief hug before stepping back. "I do not mean to be so aggravating. You know how I worry for Perry. I do not want any kind of trouble."

"Everything will be fine. Come along. Perry will be looking for us."

I stayed still while they walked in the direction of the house. It was devious to eavesdrop, yet I had been riveted to every word. The conversation was unclear, other than Marik's worry about himself, or Perry being connected to Marabelle's demise. But why should he be concerned? And what did they mean about 'her keeping quiet'? They obviously referred to Marabelle.

I turned back toward the village and home, an unhappy witness to something I did not understand. I was anxious to escape the proximity of Hollyfield. But as I walked back by the boathouse, an eerie feeling passed through me, and I turned expecting to see someone there. There was not. I was alone, or at least I seemed to be. But it was not until I reached Lake Road that I finally shook the sensation that I had been watched.

I COULD NOT WAIT TO TALK TO Dominic. I would check to see if he was home on my way back to the village. I walked briskly away from the lake towards the farm, my mind spinning like a top. A mental jigsaw lay before me and its edges were linked into a square. Now I sought to fill in the middle of the puzzle, have various parts put together so I could form one piece. This analogy seemed to help me straighten out my thoughts.

I approached the farm and saw a beautiful jet-black horse tethered outside the farmhouse. I was no judge of pedigree, but even to my untrained eye, I could tell it was a magnificent specimen of high breeding. As I neared, the steed whickered, and he turned with obsidian eyes to observe me. I reached him and gingerly held out a hand to pat his neck, then started as he turned to nuzzle his nose in my hand.

"What's this? Do you mean to steal Cressidio's affection away from me?" A friendly voice caused both the horse and I to turn. Victor LaVelle stepped closer, a smile upon his face, though he looked drained. Little wonder, he had a son in gaol and now a relative to bury.

"No, indeed," I replied, dropping my hand. "But he is sublime, Mr LaVelle."

Our eyes met, and he smiled kindly. "Call me Victor, my dear. We agreed there was to be no formality, remember?"

I nodded.

"Jillian, I am appalled that you had to witness the tragic event of last night." His expression was dour, his voice quiet. "Marabelle was not well known by many, but she was a good person and very loyal to our family." His sorrow-filled voice broke off. My heart went out to him for he could not disguise his pain.

"Victor, there is no need to say anything. I am just deeply sorry for your loss." I gave him a weak smile of encouragement. "I am here to speak with Dominic regarding new information I have recently learned. Will you come back in so I can tell you together?" I moved towards the door.

His demeanour underwent a sudden change. His green eyes brightened, and his jaw clenched. "Of course." He followed me inside.

Dominic was surprised to see his guest return, and I took some pleasure in his apparent delight at my being there also. He ushered us into the welcoming kitchen, and we automatically took our places around the table, much as we had done on my previous meeting with the two gentlemen.

"There is something I wish to share with you both, but in doing so, I break a confidence." I could feel them tense in anticipation. I looked earnestly at each man's face, uncomfortable with my dilemma. Lady Mountjoy was no friend, yet I felt allegiance to the woman regardless.

"I only do this because I want to help Billy in any way I can. But I must have your word neither one of you will breathe this to another soul." I paused.

"Of course," Victor answered promptly. "You have my promise."

"Mine too." Dominic's eyes shone with what I thought was hope. My heart warmed, for he was such a good brother.

"This morning I had a visit from Louisa Mountjoy." I recounted part of our conversation earlier in the day. I omitted many details and told the barest of facts. That Jareth was a blackmailer and most likely an ill-doer based on his reputation. They did not interrupt me and, when I finished speaking, they made not a sound. I assumed they digested the information as it related to the blacksmith's murder.

Victor was the first to comment. "I take it you deduce Flynn was killed because of a propensity for blackmail?"

"Well, you must admit it is a viable theory, Victor. Especially if we consider that scrap of paper Billy found."

"I agree with Jillian," Dominic said. "Jareth did nurture a desire to better himself. We know he gambled, so it is feasible the man was capable of threatening trouble if he did not get paid."

"All right," Victor acknowledged. "That gives us a motive for a person to want him dead. Yet I believe Lady Mountjoy as likely as Billy to murder him in cold blood."

"Yes," I interjected. "But it stands to reason Louisa may not have been his only target for blackmail. Consider, the man could have amassed large gambling debts. Perhaps there are others in the community who fell victim to Jareth Flynn's fleecing?"

"Jillian is right, Victor. I believe she is on to something."

Victor nodded, and his brows furrowed in thought. "How on earth shall we go about looking for them? One cannot exactly raise the subject cold. Imagine asking the vicar if he had any sins worthy of being bribed for?"

We all smiled at that, and the tension slipped away.

"There must be a way to unearth Flynn's antics," Dominic said. "I can start by asking around about his gaming interests. If there are others who share his love of betting, you can be sure they will be happy to talk about it, especially if I offer a coin or two for the telling."

"Excellent idea," Victor concurred. "But take caution. You will encounter some rough fellows, I'll be bound." He rose from the table and searched in his pocket. Victor pulled out a small leather pouch and tossed it to Dominic, who snatched it from the air.

"Take this," Victor gestured. "'Tis not much, but you will need to grease a few palms, and I do not want you using your own money. You need everything you have to keep the farm running for when Billy gets home."

Dominic paused momentarily and then gave a resolute nod. There was no need for theatric displays of gratitude or even a perfunctory refusal.

"Right," Victor continued. "I must leave. There is much to attend today, as you no doubt understand."

His face fell, and for a moment I felt shame that in my haste to speak of Jareth Flynn's propensity to blackmail, I had quickly forgotten the LaVelles were in mourning.

Dominic and I both rose to our feet.

"Victor. If there is anything I may do to help, you have only to say," I said quietly.

He turned his handsome face to look at me, and I was struck by the depth of sorrow in his eyes. I watched him force a smile upon his mouth as he thanked me for the offer and then bade me farewell.

I remained in the kitchen while Dominic escorted him to the door.

When he returned, Dominic came to stand behind where I sat. He leaned down and placed a soft kiss upon the back of my neck.

I sighed. "I feel so badly for Victor," I said quietly. "'Tis still difficult for me to take it in—and yet I saw her fall with my own eyes. I cannot imagine how the family must feel."

He placed another affectionate kiss on top of my head. "It is a sad situation. I don't believe I have ever seen Victor look this tired." He returned to his place at the table.

"I feel sorry for him." I swallowed. "Dominic, there is something else to tell you. I did not want to mention it in front of Victor."

His golden eyes narrowed. "What is it?"

I described my visit to the boathouse and the conversation I overheard between Marik and Evergreen.

He frowned. "Why would Marik be worried about being considered a suspect? Surely no one would think he had anything to do with Marabelle falling off a balcony. It was an accident."

"That is what everyone thinks, Dominic. Yet, if so, why did Evergreen mention her cousin potentially not keeping some kind of confidence? What could Marabelle know which would cause them worry? Think about it," I insisted. "Marik does not strike me as someone easily scared. What I heard in his voice was most certainly fear."

"What are you saying, Jillian? That Marik is worried because he has his own motive for wanting to be rid of Marabelle Pike?"

I nodded solemnly. "There can be no other reason for him to act that way. Marik must have something to hide. Something Marabelle knew and threatened to share."

Chapter Nineteen

I HAD SPOKEN WITH DOMINIC EACH day since Marabelle's untimely death. He had come to our house for tea, and on one occasion even stayed for dinner. It was uncanny how comfortably he slipped into our small family, as though he belonged there.

There was much to occupy my mind and be concerned about, yet I somehow managed to find moments of happiness whenever Dominic was around. A stolen kiss, a touch of his hand, a smouldering look from his lovely eyes. For that fraction of time, all the sorrow which seemed to have permeated into my life, would disappear.

Victor had not returned to visit Dominic, and we understood the family was preoccupied with Marabelle's funeral and the procession of visiting relatives who passed through Hollyfield House. The burial would take place on the coming Wednesday, and I believed most people in the village planned to pay their respects.

It had been strange not seeing Evergreen. Other than my glimpse of her speaking with Marik, I had not set eyes upon her since the night of the lecture and Marabelle's fall. I often thought of going to see her, but Uncle assured me it was better to give the family their privacy.

Dominic had set about questioning the men from

the area regarding the blacksmith's 'hobby', and little by little, was piecing together a better picture of Jareth Flynn and his questionable habits. That the man was a gambler was clearly an understatement. Flynn was known locally and about the Lake District as quite the 'chancer'. His primary interest was in horse racing, and he was known to travel to the racecourse in Cartmel Village at least once every month. It was a half-day's ride from Ambleside, and he usually spent a night or two there, depending upon the racing schedule.

Dominic decided it would be constructive to travel there himself and see what he might unearth. Therefore, on Saturday morning he left for Cartmel and would not return until the next day. I did not want him to go alone, but Dominic preferred not to wait for Victor to be available. He determined the quicker he left, the faster he could return. Victor was absorbed with preparations for Marabelle's funeral and was in no position to go anywhere.

With Dominic gone, it proved challenging trying to concentrate on my work at hand—I could not engage. I abandoned the task and instead spent the day assisting Mrs Stackpoole with the washing. The activity was a welcome release. By late morning, as we pegged wet clothes onto the washing line and as the sun warmed my shoulders, I had the impulse to remain out of doors.

Securing a list from Mrs Stackpoole, I retrieved my shopping basket and set off for a walk into the village. Uncle Jasper would be back at dusk, and I had been sent to purchase a thick slice of ham to be served with a salad from the garden.

Ambleside was a well-populated small village. There were generally people shopping or taking a stroll.

Today was no exception for the weather was glorious. The promise of a warm summer carried in the air. I was contemplating this when I heard someone call my name.

"Miss Jillian?" It was a child's reedy voice. I stopped and turned, then smiled as I recognised the young face of Jem Riley. I waited for him to catch up with me and we fell into step together.

"Hello Jem. How is your sister? I hope she did not catch cold." It would not surprise me if she had—the poor little mite had almost drowned.

Jem gave me a gap-toothed grin. "She's right as rain now, miss. But I got a wallopin' from my da for lettin' her run off." His face scrunched up with injustice. "It wasn't my fault. She always runs away from me when mam's not there."

"Little sisters can be a big handful, Jem."

"Yes," he agreed somberly. "She did it to me the week afore that too."

"She is a rascal. I hope she did not wind up in the lake that time as well?"

"Nope," he said cheerily. "She hid in that posh boathouse. I had a heck of a time findin' her afore mam got home from work."

I chuckled. Jenny Riley was a little scamp. But then my mind latched onto what the boy had just said. "Which fancy boathouse was that, Jem?" I glanced at him.

He looked sheepish. "I don't want to get into no trouble."

I stopped and rested a hand on his shoulder. "You will not. All you did was go in there to get your sister. There is nothing wrong with that." I noticed the quick flash of guilt ripple across his face. "Is there anything you wish to tell me?" I said in the most non-threatening tone I could muster. For some reason I instinctively felt the lad was hiding something.

He nodded glumly. "I did go there to find Jenny," he said reluctantly. He wiped his nose with a sleeve and looked up at me with wide chocolate-coloured eyes. "But once I got her, I pinched a cabbage from the garden, an' I nearly got caught." He paused, waiting for my swift admonishment and then blinked several times when I did not utter a word. I resumed walking, and he kept pace with me.

"Are you angry with me, miss? I ain't really a thief, but mam an' dad work so hard, an' there's never enough food to go 'round."

"Stealing is very bad, Jem," I said quietly.

"I know," he pleaded. "I won't ever do it again, miss. I just couldn't help myself. Then I saw the lady an' man walk up to the boathouse an' I knew I was for it. So as soon as they were busy with each other, me an' Jenny ran for it. No one followed us. We were lucky." He shook his head. "I was so scared I dropped the blasted cabbage anyway. We never even got to eat it."

I did not care about the cabbage. It was his other comment. "Jem, who was it you saw? The lady and man I mean. Did you know them?" We had reached the butcher's shop.

"Of course, I did," he said with a groan. "That's why I was scared I'd get in trouble. It was the blacksmith an' the pretty lady from the House, the one with the yellow hair."

My heart picked up rhythm. "Jareth Flynn and Miss LaVelle?"

"Yes. Who did you think I was on about?"

I ignored the question. "What did you mean by them being busy with themselves?"

His face turned a warm shade of pink. "They were kissin' an' cuddlin'." His nose wrinkled in distaste.

I could not help but smile at his expression. "And they did not see you?"

"Not at first. But then the blacksmith saw us out of the corner of his eye, 'cos he winked at me." Now his confidence returned as Jem realised I was not angry with him. "But me and Jen, we're good at hidin' from me da when he's had a drink or two. So, we hid in the bushes, an' while they were all lovey-dovey, we ran off home. Thing was though, miss." He looked up at me, and his face was racked with guilt once again. "When I heard the blacksmith was dead, all I could think about was how lucky I was. No one would find out about me an' the cabbage."

The significance of Jem's words was overwhelming. He had innocently recounted his story, placing Evergreen and Flynn at the boathouse in a romantic rendezvous. Our suspicions were correct. Though it seemed a bizarre union to me, more importantly, I now felt certain Jareth Flynn had been inside the boathouse when he dropped his watch, and it had happened right before he died.

When Dominic returned from Cartmel Sunday evening, I pulled open the front door so quickly, he practically fell inside. I had paced for so long the hall carpet could have been threadbare. My mind had been working furiously with information as it knitted together all I had learned about Jareth Flynn.

Dominic asked if Uncle Jasper was home, and at my answer to the negative, he pulled me into a warm embrace and kissed my lips. Momentarily, all thought left me as I became lost in the sensation of his passionate mouth. Then he ended the kiss and looked hard into my eyes. "God, but I've missed you, Jillian," he said, his irises burning like molten gold.

"And I, you, Dominic," I whispered, and he kissed me again. It was a struggle to disentangle our lips and quell our desire. But there was much to discuss, and I was anxious to begin. I brewed a pot of tea and we sat in the kitchen.

"What is it, Jillian? You seem quite agitated." Dominic smiled at me. "I'd like to think my kiss is the culprit, but somehow I fear I would be wrong."

"I do have something to tell you. But first, I want to hear what you discovered in Cartmel Village. Did you learn any more about Flynn and his gaming habits?"

Dominic gave a wry smirk and set down his mug. "Indeed, I did. I had the misfortune to spend an entire evening at The Pig and Whistle Inn. A veritable den of horse gaming thugs and crooks if I ever saw one."

"Oh no. I hope there was no trouble?"

"None at all. But Flynn was well known among the patrons and not in a particularly good way."

"Why is that?"

"According to the men I spoke with, our blacksmith had run up some serious debts with several of the local betting men. Many of the sums quite large for a man of his meagre income."

"Then that explains additional motives for someone to kill the man."

"Yes it does. However, the news of Flynn's death did not even reach Cartmel until several days after he died. And though I am no expert on criminals, the men I met were capable of stealing wallets and other petty crimes—but not murder. It strikes me that Flynn was at risk of being roughed over by someone wanting to get repaid. Yet there would be no hope of restoration if you killed the very person owing you money."

He made a valid point. What use was Flynn dead? I quickly agreed. "You are right. Unless it was a random act of anger, I tend to think it someone who needed him silenced."

"And judging by his debts," Dominic added. "Jareth needed to get his hands on a great deal of money."

"We know he blackmailed Louisa Mountjoy." I chewed my bottom lip. "But I do not think her the murderer. Lord Mountjoy had no idea of the affair or blackmail, so he is an unlikely suspect." Our eyes met, and then his gaze lowered to rest on my mouth, and he smiled, his thoughts evidently returning to our kiss of minutes ago. I raised one eyebrow and endeavoured to look stern. "Dominic?"

He blinked. "Sorry."

"Who else could Jareth have been blackmailing?

Dominic ran his fingers through his thick dark curls. "I wish I knew. Kemp says we have about three weeks until Billy's trial begins and still much to do. I will speak with Victor, after Marabelle's funeral. Then we can formulate our next move."

At the mention of Billy's trial, my heart sank. The enormity of our task sometimes overwhelmed. "Let me tell you my news." I could not wait to share little Jem's story. Quickly I told Dominic the gist of what the child had said and, as I anticipated, he was pleased to have the information yet there was something about his expression which caused me to think Dominic did not welcome the fact Evergreen was romantically involved with the man.

"You think Evergreen another target for blackmail?" he said.

I nodded. "If she was involved with Jareth and met him in secret, then it is possible. After all, he did the same thing to Louisa, so why not Evergreen? She is rich. Perhaps Flynn discovered she was sent to Ambleside as a penance for her indiscretions in London. What might Victor do if he found out she was still misbehaving?"

"Send her away I imagine."

"Then what better avenue to get more money. Lord knows, Evergreen could pay handsomely for his silence." I still sensed Dominic's dislike of acknowledging Evergreen's penchant for dalliances. It was beginning to trouble me more at each observation.

"But what about the note Billy found? It referenced something unnatural. Flynn would not have written the letter to Evergreen if he was the person involved in her secret." Dominic asked.

"Ah," I said triumphantly. "But what if *that* note was not meant for Evergreen?"

WEDNESDAY HELD THE PROMISE OF sunny weather. The birds sang brightly, and there was not a stir of wind upon the air. It seemed incongruous to have a funeral on such a lovely day, emphasising how sad it was that Marabelle would never see the beauty of nature ever again.

By the time Uncle Jasper, Mrs Stackpoole and I arrived at St. Mary's, it was filled to capacity. Fortunately, we had asked Dominic to save a place should he arrive before us and this he had done.

The LaVelles and their relations were seated where the choir usually sat, affording them some privacy. Reverend Fothergill delivered his sermon, and Marabelle's eulogy was short and to the point. The selection of hymns was sung, and as the service concluded, we rose and watched the family walk down the aisle. Their eyes remained straight ahead, their countenance stoic. Victor was sombre and Evergreen's face hidden behind a veil. Only Perry glanced our way as they passed.

Out in the sunny morning, the family did not wait to greet the mourners. Instead, their carriages departed back to Hollyfield. Dominic told me there was a small family vault in the grounds at the back of the House, and it was there Marabelle would be interred. To be truthful, I was glad there was no public burial. Being at the funeral was too close a reminder of my own recent and painful loss.

Walking back home, Dominic and I followed behind my uncle and Mrs Stackpoole. After our conversation when he had returned from Cartmel, we still had much to consider. Dominic had spent the past two afternoons in Kendal with Billy and the solicitor. But no real progress had been made. It was imperative we find out as much as possible before Billy went to trial—time was running out.

"What are your plans for the rest of the day, Jillian?" Dominic broke the silence.

I sighed. "I do not feel much like working. I think I would rather be outside. It is so lovely."

"It is." He looked at my face. "And perhaps more so after attending a funeral. Life is so precious, Jilly, yet we fritter our time away until it is too late."

"That is quite morose, Dominic. You are glum, indeed."

"Not really. The death of a person at so young an age should be enough of a lesson to ensure we not waste what little time we have." His expression was serious. "There has been too much sorrow in Ambleside, of late. More than I wish to deal with."

Without a care who saw, I took his hand and gave it a squeeze. "I am sorry. You have not had an easy time of it, Dominic. Take comfort in all we have learned. I feel certain we will get to the bottom of this horrible business."

"What do you think, Jilly?" Uncle Jasper came to a sudden stop and turned to look at us. I quickly released Dominic's hand, but he had not missed it. His pale eyes met mine for a brief moment, and I could not decide what he thought about my display of affection.

"Mrs Stackpoole has a nice pork pie to share with us for lunch. Hurry along, you two."

AFTER LUNCH, DOMINIC ACCOMPANIED me, and we set off walking towards the lake.

"How was your brother, yesterday?" I usually waited for Dominic to raise the subject of Billy. I was not sure if it made him unhappy to be reminded of their bleak situation.

"He does surprisingly well. Billy likes things to be familiar and the same. He has been in gaol long enough now that I believe he has become less frightened. The wardens understand him better, and therefore are kinder than they were in the beginning. But Billy still cannot comprehend the gravity of his situation." He shrugged. "Perhaps that is for the best."

"Has Mr Kemp said much about his strategy for the trial?"

"No. Though I believe he converses with Victor regularly. Kemp is an intelligent fellow. He is sincere about wanting to help my brother. But it still all hangs on the blasted knife used and Billy not having an alibi." He stopped as we reached the end of Lake Road.

"Would you like to walk a little further? We could venture down to the trees?" He gestured along the shoreline where the woods began. Three benches were placed in scenic spots where one could rest and enjoy the panorama of the water. I nodded, and we made our way to one of the seats.

The afternoon sun was intense and bright. I sat back against the seat with my face upturned. Freckles and a dark complexion were not in fashion, but I cared not one whit. The soothing blush of warmth kissing my skin was relaxing. Beside me, I sensed Dominic mirrored my actions.

"We are like a couple of lizards basking in the heat, Jilly. This is pleasant, is it not?"

"Yes," I sighed. "I imagine it must be just like this all the time on the continent. Little wonder it is popular to travel there during winter. Just think how much warmer it was when the LaVelles lived in India? It must have been strange for the family to get used to the climate here. I expect Marik misses his home."

"I believe he is happy enough. From what he has

said, it was a big adjustment coming to England, but he has embraced our culture and traditions wholeheartedly."

I turned to look at Dominic. He was such a handsome fellow. His head was tilted towards the sun, and I watched in fascination while the light played across his strong jaw, thick brows and sensual mouth. His dark hair fell back in a mass of waves, and I wondered how a man could look so masculine and beautiful at the same time.

"Do you study me, Jillian?" Dominic opened his eyes.

Caught, I gave him a nervous smile. "Yes."

"And have I passed inspection?" A lazy grin slid across his face, and my breath caught in my throat. How could another human being elicit such a reaction from me?

"You will do." I chuckled, and Dominic snatched up my hand and pressed it to his lips.

"Well, you are stuck with me now, Miss Farraday, so you had better learn to live with it." His gaze went to my mouth, and though our faces were not close, the intimacy radiating from his eyes made me feel as though he had kissed me.

The bark of a dog pierced the moment, and I quickly gathered my composure. "When will you see Victor?"

"I plan to call on him tomorrow. His company will have departed by then." There had been a succession of relatives visiting Hollyfield. "He deserves much longer to mourn, but time is something we do not have in abundance. In light of your discoveries, we need his help." Dominic tensed at the thought, straightened his spine, and ran his fingers through his hair. "Come, let us walk along further." He gestured to the wooded area. "There is a small waterfall close by. Would you care to see it?"

"Yes." I rose to my feet. "Lead the way."

THE TRAIL THROUGH THE WOODS was narrow, and consequently we walked in single file. Dominic remarked upon various points of interest and then regaled me with an old folk tale about a local wizard who had lived in these woods. When he said the man's name was Jacob Nash, I interrupted.

"Is he related to Peggy Nash?"

"He was her father."

"I wonder why they lived out here."

"Jacob was a Druid. The old man was eccentric, and no one knew exactly where his dwelling was. But somehow, he managed to support both himself and his daughter by selling medicinal potions. Whether or not the remedies worked, I do not know."

"I wish Peggy was not Billy's only alibi. What a shame she is so odd. If she were any other villager, Billy would be released upon their testimony."

"Do not remind me," Dominic said in a low voice, and I immediately regretted the comment.

We had walked for some time when I detected the sound of water. As the trail widened I drew level with Dominic and he reached for my hand.

"We are close now. It is a lovely spot—one I have painted several times for my postcards." He was leading me past thickets of bushes, when I heard the unmistakable babble of voices. Dominic must have noted them too, for his pace abruptly slowed.

"It seems we are not the only ones seeking a beautiful place today, Jillian." As he spoke, we reached a clearing in the woods and the trail led to the bank of a small lagoon. A rocky hillock supported a steep fall, which cascaded plumes of rushing water down into the pool. The voices came again. My eyes were drawn across to the naked figure of a tall, lean man. As I watched, he dived from the rocks and into the water.

I blinked and then felt heat rise in my face as I realised whose nude body I had seen. There was no mistaking that dark skin for a pale Englishman. It was Marik Singh.

"Oh, dear," I stammered.

Dominic grinned widely, not in the least perturbed. "Don't be alarmed, Jilly. It is just a body as nature made it."

Another shout, and this time I saw Perry LaVelle climb onto the rock his friend had just vacated moments before. I turned away with embarrassment.

"I am sorry," Dominic said kindly. "I did not consider anyone else would be here." He looked up to the blue skies. "But it is a particularly lovely day, and warm too. No wonder Marik and Perry escaped here to cool off. They were probably trying to get away from a house full of people."

"Dominic, they have just buried their cousin. It seems somewhat inappropriate to be here having fun under such sad circumstances."

"You must not think ill of them for behaving like healthy young men. Being unhappy will not bring Marabelle back. They just want to release some energy after all that has transpired. I cannot fault them for it."

We both turned to stare at the blue water. It did

look inviting, and part of me really could not blame them at all. Perry swam over to the base of the waterfall where Marik trod water. Perry splashed his friend, and we heard them both laugh. Perry then swam towards the handsome Indian. Marik opened his arms and Perry drew closer. Puzzled, I watched them embrace. And then all the breath suddenly disappeared from my lungs, as their mouths joined together in a passionate kiss.

Chapter Twenty

"WAIT, JILLIAN." I IGNORED DOMINIC'S request as I rushed to put as much distance between myself and the lagoon. I all but ran, though I did not know why.

"Jillian," Dominic said louder, and the tone in his voice made me slow down and allow him to draw level with me. He took my hands and pulled me to a stop. "Come on, Jilly. Do not be troubled by what you saw."

The image of the two men kissing found its way to my mind and I shuddered. "But they were together—like a man and a woman. It was all so—wrong."

He gave a heavy sigh. "I grant you 'tis shocking to see two men in that way, especially when it is the first time. But you have to understand it is not so unusual. Some men cannot feel an attraction to a woman, by no choice of their own—and that is the case with Perry and Marik. I have long thought it odd Perry has not been attached to anyone nor married. But I never guessed it was because of this. They have been careful to hide their relationship." Dominic's expression was thoughtful, and he showed no disgust or condemnation.

"They were not hiding much just then," I snapped. "To behave that way—in public."

"Yes, Jilly. It was foolish."

And he was right. Even I knew such behaviour was against the law.

"They were reckless," he added. "For anyone could

have seen them and then there would be trouble. Come." He tugged me to begin walking again. "Let us go back to the farm, and we'll have some refreshment. I am parched from the heat, and you must be too."

THE WALK BACK TO WOLFE FARM was quiet. I still filtered through what I had witnessed at the lagoon. I was surprised by how shocking I found their actions. Of course, I was aware there were men who did not seek the company of women, but I had never witnessed it first-hand. Images of Perry and Marik at Hollyfield, and on the few occasions I had been in their company, whirled around my head. I replayed the scenes, searching for a glimpse of something I had not registered before. It was not repulsion or disgust which consumed me. I was quite simply shocked.

After a tall mug of cool water, I calmed. Standing in the kitchen with my back resting against the mantel, I watched Dominic pour himself a drink.

"I am sorry," I began. "I do not know why I overreacted. It was wrong of me."

Dominic smiled and came to stand before me. He cupped my chin in his hand and tilted my face to look into his own. "Oh, Jillian," he said softly. "I understand. For most people, witnessing two men acting in a romantic way would be unsettling because they are unused to it." He bent his head, and his lips brushed my own. Then he stepped away. "In London, I knew many men like Perry and Marik, especially within the artistic community. I learned long ago to think of it as natural. 'Tis just one human being caring for another when it comes down to it, after all. "

I could agree with that, but yet the notion was still

foreign to me.

"Imagine," he continued. "How it must feel to love another and live within a society which condemns you. Indeed, it was not so long ago, men were put to death for engaging in a relationship with another of their sex. A cruel and unjust punishment, and I am glad it is no longer so."

"You are right," I said. "No person should die because they care for another. Yet it is still against the law for two men to conduct an affair, is it not?"

"Yes. In the eyes of the world, or at least most countries, it is considered an unnatural act for the same gender to feel passion. Perry is foolhardy displaying any sign of affection to Marik while in public."

"Will you tell Perry we saw them?"

"I shall say I was there, but I prefer not to mention you, Jillian. It is right they should know so in future they'll not be so reckless."

I finished my water and placed the mug in the sink while I mulled over Dominic's words. He was far more liberal-minded than I, yet I agreed with his opinions and I had no right to judge them. There had never been the need to think about the subject before. But how would I feel when I saw Perry again? Would I think of him differently now? Perhaps.

Dominic walked with me from the farm back to the road. "Do this one thing for me, it might help you understand. Imagine if you will, a world where you and I could show one another affection in public. If it were so, I would embrace you and kiss you farewell right now. But society dictates if would be improper, that we cannot show our affection without a ring. If I kissed you here and now, your reputation would be tarnished should we be seen. Perry and Marik can never have a ring to bind their love. They are forced to hide their feelings for one another. In the eyes of the world their love is considered an unnatural love. That is how it is to be a homosexual."

Something in my mind suddenly clicked into place. I gasped.

"What is it?" he asked with concern.

"In the eyes of the world, it is unnatural," I repeated Dominic's words. "Remember, the note said *unnatural*." Dominic's face was blank.

"Dominic, Billy's piece of paper was from a blackmail note. Whoever wrote it referred to an unnatural act, and—"

"Dear God, you are right," Dominic said in wonder. "Flynn must have been blackmailing Marik and Perry as well."

THE NEXT DAY UNCLE JASPER LEFT for Wadham University in Oxford and would be gone overnight. Dominic planned to contact Victor, and visit Billy, but promised to stop by on his way home later in the day. There was nothing more to be done regarding Flynn until Victor had been brought up to date. By mutual agreement, we determined it was better for Victor to remain ignorant of our suspicions that Perry might be another victim of Flynn's blackmail. Instead, Dominic would speak with Perry at the first opportunity, rather than cause the family any more trouble. They had already endured enough.

I was finishing up with a particularly tricky transcription when I heard a carriage outside, and I got up to look out of the study window. It was Evergreen

LaVelle come to see me. I opened the front door before she had a chance to knock and bade her come in.

She was dressed in black, befitting for her state of mourning. Yet the jaunty angle of her little hat mocked the solemnity of her costume. Evergreen dropped into the armchair facing my own, waved away my offer of tea and gave a theatrical sigh.

"It has been abysmal at home," she complained, her brow knotted with annoyance.

"I can imagine," I soothed. "Losing a family member is never easy."

"Nonsense," she snapped. "I wasn't referring to my clumsy cousin falling off a balcony, but the herd of miserable, boring relatives who came to pay their respects to Father. I cannot believe I am related to such a dull set of people, Jillian." She rolled her eyes in distaste. "Of course, they are all Mother's side of the family. I much prefer the Symingtons in India. Only the stodgy ones live in England."

I shook my head and swallowed my admonishment. It would serve no purpose. Evergreen LaVelle might be educated and rich, but she sorely lacked manners. Instead, I asked after her father.

"Oh, he is busy as usual. Dominic came to the house this morning, and they've been closeted in the study the entire time." She spread her gloved hand on her lap and stared at it. "From what I hear, you are spending a great deal of time with our bohemian painter, Jillian. I have known Dom long enough that I can help you if there is anything you want to know about him?" She smiled, but it was feline. I wondered again if she harboured feelings for Dominic.

"No, thank you. I do not require your assistance.

Dominic and I are friends—lord knows he has needed them in abundance since Billy's arrest. There is no peace to be had for him, well, not until Billy is acquitted."

"Acquitted?" She was aghast. "Why would that happen? The boy killed Jareth Flynn, and he'll swing for it." Her voice carried no compassion. Indeed, I even detected a small gleam in her eye. How could Evergreen be pleased Billy Wolfe might hang?

"The fact his knife was used does not constitute his guilt." I chastised. "A thorough investigation is still ongoing. Billy deserves a fair trial."

"Jillian, you are new around here, and consequently, I bear that in mind when I listen to what you say. But mark my words, that idiot boy has always been strange. As a matter of fact, he has even scared me a time or two, though I never told Father, nor Dominic, for that matter."

I stared at her pretty face in disbelief. Was she being honest? I could not tell, yet instinctively I did not believe her. Evergreen LaVelle would never be easily scared. I doubted she would hesitate to report Billy's behavior if he had made her uncomfortable. I decided to change the subject. "How well did you know Jareth Flynn?"

Her shift in posture was noticeable, and I sensed her discomfort. This pleased me.

"Why on earth are you asking me that? You know, Jillian, your propensity for bluntness can be most disconcerting, but sometimes it is insulting." She was profoundly displeased.

"I do not mean to offend you," I placated. "But I would like to know about your relationship with the blacksmith."

Evergreen got to her feet and walked over to the parlour window. She stood with her back to me for a few moments and then turned to face me. I could see her irritation by the rigidity of her posture, and her colour was up. "I take it you have a good reason for this impertinent question?"

I nodded.

"Oh, all right, I will tell you. I knew Flynn as a friend. But you cannot tell another soul because my father would kill me if he found out." She walked back to take her vacated seat. "Look, Jillian. I got myself into a little predicament in London. Nothing too terrible, but Father was livid about it. He sent me to Hollyfield to keep me out of trouble and for me to pay penance. I was bored out of my mind. I met Flynn when my horse threw a shoe. Of course, he was not the kind of person I would ordinarily associate with, but then, I could say the same about you."

I ignored her barb.

"The man was friendly, handsome, and he made me laugh. We became friends. And that is all."

"How often did you meet?"

"I beg your pardon."

"Jareth. Did you and he meet up as friends from time to time?"

She had the decency to blush. It answered my question, but I was not yet finished. "When did you last see him?"

"The day before they found his body. We met near our boathouse as he had business at Hollyfield." I wondered what that business was but did not press her. Frankly, I was surprised she had told me even this much.

"Jillian, I had nothing to do with what happened to the man. I admit to being guilty of a little flirtation, but that is all."

"Yet you are convinced Billy Wolfe killed him. A boy in a man's body, who had no motive to kill Flynn."

"Yes, he did." Her voice was firm. "Jareth teased Billy all the time, and he probably just snapped."

"If that were the case, he would have hit the man, not killed him."

"Oh, so now you are a sleuth? It seems you are bent on putting the blame elsewhere."

"Perhaps it is that I do not understand your intense dislike of Billy. How can you think him a lower life form because he has an affliction which he was born with?"

"What would you know about my feelings?"

"I know you are harsh whenever you speak of him, that you despise his condition. But why? What has Billy ever done to you?" I already knew. Billy had the audacity to be an unwelcome, unwanted half-brother. I did not tell her I was privy to the family's secret. I wondered if she would tell me herself.

She returned to her seat. "Jillian, you know nothing of me or the LaVelles, yet you are very swift to judge. I come from an ambiguous family. On my father's side, we are from hardworking-class stock. My mother's family were aristocratic, and frankly prone to nervous dispositions, especially the women." She sighed. "Mother lost two children before Perry and I were born. Vincent was stillborn, and Lucien lived for six weeks. By the time she gave birth to twins while living in India, it took much out of her. According to our ayah,

Simka, Mother often spoke of her lost boys as though they were still alive. She spent much time in her sickbed, and Simka took care of Perry and me. I do not know what was wrong with our mother. It was most likely depression. Because she committed suicide when we were two years old."

I gasped, "Oh, no." I felt shame in goading her. The poor girl was unhappy and with good reason. To lose her mother at such a young age was tragic.

"So, you see, Jillian, I have experienced what mental illness does first-hand. If I am cruel in my opinion of Billy, then so be it, I make no apology. Now—" she rose to her feet. "I must be off. I really did just need a break from the miserable house. That is why I came."

I stood up, wracked with guilt. "I am sorry for making you feel worse by dragging up the past. Please accept my apology, Evergreen. I hope I have not made you unhappy."

"Do not concern yourself," she said, reverting to her usual flippant tone. "I have lived with the consequences now for nineteen years. I believe I can manage a little conversation like this."

I walked her to the hallway.

She stopped at the door and turned to me. "Would you be able to visit Hollyfield on Friday? Come for luncheon, Jillian, and spend the afternoon with me." She sensed my hesitation. "Oh, say you can, please, else I shall go mad with being alone."

I desperately wanted to refuse, yet after my indelicacy with her mother, I could not bring myself to decline.

DOMINIC CAME TO THE HOUSE late in the day and I felt ridiculously pleased to see him. We went straight into the kitchen where he gratefully accepted a thick ham sandwich and a frothy mug of ale. Mrs Stackpoole was out visiting a neighbour and we had the house to ourselves.

There were many questions I burned to ask but thought it better to let him sate his hunger first. I initiated the conversation. "Evergreen called today. She was bored from having family company so long and sought to be entertained by me instead."

Dominic frowned. "How did that go? I'll warrant she was as pent up as a caged beast."

"You could say that. I shocked her because I asked about the relationship she had with Flynn."

Dominic raised one thick brow. "You were feeling brave."

"Apparently. Although I was rather surprised because she actually answered my question. Of course, she did not confess to having any type of romantic attachment to him but said it was a light flirtation and that he made her laugh."

"Is that the secret to making a woman yearn for a man, then? Dear me, I shall throw down my paintbrush and learn to be funny." He grinned devilishly, and I smiled back in amusement.

"She also spoke about her mother. I was quite hard on her for the way she talks about Billy, but it seems she has a deep-rooted fear of any type of mental indisposition." I watched Dominic take a sip of ale. "Did you know what happened to her mother?"

He nodded. "Yes, it is no secret, though most people don't speak of it out of respect for the family."

"I was ashamed of myself for being so inconsiderate. Yet Evergreen brushed it off and went on her way. But I did discover she saw Jareth the night before he died. She said he was near the boathouse as he had business at Hollyfield."

"Well, that explains the watch being there. I wonder what business a blacksmith could have with the LaVelles?"

"She did not say. I still think the watch must have come off in a struggle. What if Jareth was there the night before and Evergreen saw something. She will not step forward in order to protect her reputation. For some reason she is intent on naming Billy as the villain, and I wish I knew why."

Dominic pushed away his empty plate. "Evergreen was incensed with Victor when she discovered he was Billy's father. I think she feels tainted by his condition, that it somehow makes her pedigree ignoble. She might not show it, but she is fiercely jealous of anyone receiving her father's attention."

"Really? I would not have guessed that. Evergreen seems to antagonize him at every opportunity."

"A sure way to earn his attention," Dominic said. He was right. It was working. There was far more to Miss LaVelle than met the eye.

Dominic pushed his chair back from the table but did not rise. I got up and went around to take away his plate, but he grasped my wrist and pulled me onto his lap. His thighs were firm and strong as he easily supported my weight. His arm encircled my waist while mine slid up to wrap around his neck. I savoured the sweet moment of anticipation before his lips met mine and lost myself in the warmth of his kiss. It was

The Secret of Hollyfield House

endless, and when we finally broke for air, my mouth felt deliciously stung and swollen.

His breathing matched my own, and as we looked into one another's eyes, he gently traced a line down my cheek with a finger. "You are so beautiful, Jilly. You are like a siren, with your cat's eyes and sable hair. My god, I am tormented with the need to either take you to my bed or paint you."

Warmth enveloped my cheeks. No one had ever spoken to me in this manner. Desire pulsed through my veins as I relished the flattery while simultaneously feeling shy. "I am unsure how to respond and maintain my ladylike reputation," I stammered weakly.

Dominic stared at me for a moment and then gave a short laugh. "Oh, I have embarrassed you? I am sorry." He leaned back to see my face better. "I meant it as a compliment sweet Jilly. It was not my intention to make you uncomfortable."

He was so sincere. I moved my face closer to his, while the stirring in my body throbbed like a drumbeat. Much to my own surprise, I initiated a passionate, deep kiss.

When the kitchen door handle turned, I leapt to my feet and hit my knee against the table.

"I'm back, Miss Jillian—" Mrs Stackpoole stepped into the kitchen and stopped in her tracks as she saw Dominic at the table, and me red-faced, rubbing my knee.

"Oh, I'm sorry. I didn't realise you were keepin' company this evenin'." Her face registered disapproval, enough for me to recognise her opinion of my being unchaperoned, alone in the house with a man.

"It is only Dominic, Mrs Stackpoole. He is back

from Kendal and thought to see my uncle. I shared a sandwich with him. We were just speaking of the funeral yesterday."

The mention of the funeral did precisely what I had hoped. Mrs Stackpoole's judgmental expression changed instantly as the insatiable village gossip within her took charge.

"Now that was a strange affair, was it not?" The older woman settled herself across from Dominic. "I never before saw a family in such a hurry to put a body in the ground. Didn't even stay to see all the mourners as we came out of the church. Shockin' manners if you ask me. An' them the gentry."

Dominic pretended to agree. I could see him preparing to stand and make his escape. I did not blame him. His day had already been long, yet I was reluctant for him to leave without telling me about his meeting with Victor.

"I'll not tarry. If you will excuse me, Mrs Stackpoole." He rose and gifted her with a smile.

"I haven't chased you off now, have I, Dominic? 'Twas not my intent I assure you." She gave him a beguiling glance.

"Not at all. I have been gone the better part of the day. I should get back to the farm and tend the animals before they run away to find somewhere else to eat their dinner." He glanced my way. "Can you stop by tomorrow at your earliest convenience, Jillian?"

"Yes, of course."

"Well, then I bid you ladies both a good night." He turned and went out of the kitchen door, leaving a vacuum in the room where he had been.

WITH THE HOUSE SECURED FOR THE night and the lamps doused, Mrs Stackpoole bade me goodnight and we retired to our respective rooms. I lay in bed. Undulating thoughts filled my head, most centred around Dominic and our time together. I examined the catalogue of memories I had already amassed with him. Had it been just a few weeks since we had met? Strange, but it was difficult to picture my life without him being a part of it now. How different might it have been, had Billy not been arrested? Indeed, it was surprising our relationship had managed to even start under these terrible circumstances.

I reached over to my night table and on impulse did not extinguish the lamp but opened the drawer to retrieve the tin containing the moonstone. Its presence had slipped my mind with everything else going on in the past week. But now I held it in my fingers and studied its bright iridescence. Who had given this to my mother? Was it a man she truly loved? My thoughts went to Dominic. Had she felt as strongly for this stranger as I did for Dominic Wolfe? The idea surprised me. What did I feel for the handsome artist? Love? Affection? Compassion?

I closed my eyes. I did not want to love Dominic Wolfe. For everyone I loved always left me.

Chapter Twenty-One

I WALKED TO WOLFE FARM AND my fingers toyed with the moonstone in my pocket. I had fallen asleep with the gem in my hand, and for some reason felt the compunction to keep it on my person today. There was such significance to the stone, or at least there had been to my mother at one point in her life. Regardless, somehow it made me feel closer to her.

It was early, but I knew Dominic would already be up and busy tending the livestock. I was certain he would not mind my coming. The morning promised yet another beautiful day. Birdsong trilled in the air. Even the creatures were happy it was almost summertime.

I found Dominic in the stables, mucking out the stalls.

"Good morning, Jillian." He paused and leaned on the pitchfork. "I'd greet you more warmly, but I smell of manure."

I laughed, noting the sweat beading upon his brow. He had clearly been working for some time.

"Can I help?" It seemed a feeble offer, but I made it anyway.

"Not out here. But if you've a mind to put the kettle on, I'll come in presently and share a mug with you?"

I nodded and left him to his work.

By the time Dominic joined me in the kitchen, the

kettle had boiled, and sausages sizzled in the frying pan. I was not sure if he had breakfasted, but the look of delight he threw my way told me he had not. I had warmed a pan of water, and I poured it into a tin bowl so he could clean his face and hands. It did not take long, and while he washed, I fried eggs and a piece of crusty bread.

I joined him at the table with a hot mug of tea and watched with interest as he devoured the plate of food I placed before him. While he ate, I showed him the moonstone.

"Where did you get that?" he asked, taking it from my hand. He examined it carefully and held it up to the light. He frowned. "It is a pretty pendant. You don't have an admirer I should know about do you?"

I laughed. "Of course not. It belonged to my mother. It seems she was the one with an admirer, before she met my father. Apparently, a mysterious man gave her the moonstone, and when their relationship ended, Mother left it in my uncle's care. I found it tucked into the back of a wardrobe, and Uncle Jasper told me its history."

Dominic handed it back. "Well, now you have unearthed a hidden treasure, you should let me find you a chain so you can wear it as a necklace. My mother had inexpensive pieces of jewellry. I will look and see if I can find one which might fit."

"Oh no, Dominic," I said quickly. "I couldn't take something that belonged to your mother." I put the stone back in my pocket and met his even stare. He looked as though he wanted to say something else and then changed his mind. The moment was awkward.

"I am curious about your meeting with Victor

yesterday." I changed the subject, anxious to get on a more comfortable footing with him.

He took a sip of his tea. "Yes, it was unfortunate Mrs Stackpoole decided to interrupt us last evening before I could tell you." He grinned, and a wicked light shone in his amber eyes. "Though perhaps it was fortuitous, for I might not have behaved myself at all."

My cheeks grew warm, but I was not embarrassed—in fact, quite the opposite. I liked this man's attention and praise.

"How did you find Victor?"

"Suffocating in a houseful of well-meaning relatives who are sorely trying his patience. However, we had a good conversation, and he brought me up to date with Kemp's findings."

"What did he say?"

"Kemp plans to introduce the idea that Billy's knife was used by another to kill Flynn. Therefore, either intentionally or by chance putting Billy in the frame for murder. He will introduce Peggy Nash's information, though he does not expect it to hold well because of her mental state and lack of credibility. But it lends itself to support the theory of his innocence. With the discovery of Flynn's financial obligations to a few dubious characters, it provides other candidates with motives far outweighing my brother's. Whenever there is violence, it is common to find money issues at its heart."

"And what of the blackmail?" This was shaky ground.

Dominic leaned back in his chair with a deep sigh. "That is where things become murky, Jillian. There is evidence in the scrap of paper found that Flynn was a blackmailer. But as Victor points out, we would have to compare the writing to identify him as its author. If it is proved he wrote the note, then who was it sent to? As far as Victor is concerned, Louisa Mountjoy is his only victim. We cannot name her in a court of law and expose her relationship to the blacksmith."

It was my turn to sigh. "And you cannot tell Victor about Evergreen and Flynn's relationship, or what we know of Perry and Marik, all three potential blackmail victims, without exposing everything and disgracing the family."

"Not to mention Perry and Marik breaking the law. That type of scandal could ruin Victor, and possibly be the downfall of his business too."

"But those are the most incriminating reasons for Flynn to have been killed—wouldn't that, and other evidence of his gaming debts be enough to introduce doubt of Billy's guilt?"

"Yes." His tone was resolute. He assuredly had dwelled on this information since speaking to Victor.

"So, we are stuck."

"It seems we are. At least for the time being. The trial date is coming up. If only we could find another person besides Peggy who saw Billy that day, and could place my brother away from the murder scene—" The utter frustration in his voice tore at my heart.

"Well then, Mr Wolfe." I smiled with a forced bravado I did not feel. "I suggest we get busy."

MY UNCLE HAD COME HOME WITH a new project from Leicester University which totally absorbed his thoughts. Upon his return he gave me a perfunctory kiss on the cheek and then disappeared into his study, simultaneously exclaiming, "I shall take all my meals in here until I am finished with this damnable essay." True to his word, he remained closeted for the entire evening, even chasing away Mrs Stackpoole, who was completely affronted by the rejection. I soothed her frayed ego with a cup of tea and kind compliments about the fabric of her dress, counting each moment until she would settle. I desperately wanted to go up to my room and think without interruption. Perhaps I was a little like my uncle, after all.

Later that evening, I sat at my small writing table studying the blank piece of paper before me. I was not sure where to start. There were so many loose ends to this puzzle. If I could just write it all down, then I might see a pattern. I began to note everything I had learned since first meeting Evergreen. As I listed the names of the people I had met, and the events which had taken place, I noticed her name more than any other kept cropping up. Could Evergreen LaVelle be the link between everyone?

There were obvious people with reason to take issue with Jareth Flynn and subsequently wish him dead. But wanting someone dead was still a far cry from perpetuating murder. I sighed. This was a messy tangle indeed, and the days were passing swiftly. Before too long, Billy Wolfe would be on trial, and his life hung in the balance.

If I had ever suspected Billy of murder, those suspicions had been vanquished time and again as we discovered many others had their secrets. It was despicable for the killer to target the poor boy, lay the blame at his feet, knowing he would have no chance of proving his innocence.

Therefore, I should look at it this way. Who stood to gain by getting rid of Billy? Were they killing two birds with one stone? I made a mental note to talk to Dominic about this new theory. After all, it really did make sense to look at it from a fresh angle.

Billy Wolfe. I had met him only briefly, and I did not know his personality other than what had been relayed by others. But if I could speak with him, then surely I would get a better understanding of who he was? That, in turn, might help me determine who his enemies were.

It was apparent the LaVelle children did not care for his association as half-brother to them both. Neither Evergreen nor Perry acknowledged Billy. Moreover, Evergreen made no secret of her disdain for the boy. But it would be an exceptionally cruel and vindictive person who would label him a murderer and watch him hang on the end of a gibbet. Owning a blood relationship to a mentally challenged sibling might be burdensome for a perfect family like the LaVelles. But watching an innocent boy swing was evil beyond redemption.

I concluded that I would ask Dominic to take me with him on his next visit to the Kendal Gaol. Would he be comfortable with my request? I did not know. Perhaps he might enjoy the company on what must be such an emotionally arduous task.

Dominic's visage filled my thoughts. I held great admiration for him. Other than the undeniable pull of attraction between us, as I watched him navigate this worrisome and challenging time with his brother, it brought home to me what an unusually good man he was. Dominic had lost his only opportunity to become a successful artist in London by returning to care for Billy after their parents' death. Now he faced a terrifying consequence should Billy be found guilty. Yet, somehow, he still maintained a sense of decency and tried to keep things as normal as possible. Was I in love with Dominic? Did I see him through the bewitched eyes of one under his spell? Possibly.

It was little wonder a man like him could interest me. I knew myself to be on the precipice of a new journey in life now both my parents were gone. I had no family, save Uncle Jasper. And by the looks of things, his relationship with Mrs Stackpoole continued to prosper. At some point, I would need to reconsider my prospects and where I might live, should the two of them form their own union.

There was much to think on. I set down my pen and stared at the paper with my scribbles. First, I would talk to Billy Wolfe. There was something both Dominic and I were missing in this story. Though I could not see it, I was aware it lingered in the corners of my mind and knew it was only a matter of time before clarity came. For now, I would focus upon the mess at hand. In that precise moment, something inside me budded. Finally, I felt as though I had real purpose. I closed my eyes, making a promise to myself. I would determine what had happened to Jareth Flynn and Marabelle Pike, if it were the last thing I would do.

DOMINIC CALLED BY LATER IN THE day. I waited until we were sat in the kitchen before I asked permission to see his brother.

He was surprised by my request. "I am not sure if that is wise, Jillian. After all, Billy is in a state of flux as it is. He might be confused as to your intent."

I had already considered this. "I realise that. But I can tell him I have checked on the calves to make sure they are faring well. Billy would like that, don't you think? I also have a new book for him to read. He might even enjoy seeing someone different for a change?"

He was not convinced. Dominic was extremely protective of his younger brother, which was commendable. Yet at this stage in our investigation, we needed anything we could grasp.

"Look, Dominic. What is there to lose at this point? We have been so focused upon the victims in this crime that we have not considered Billy a victim himself. How could it hurt to explore the theory, see if there is another angle we have missed? I do not know Billy well, so I will not be as biased in my appraisal of him, as you and even Victor are. I will not be threatening either, so he should feel comfortable talking to me. Especially if you tell him I am to come ahead of time."

Dominic's shoulders sagged. I felt badly for him. I laid a hand on his forearm. "Dear man, I have naught but the desire to help you. I believe your brother is innocent, and I only want the chance to see what I can do to prove it."

He looked up at me then, and my breath caught in my throat when I saw the pain shining in his beautiful eyes. Dominic had already borne so much. How brave he was keeping his emotions in check, concealing the weight of his concerns each and every day.

"Then you may see him, Jillian. I will ask permission at the gaol today."

"Thank you." I smiled with as much reassurance as I could muster. He was exhausted, and my heart went out to him. But as I looked at his face, a knot of fear gnawed in the pit of my belly. Because I realised that if Billy Wolfe hanged for a crime he did not commit, I did not know what Dominic would do.

Chapter Twenty-Two

DOMINIC JOINED US FOR DINNER on Sunday evening. I found his appearance worrisome. I comprehended that as the days drew closer to Billy's trial, so Dominic's concerns and fears increased. This was evident in the harsh set of his features, the shadows under his eyes. Dear God, I hoped I could ease his distress.

After dinner, Dominic seemed in a hurry to leave. This would have been disappointing except when he bade farewell to Uncle and Mrs Stackpoole, he asked me to go along with him, at least to the end of our street. It was a beautiful night, and I readily agreed. I took my shawl to wrap across my shoulders as there was a little chill in the air.

As soon as we were outside, he spoke. "I go to see Billy in the morning, Jillian. I have permission from the gaol for you to come with me."

I linked my arm through his. "That is good news, Dominic. What time shall I be ready?"

"We can meet in the village for the ten-o'clock coach, if it suits you?"

"Yes, that will be fine." We had already reached the last house in the street.

Dominic stopped under the gaslight and then turned to face me. "Jilly," he said softly. "You are the kindest, loveliest person I know. I'll never be able to thank you enough for all you have done—*are* doing to help my family." He leaned forward and placed a soft kiss on my lips.

The sensation was tender, and tears pricked my eyes. As Dominic pulled back, I studied his face intently.

"I wish I could make your problems disappear. You and Billy are so undeserving of all that has happened. I cannot tell you how I admire the way you have dealt with this dark episode in your life. Your kindness, dignity, and grace in such a time of turmoil are an example to the rest of us. I am so fortunate to count you as my dearest friend." My voice wavered.

Dominic reached up and wiped a tear from my face with the pad of his thumb, and then slowly caressed my bottom lip. "And you are mine, Jilly. I could not endure this without you by my side." He became quiet, yet his eyes told me his desires. I kissed his thumb, and we both smiled.

"Until tomorrow," he said softly.

I RECOGNISED MANY OF THE landmarks on our way to Kendal, for I had accompanied Evergreen not so long ago. But where the town had brought joy and a happy day of shopping, visiting the gaol brought me low.

The constabulary was a dreary old building, and though the attached gaol had been added on in later years, it was shabby, dismal, and unclean. Dominic preceded me through the myriad of locked gates until we finally arrived at a row of cells. The air was damp, and there was an odour of unwashed bodies and unsanitary conditions borne in the air.

As the young constable stopped in front of the first metal door, I composed myself and fought against the acid in my throat, bobbing in protest at the disgusting smell of the place.

He pulled a large circlet of keys from his belt and banged on the door. "Step away, Billy, you've visitors here." He unlocked the door and then pushed it open. "In you go then, an' mind you don't upset him. He kept us up half the night with his shoutin'."

Dominic nodded assent, and I followed him into the cell.

Billy lay on his side upon a narrow cot, his arms wrapped around bent knees which he hugged to his chest. At the sight of Dominic, he sat up, and I was shocked at how thin he had become. The robust chubby boy I remembered had been replaced by a hollow-cheeked youth, and the light in his eyes was snuffed.

"'Tis you, Dom," he said, getting to his feet. The brothers embraced, and the sight was so moving I swallowed hard to compose myself.

"Look, Billy. Miss Jillian has come to see you like I promised. Do you remember her?" Dominic gestured to where I stood. The boy stared at me for a moment with a puzzled expression on his face.

I smiled broadly. "Hello, Billy," I said. "I wanted to come and tell you I have visited your cows and they look very well."

He blinked. "Did you see 'em babies too?"

"Yes," I reassured. "They are getting very fat and growing taller each day."

"I miss 'em, I do." He looked crestfallen, and at once, I felt guilty.

"Do not be sad," I said with as much assertion as I could muster. "They will still be there when you come home." I caught Dominic's quick glance my way and understood he was chastising me for making false promises.

"Billy," Dominic said. "Miss Jillian wants to ask you some questions. Would you mind?" He led his brother back to the bed, and they both sat down. "I know you've had to talk to a lot of people. But Jillian is my dear friend, so that makes her your friend as well. She's trying to help us."

"Tired of talkin', Dom. Makes my head hurt, it does."

"I understand. But Billy, you know I wouldn't ask you unless it was really important."

Billy nodded, and Dominic looked my way. There was a small wooden stool over by one wall. I set it near the bed and sat down. I had to look up to meet the stares of the Wolfe brothers, but I thought it a good idea to have my head lower than Billy's—I would seem less intimidating that way.

"Billy. I want to talk to you about your work at Hollyfield."

He gave a nod.

I smiled. "I know you work very hard for the LaVelle family."

Another nod. "That Victor, I like him—he's da number two. Right, Dom?" He looked at his brother.

"Yes, Billy."

"Are you friends with the rest of the family?" I said gently. "Or the other people who work at Hollyfield?"

Billy gave a little grin. "I like that pretty girl who dusts an' mops. She's got yellow hair an' sometimes gives me a biscuit from the kitchen."

"That's lovely," I said. "She is nice to do that. What about the other ladies at the House? Do you know

Miss Marabelle?"

He nodded. "Her face is always sad," he said. "An' she don't say much to me."

"And Miss Evergreen?" I added.

Billy's expression changed entirely, and his demeanour became agitated. His eyes started to look around the cell, not settling upon anything in particular. The mention of his half-sister's name had provoked a strong reaction.

"Does Miss Evergreen ever speak to you, Billy?"

He did not reply.

"Come, Billy," prompted his brother. "'Tis all right to talk to Jillian like you are talking to me. Don't be afraid." He squeezed his brother's hand.

Billy's eyes met mine, and at once, I saw how troubled they were. What was this then? Something had definitely happened to make him so reluctant to speak of her.

"Please, Billy, it is so helpful if you answer my questions. You won't get in any trouble by talking about Miss Evergreen to me. I promise."

Billy licked his lips. "She don't like me," he said. "She calls me bad names."

I steeled myself. I could not show how his words affected me. The time for empathy would come later. "What sort of names?" I asked.

"She says I'm stupid an' a fat idiot. She don't want me near the house."

Dominic stiffened—this was difficult for him to hear. I hoped he would remain quiet.

"Why do you think Evergreen says those nasty things, Billy?"

"'Cause, she don't want to be my sister. She only

likes Perry an' Marik and Dom. She don't like Miss Marabelle neither. I heard her shoutin' at her I did." He looked at Dominic as though he had just shared a secret. Dominic said nothing but put an arm about his brother's shoulders.

"Is Miss Evergreen mean to anyone else?"

Billy looked as though he was thinking hard. Then he gave a sly grin. "Well, I thought she was being mean, 'cause it looked like she was tryin' to squash him. But then he started laughin', so I thought she was ticklin' him instead." Beside him, Dominic frowned. I pressed on.

"Who was it you saw her with, Billy?"

"She was playin', and her top come down. An' he just laughed an' tickled her as well. I ain't never seen Miss Evergreen like that afore. He must be her best friend."

"Who was she playing with?" This time it was Dominic who asked.

Billy turned to him and grinned. "Jareth. They was rollin' on the ground getting' grass stuck in her hair. They was havin' fun until they saw me."

"What happened then?" I asked, holding my breath.

Billy's face grew frightened. "He's a big bully. He did chase me through the woods, an' I got away, an' he never caught me. I hid near the bunnies."

"That was clever, Billy," I said. "Were you scared the blacksmith would come and find you later?"

"I were at first, but I never saw him. Then she come an' seen me in the woodshed after that day. She called me bad names, an' I was frightened she might tell on me."

"Miss Evergreen?" I prompted.

He nodded vigorously. "I never hurt her ever, but she said if I told about the blacksmith ticklin' her, she'd tell Victor I hurt her. Said I'd get in lots of trouble an' be sent to the madhouse and then she'd kill all the baby bunnies too." His eyes grew teary, and he looked at his brother. "Don't let her kill the bunnies, Dom. Them are just little babies."

"The bunnies are safe," Dominic said quickly. "No one has hurt them."

I had an idea. "Peggy Nash is looking after the bunnies, Billy. You know Peggy, don't you?"

"My friend." He smiled. "Gives me honey drops an' I like 'em."

"Do you remember the last time you saw Peggy?" I continued.

He thought for a moment, and I knew it would be hard for Billy to parse time into real events, but it was worth a try.

"We was lookin' at the bunnies."

"She sounds like a nice friend. Were you looking at the bunnies with Peggy before the bully chased you, or was it after the bully chased you?"

"Oh, it were after. Peggy saw me an' I was out of breath. I told Peggy the blacksmith's a bad man an' he chased me. She don't like him neither. He calls her names too." He looked at Dominic. "Did you bring me humbugs, Dom?"

Dominic gave me a swift look conveying the questioning needed to be at an end as he rummaged in his pocket and handed Billy a small twist of paper containing several of the flavoured sweets. As the boy sucked on the mints, he looked at the book I had brought him and told us how much he liked the pictures of the train.

I kept quiet for the remainder of our visit. I watched closely as Dominic calmly conversed with the boy showing such dedication towards him. What other man would be so kind?

At length, Dominic rose to go. I left the cell first to allow them privacy as they said their goodbyes. Neither of us spoke until we stepped back into the fresh air with the gaol behind us.

"I cannot believe Evergreen has been so cruel to your brother." It burst out of me before I could censor my tone. I was angry with her for picking on a boy who was unable to defend himself or articulate his feelings.

"It is typical of her," Dominic said in a monotone voice. "She has always been frightfully nasty to anyone she is jealous of."

I stopped in my tracks. "Evergreen jealous of your brother? That is a ridiculous notion." Dominic was not thinking straight. I caught back up with him. "I don't understand your meaning."

"'Tis simple." He said as we moved aside to allow a woman with several children room to pass on the pavement. "Evergreen has always detested seeing another as the recipient of her father's attention. She disliked Marabelle for the same reason. It incenses her that Victor acknowledges Billy, because in her eyes he is a simpleton and unworthy of that privilege." He grasped my arm and guided me across the street towards where we would wait for the Ambleside coach.

"Yet you do not sound affected by her opinion, Dominic?" And he did not. There was no outrage, He was curiously quiet.

"I have long since stopped being shocked by the behaviour of women like Evergreen. Remember," he added. "I was in London while she was the toast of the town. Nothing she does surprises me."

"Even her affair with Jareth Flynn?"

This time he stopped, and I did the same. I looked hard at his face and saw a mixture of emotion pass through his eyes. Something shifted inside me. What was this about?

"It appears our blacksmith was a target for many bored and lonely women in Ambleside," he said. "That Evergreen partook is no surprise to me. What bewilders me is that she would be so careless. It was a similar affair which brought her to Hollyfield in the first place. If Victor ever finds out about Flynn, he will no doubt send her away and she'll lose her inheritance." He began to walk again. "Come Jillian. I see our coach; we must hurry else we will miss it."

THE CARRIAGE WAS FULL, AND NEITHER one of us had much to say as it rumbled through the countryside. When we arrived in Ambleside, Dominic invited me to eat lunch with him, and we made our way to a tearoom across from the pub.

We ordered cheese sandwiches and a pot of tea. The place was quiet, and we were seated out of earshot from the other patrons.

"Thank you for visiting my brother," Dominic said earnestly. "The gaol is no place for a lady, and I know how abhorrent you found it." He reached over the table and took my hand. "The way you questioned Billy was both compassionate and brilliant. You instinctively seemed to know the best approach. I am pleasantly shocked by how open and responsive he was to your gentle coaxing." His eyes shone. "Well done, Jilly. Well done indeed." He released my hand.

"Thank you," I replied. "Billy is a bright boy—his brain just uses information differently than most. I kept that in mind while I spoke with him."

The waitress brought over our plates of sandwiches. We thanked her, and she left us to it.

I continued, "Billy's memory of being with Peggy confirms everything she told me about seeing him the day Jareth died. I think Jareth chased Billy away when he was caught with Evergreen. He must have gone back to the boathouse and that is when an altercation occurred. One which made him lose his watch and then ultimately, his life. Billy was nowhere near the boathouse; I just wish we could convince the authorities. It is obvious someone else murdered the man. Lord knows he had enough enemies."

"This situation gets more complex at every turn." Dominic sipped his tea. "I wish we could confide all we know to Victor. I would welcome his expertise to sort it all out."

"Then perhaps it is time you were honest with him? What of Evergreen's threats to Billy? You cannot ignore what she said to him. At some point, you will have to tell Victor everything. Keeping secrets now is simply not worth it. You must put it all on the table and prevent your brother from being found guilty. I know we do not yet have all the answers, but surely this information is sufficient enough to cast doubt for the jury."

"You are right," he agreed, yet his brow furrowed. "But I do not relish having to tell the man his daughter has been cavorting with a blacksmith and that his son loves another man. It will devastate him, Jillian. Victor is a strong and resilient person, but he is only human."

"Who is only human?" We both glanced up at the unexpected interruption. Evergreen LaVelle raised one eyebrow as she stared at Dominic, and I wondered how much of our conversation she had overheard.

Chapter Twenty-Three

"WHY MY UNCLE, OF COURSE," I said quickly. "We were speaking of his growing affection for our housekeeper. Dominic just finished telling me he thought Uncle Jasper was softening as he aged. I implied we humans are not meant to be alone. We crave the companionship of others. Wouldn't you agree?"

Evergreen rolled her eyes. "Goodness, Jillian, what a lot of rubbish. Honestly, you do think the oddest things." She scanned the table. "This is rather cosy. I had no notion the two of you were this well acquainted." She gave a malevolent smile.

"Ah," Dominic replied. "Miss LaVelle isn't always privy to everything going on in Ambleside, after all." His voice was stern.

"Oh, stop," she pouted. "I was passing and saw you through the window. I wanted to ask if you had received your invitation from the Mountjoys?" She glanced first at me and then Dominic. We must have looked blank.

"To their dinner party!" She sounded exasperated. "Really, where have you both been? The invitations were delivered today. It is this coming Saturday. Doesn't that sound marvellous?" Her lovely blue eyes shone.

"No. It seems inappropriate considering recent events," Dominic said disdainfully. "Surely you do not plan to attend. You are in mourning after all."

"Nonsense," she snapped. "It's not as though Marabelle was a close family member, is it? Besides, we have to go. Wilkie Collins has accepted an invitation for the weekend, and the dinner is in his honour."

"The author, Wilkie Collins?" I could not help responding. He was a brilliant writer.

"Yes, who else?" she replied flippantly.

A figure appeared at the window—it was Perry. He knocked on the glass and waved, then gestured to his sister to hurry. Evergreen rolled her eyes. She turned to leave and then paused to look back at me. "Jillian, call on me in the morning, please. There is something important I wish to discuss with you."

Before I could respond, she disappeared in a whirl of skirts. Dominic stared out of the window watching her retreating figure, his expression guarded. I fastened my eyes upon her, and the image of Jareth Flynn formed in my mind, then Billy. My emotions were mixed now I had learned more of who Evergreen LaVelle really was. I was unsure if I even wanted to be her friend.

I WALKED HOME RE-EXAMINING THE remainder of my conversation with Dominic after Evergreen had left the tearoom. He was adamant we refrain from telling Victor everything, at least for a few more days. He reasoned we should have more proof, see what else there might be to discover first. I disagreed. But this was his decision—Billy was his brother, not mine.

Upon arriving home, Uncle Jasper called out a cheery hello, closely followed by a chuckle which sounded very much like Mrs Stackpoole's laugh. I left them to themselves and went up to my room and sank down onto my bed with a sigh. What a strange day. My first and hopefully my last experience visiting a gaol, and then the subsequent information from Billy to think about. It confounded me. All at once I felt drained of energy. A light breeze wafted in through my open bedroom window, and I closed my eyes.

I awoke and found I had slept through the entire afternoon. I rose and hurried downstairs, where Mrs Stackpoole prepared dinner. She cooked mashed potatoes, fresh peas and beef rissoles, with rhubarb and custard for pudding. I ate heartily.

Uncle Jasper showed me our invitation to the Mountjoy's dinner. Our conversation fastened around the subject of Wilkie Collins, the famous author who would be in attendance. Though I did not relish going to the same location where I'd witnessed Marabelle's death not ten days hence, I was enthralled at the notion of meeting a writer of such renown. No doubt Mr Collins was a friend of Louisa's. I would be so honoured meeting the man who had penned a book with the same title as the pendant in my pocket. *The Moonstone* had been a thrilling read from start to finish. I still had my copy, and with thoughts of reading it once again, much to Mrs Stackpoole's, and Uncle Jasper's surprise, I excused myself and had an early night.

AFTER LUNCHEON THE FOLLOWING day, I was alone in the house when I heard a carriage stop outside. I opened the door and found Evergreen standing on the step.

"Evergreen? What brings you here?"

Without answering, she pushed none-too gently

past me and marched straight into the parlour. Fortunately, Uncle Jasper was out on the hills, or she would have made him jump out of his skin.

"I suppose you think yourself too important to do my bidding now, Jillian?" She rounded on me angrily as I followed her into the room.

"I beg your pardon?" I was taken aback by her venomous tone. "Is something amiss, Evergreen?"

"Amiss?" She rounded on me. "Oh, indeed it is. Do you not recall accepting an invitation to Hollyfield House for this very morning? Yet you saw fit not to come? I waited for two hours, and still, you did not appear. I presume there is good reason you did not send word to tell me you had changed your plans?"

I frowned, her words sounding like nonsense to my ears. Then I remembered what she had said at the tearoom. I sighed. "Oh, I am so sorry, Evergreen. It completely slipped my mind. I—"

"Slipped your mind?" she said with disbelief. "An invitation to Hollyfield is so irrelevant it cannot stick in your thoughts?" She glowered at me. "Were you so besotted with Dominic Wolfe that you only had time for him and not me?"

I took a step towards her as my anger sparked. "How dare you speak to me thus, Evergreen. You are not the only person living in Ambleside with whom I am acquainted. If I forgot an invitation so quickly mentioned, then I am truly sorry. That does not give you leave to speak so disrespectfully to me. You might think you are important because you are rich, and live at Hollyfield House, but at this moment all you resemble is a spoiled brat." I snapped.

Her shoulders sagged; the fight gone out of her.

And then she did the unexpected. Evergreen burst out laughing. I had not expected that response, and all at once I found myself laughing too.

"Oh, Jillian," she sighed after we had calmed. "Only you have the gumption to speak to me like that. 'Tis why I am so fond of you, I'm sure."

"Yet you have a strange way of showing it. Look, Evergreen, I really did forget your invitation. Has it occurred to you, that even I get tired sometimes? After seeing you yesterday, I came home and slept the day away. I was so weary."

"You did look a little peaky." She conceded and took a seat by the hearth. "Why don't you make us tea and then I can tell you my plans."

I bade her sit and went to organise refreshment. As I readied the cups and saucers, I thought about my outburst. I wondered if my eagerness to shout at her came not from her tone with me, but rather from what Billy had told me of her dealings with him. I was sure of it. My feelings toward Miss LaVelle had metamorphosed into something I did not yet recognise.

I returned with our drinks and a small plate of blackcurrant tarts. I sat across from Evergreen, and we sampled them. They were delicious.

"Are you going to tell me what important matter warrants all this fuss?" I asked.

She set down her empty tart plate on the side table. "Why the Mountjoy dinner, of course. Jillian, I want you to come to Hollyfield to dress for it."

"What?"

Her eyes gleamed with excitement. "You have been to Hollyfield twice for dinner and worn the same outdated dress."

I gasped. "How dare—"

"Wait." She raised her hand. "I am not trying to insult you. I am being completely frank." She grinned. "Not unlike yourself. But that's beside the point. I have so many things I do not wear, and I would love for you to pick out something for the party."

I cringed. "No, Evergreen. 'Tis kind of you, but I would rather not."

"Why?" She was horrified at my refusal. "What is wrong with you wearing something more befitting a woman of your age? Jillian, your dress is decent enough, but better suited to an old maid than someone as young as you."

I did not reply.

"Look," she said. "Humour me for a moment. Do not take this so personally. The fact is I have many clothes, and you do not. We are friends, so why not stop being proud and say yes. It would be so much fun helping you pick something out. Especially as I have to wear blasted black for the next three months."

I studied her face as she spoke, noticing how agitated she became in her effort to convince me to do her bidding. As she continued her argument, I thought of all I knew about her, and the information which had recently come to light. Evergreen was the one person linking all the recent events together. Spending more time in her company could help me discover some of her secrets. If there was anything to learn which might help Billy, then it was worthwhile indeed.

"Perhaps you are right," I said suddenly, stopping her mid-sentence.

"You'll let me dress you?" she said excitedly.

I nodded in agreement. "But just so we are clear, I

refuse to wear anything pink."

Evergreen clapped her hands together with delight. "Oh, this shall be such a lark. I promise you, Jillian. You shall not regret it!"

I sincerely hoped I would not.

I SET OFF FOR HOLLYFIELD THE NEXT morning without stopping at Wolfe Farm. Dominic had much work to do in the fields, and I did not want to be a distraction. But the walk down Lake Road was pleasant even so, and as usual, I enjoyed watching the livestock in the green fields.

Evergreen was in high spirits, contrasting greatly with the atmosphere of the house, which lay deep in mourning. Black crepe paper adorned the doors and windows of each room, and the servants wore black armbands over their uniforms. Evergreen herself was in a dark grey gown but wore bright ruby earrings in defiance.

"Come up to my chamber," she announced merrily, grasping my arm and tugging me up the vast staircase. I had not been to the second floor at Hollyfield and was at once impressed by the lavish furnishings and beautiful paintings strewn across the walls.

When I followed Evergreen into her bedchamber, I let out a gasp of delight. Her room was so magnificently decorated, I thought I had walked into Aladdin's cave. Such rich colours I had not seen before, and what fabrics! Her bed was adorned with vibrant orange and pink silks, and an abundance of satin pillows. Curtains floated at the open window, as sheer as clouds, adorned with tiny jewels, which twinkled as they caught the sunlight. Sheets of silks hung from the ceiling above the bed, and it was like stepping into an exotic land instead of the heart of the English countryside.

"Oh, Evergreen. This is the loveliest room I have ever seen." I was spellbound. It was magical.

"Nonsense. 'Tis only India silks and such to remind me of when we lived there. I much prefer the eastern colours. The British are so dull, don't you agree?"

I laughed. The girl had more English blood in her veins than I did. Her family probably went back to the Crusades. But I did not comment. I followed her to one part of the room where there stood a massive ornately carved wardrobe.

"Goodness me," I said. "This is a wardrobe? I thought it another room." I grinned and received a glare.

"Stop being silly. I want to show you the dress I have in mind for you to wear. It shall be the perfect complement to your hair."

She swung open the doors to reveal a startling variety of ball gowns hanging inside. I could easily have been standing in a dress shop. Every conceivable colour and fabric greeted my eyes. Though I had not been excited at the prospect of borrowing a dress, now I saw the beauty before me, I was quite swept up in the moment. "Oh, these are stunning, Evergreen. You have such lovely things," I said in admiration.

She all but purred under my flattery. "They are superb, are they not? I suppose that is one advantage to having a wealthy father. He does not complain about my dressmaker's bill. Now—" She reached inside and plucked a garment from the centre. "See what you think. This is the one I selected. Do you like it?" She held out the gown, and I caught my breath.

The silk dress reminded me of a piece of dark jade I had once seen in a shop window. A shade so rich it was almost iridescent. "Evergreen, it is simply gorgeous." I ran my fingers down the length of the fabric. It was soft and cool on my skin. I glanced up at her face, which radiated pleasure.

"I cannot possibly wear something as fine as this," I said wistfully. "'Tis far too pretty for me."

"Nonsense," she snapped, guiding me to stand before a full-length mirror where she held the dress up against me. "Now look. I am right. With your dark hair, the green silk works perfectly, wouldn't you say? We can braid your hair into a loose knot, and you will look wonderful. Well?"

I hesitated. I was torn. My vanity ran on full steam while my common sense hid out of sight. But the truth was, regardless of everything, I wanted to wear the dress. I could at least try it on—where was the harm in that?

Evergreen helped me out of my clothes, and I stood in my undergarments facing the mirror. I felt a little self-conscious as I had no maid and was not used to having another person see me so undressed. Evergreen had grown quiet. I turned to look at her. She stood staring at my reflection, her eyes upon my birthmark.

"Good lord, what on earth is that?" she asked.

I was embarrassed. "A birthmark. One I keep hidden. Do you think it ugly?" I automatically covered it with my hand.

She blinked. "Not especially, I was wondering if the neckline will be too low on the dress. But I think it will conceal it."

"Good, I prefer no one sees it."

She helped me into the gown. "I think that wise. It would only serve to distract." She examined the bodice. "Ah, yes. The neckline is perfect." She fastened the buttons at the back of the dress. "Now, let us take a look at you."

I stepped before the mirror and though my mouth opened, no sound came out. The dress was magnificent. Tight in the bodice, the modest neck square and high. At the waistband, the material fell away in waves of deep green silk, so lustrous that the fabric looked wet. The sleeves were full at the top and narrowed to the wrist where they were secured with tiny pearl buttons.

"I think this suits?" Her voice had lost some enthusiasm.

"Yes, I like it very well."

"Then it is yours to wear on Saturday. You must come here to dress and get ready. My maid, Peters, can do your hair. Then you may ride with us to Mountjoy House. It shall be such fun and we shall make a jolly night of it!"

There followed some hair arranging ideas and after that an enjoyable time of selecting accessories. In truth, I enjoyed myself immensely, and by the time I set off for home it was almost four o'clock in the afternoon. I walked back as though I floated on the air. My head spun with silly delight at the prospect of wearing the pretty dress.

It was only as I went up to my room and looked at the contrast of my bare, dull chamber to Evergreen's sumptuous bedroom that I realised I had forgotten my quest. I had been so wrapped up in silliness and fashion,

I had forgotten Evergreen's cruelty to Billy. Was I so shallow that a fancy gown could sway me from my goal? I had failed in my task, and I was not happy.

Chapter Twenty-Four

DOMINIC HAD BEEN SCARCE ALL WEEK for he was busy with the farm. We had seen one another as frequently as possible but were restricted to meals together, and a stolen kiss here and there. Tonight, I looked forward to seeing him at the grand dinner party almost as eagerly as I anticipated meeting Mr Wilkie Collins. Uncle Jasper was invited and would escort Mrs Stackpoole while I went with the Hollyfield group.

Unlike my previous experience at Mountjoy House, and perhaps in an effort to erase unhappy memories, the place had a festive and jolly air. No society lecture tonight, but rather a gathering of people with a common love of art and literature, not science.

It was thrilling putting on the lovely gown at Hollyfield. Evergreen's maid styled my hair in a loose chignon and dusted a light amount of rouge on my cheekbones and my lips. I felt transformed. But I looked nothing as exotic as my friend. For when Evergreen descended the stairs down to the hall, we collectively gasped. Still respecting the colours of mourning, she was attired in a magnificent black silk Indian sari, the fabric shimmering under small beads of jet. She looked particularly stunning. Her hair was swept into an elaborate arrangement of curls with pieces of jet liberally placed through her gold tresses. The tunic was tailored to hug her body and reached just above her knee. Matching trousers clung to her shapely legs, and on her feet she wore ornate slippers.

As we entered the house, Evergreen elicited much attention from both the ladies and the gentlemen, though for different reasons I knew. I did not mind. I was happy to bask in her shadow as long as Dominic liked how I looked this evening.

In the drawing room, Mr Wilkie Collins, the guest of honour, struck me as a formidable looking gentleman. He held court with a number of his admirers while Louisa stood sentry at his side. Lady Mountjoy looked lovely tonight. Her dark beauty was complemented by a ruby gown, her eyes warmed to the colour of brandy in the soft light of the room. She saw me come in and gestured for me to approach.

I joined her with some trepidation. I had never before met anyone of Mr Collins' ilk. Not only was he famous, but someone I greatly admired.

"Wilkie, here is a dear friend. Jillian Farraday, please meet Mr Wilkie Collins."

He extended a hand, and I shook it. He peered at me through his spectacles, and his eyes went straight to my neck.

"Why, is that a moonstone you have there, Miss Farraday?" He was smiling. I automatically reached to touch the pendant. I had fashioned a chain of sorts so I might wear it. It hung on a thin piece of leather.

"It is, Mr Collins. Though I do not know its origin, it belonged to my mother. I believe it is from India."

He nodded enthusiastically. "Most likely, I'll be bound. They mine for 'em, near Kashmir. My favourite stones. Find 'em fascinating."

"Yes, dear," Louisa agreed. "Hence the title of

your book. Have you read *The Moonstone,* Jillian?"

"Oh, yes. It is a wonderful book. I have read it more than once. I do enjoy your work, Mr Collins and should like to thank you for it."

"Pleasure, my dear," he said kindly. I was then aware of others waiting to meet the author. I made my excuses and stepped away.

When Dominic arrived, I sensed, rather than saw him. I smiled at him as he stood speaking with Perry, and they both approached.

"What do you think of our Miss Farraday, Dom? Does she not look elegant?" I looked at Dominic's face to see his reaction and saw his eyes darken as they raked over my costume.

"Jillian, you look stunning," he said quietly, and I could not help the smile that found my lips. "The colour," he continued, "It brings out the copper in your hair, and your eyes are shining like emeralds. You look like someone from a mystical world."

"I am sent from Merlin's court, perhaps." I laughed, enjoying the attention and feeling more feminine than I ever had before.

"And what do you say of my outfit, Dom?" A voice purred from behind. Evergreen stepped forward, and I watched Dominic's face register surprise. He took a few seconds to respond, and I felt a twinge of jealousy.

"What a lovely sari. Most unusual to see in this part of the world. You look wonderful. I am sure you will be the talk of the village," he said.

"I believe that's the intent, old boy," muttered Perry. "She does like getting the tongues wagging, does she not?"

"Oh, bother to the both of you," Evergreen snapped. She took my arm. "Come, Jillian, let us go and find someone interesting to talk to. These boys are tiresome." She led me away before I could protest. I glanced over my shoulder at Dominic and raised a brow. He grinned.

After much conversing with several of the other guests, we made our way to the dining room when dinner was announced. I found to my relief, that I was to sit next to Uncle Jasper. Victor LaVelle would be directly across from me.

I counted at least twenty for dinner, and I had never attended such a grand affair. Mr Collins was feted and praised, and the food was outstanding. I did not speak to Victor, for the table was too broad and full of dishes and concoctions. He seemed busy engaging with the people next to him. But I noticed on more than one occasion that when I happened to look up, I would find Victor's eyes on me, his expression curious as though he thought something odd. Was it my dress? Did I indeed appear so changed that he did not like it? Dominic was seated several places down the table from me. I was disappointed not to have his company, but I knew he would not be bored as he sat next to Evergreen, whose laughter I heard throughout the meal

After dinner, we ladies left the gentlemen to their cigars and Evergreen came instantly to sit by me. "Is this not fun?" she said with a twinkle in her eye. "I am so relieved to be out of the house. Are you enjoying yourself, Jillian? Have you been much admired?" She was proud of her handiwork in my appearance, and I thanked her once more.

"Nonsense," she said. "It was entertaining to see

you go from duckling to swan." And there it was again. Evergreen's uncanny knack to let the needle pierce the veneer of friendship. As I sipped on my sherry, I wondered what kind of relationship we might have had were it not for her cruel tongue. I thought of her comments about Billy. Despite her kindness to me, Evergreen had such a horrid propensity to wound.

I watched while across the room, Mrs Stackpoole spoke with one of the other guests. Prunella was fetching in her lilac gown, her hair up in a tidy bun. It was kind of Louisa Mountjoy to include people such as us. Had we lived in London, the paths between our social classes would never have crossed.

"And here are the lovely ladies." Lord Mountjoy entered the drawing-room with the rest of the gentlemen, along with wisps of cigar smoke. My eyes hungrily searched for Dominic, but he was not there. It was Victor who came over to where I sat.

"Are you enjoying the evening, Jillian?" He smiled pleasantly, and Evergreen stiffened beside me. I remembered Dominic's remark that she sought her father's attention.

"Yes, thank you. It is a nice gathering, is it not, Evergreen?" I attempted to include her in the conversation.

"Anything is better than being cooped up at Hollyfield." Her voice was petulant.

"I could not help but notice your pendant earlier," Victor said. "Is it not a moonstone? If so, I assume you wear it in honour of our guest?"

"Yes," I replied, realising *that* had been the object of his perusal at the dining table. "It belonged to my mother, and now me. I know little about the stone, but I find it pretty and comforting to wear as it was hers."

Victor frowned. "I understand your mother passed away not long ago, and that is how you came to be in Ambleside."

I was distracted as Evergreen abruptly rose from the settle and moved away. I looked up at Victor. He wore a thoughtful expression. His pallor was somewhat pale. "Are you feeling unwell, Victor?" I asked, getting to my feet.

"I am sorry," he said, clearing his throat. "I fear the cigar was a little strong and has upset my constitution. I must go and find a glass of water. Please excuse me."

I watched him walk away and scanned the room to see if Dominic might have joined us by now. He had not. I found his absence unsettling. There was nothing for it but to seek him out.

At length, I discovered him in the billiards room, engaged in a game with both Perry and Marik. Much to my surprise, Evergreen stood in one corner, a brandy glass in her hand.

There you are, Dominic," I said. "I thought you gone home."

He set down his cue and came to where I stood. "I am sorry, Jillian. These two ruffians kidnapped me after dinner and challenged me to a game."

"We wanted to play against someone we could beat," laughed Perry, who pocketed a red ball into the side net.

"Good shot," exclaimed Marik as he poured himself a drink from a decanter. He looked over at me. "Miss Farraday, you are quite lovely tonight. The green of your gown sets off the richness of your hair."

"Dear me," Evergreen said. "You wax poetic

tonight, Marik. I did not think Miss Farraday your—type." The room tensed for just a moment, and then it passed. I understood her reference, though the LaVelles and Marik were unaware Dominic, and I knew their secret.

"Thank you for the compliment, Marik. Evergreen was so good as to lend me this dress and the use of her maid. She has been most kind."

"Not an adjective I'd use to describe my fair sister," Perry announced, and I noticed a flash of anger from his twin.

The atmosphere in the room was unsettling, edgy in a way which one expected something was about to happen. I did not want to remain and promptly decided to leave the men to their billiards. Dominic appeared to have finished his game, and I told him I was returning to the drawing-room, assuming he would offer to escort me. But instead, he smiled and said he would see me later.

I left the room in irritation. Dominic, normally so attentive, had behaved indifferently. What was wrong with him this evening? I thought he would spend a little of his time with me. Indeed, had I not dressed in finery purely to turn his head? All my hopeful anticipation of the night dissolved, and I could not dam the flood of disappointment.

I returned to the party, but as I sipped sherry and spoke with the other guests, my heart was not in it at all. It travelled to the billiard room, where Evergreen LaVelle and Dominic remained.

I watched the mantel clock as an hour passed by. As it struck eleven, Uncle Jasper summoned me to join him and Mrs Stackpoole. It was time to take our leave.

Lord Mountjoy's carriage would deliver us home, and I had little option but to do his bidding. We collected our wraps, and though I yearned to find Dominic to say my goodbyes, I was ushered outside and into the carriage.

As we pulled away, I turned to take another look at the large house illuminated by gaslights burning bright. Why had Dominic not spent time with me? Did he no longer care?

MY STATE OF MIND WAS NOT GOOD. After a fitful night of sleep, I had awoken to heavy rain pounding on the roof, a slight headache, and the uncomfortable feeling that my life had shifted position. I lay under my blankets, loathe to get up, while I replayed the events of the evening for at least the fourth time.

What had made Dominic behave so strangely? Usually affectionate and always attentive, last night he had behaved like a mere acquaintance, not a man who had shown me his love. What could have happened to bring about the sudden change? Evergreen's face popped into my head and again a twinge of discomfort gnawed at me. Was there something between the two of them? I always picked up on a subtle shift in Dominic's demeanour whenever Evergreen was with us. Part of me desperately wanted to ask him, yet I was afraid of his answer. I had to believe Dominic was a truthful man. Surely, he would not have encouraged my affections if his own feelings were for another?

UNCLE JASPER'S MOOD WAS LIKE day to my night. He worked most of that morning, yet on several occasions I know I heard him whistling. For some reason, his joy enhanced my lack of it, and by the end of the day, I was low.

Would I see Dominic? Though I knew he would be in Kendal with Billy, I half-expected him to knock at the door on his way home, as he was wont to do. He did not come. At dinner, I barely touched my food.

"Jilly, what ails you?" Uncle Jasper asked with a concerned frown.

"Nothing," I lied. "I am a little under the weather. I think perhaps the rich food and fine wine at dinner last evening were too much for me."

"Well, that would explain it," he stated. He then embarked upon a story where he had over-eaten and the dramatic effects it had taken on his body. Mrs Stackpoole seemed riveted. I did not listen to a word.

My uncle retired to his study while I helped Mrs Stackpoole clear away the dinner plates. My mind jostled with many thoughts, yet they kept returning to Dominic and his treatment of me at the Mountjoy's. Finally, I had enough. It was not my nature to dwell and worry. I would rather speak my mind and have it out. I took off my apron, hung it on the peg and told Mrs Stackpoole I was taking a quick walk before it got dark. I did not wait for her reply.

DOMINIC WOULD NOT EXPECT ME this late in the day. I knew it was foolish on my part to go to Wolfe Farm unannounced, but I could not help myself. I was desperate for answers.

The farm took on a different persona as dusk gave way to the night creeping slowly across the land. Shapes so familiar in the light of day were at once foreign and shadowed. But I chased away my concerns and approached the farmhouse, drawn to a lit kitchen window like a moth. Thank goodness it appeared Dominic was home.

As I reached the kitchen door and went to knock, the sound of voices stilled my hand. Dominic was not alone. Loathe to be a bother and interrupt, I put my ear to the door and listened intently. I heard a woman speak, and I froze. Who was with Dominic at this hour?

I moved away towards the kitchen window. When I reached it, I debated how I could look through without being seen. Slowly, I peered around. Two figures stood facing one another in front of the hearth.

Their voices became louder. I could not hear what was being said, but their tones grew hostile. I wanted to know more. Bolder now, I stepped in front of the window at the very moment Evergreen LaVelle moved nearer to Dominic. My stomach convulsed with what I could only know as jealousy. My blood raced through my veins at a gallop. What was Evergreen doing here?

At first, I thought she meant to strike him. Even from my poor vantage point I could see the wildness of her expression. But as she neared him, the breath left my body as Evergreen placed her arms about Dominic's neck, pulled him close and kissed him.

My heart lurched, I felt sick and my mind raced. I looked away in utter disgust, tears streaming down my face. So, my suspicions had been correct. I had been played the fool the entire time. Evergreen and Dominic were obviously involved prior to my moving here. Dear God, Dominic Wolfe had toyed with me like I was a lovesick child.

I moved away from the repugnant scene and ran from the farm. I do not remember how I arrived home or how long it took me to get there because I was too distraught, too broken-hearted to pay attention or see through my tear-filled eyes. I went into the house and directly upstairs to my room. I threw down my cloak and fell onto the bed where I buried my face into my pillow and soundlessly wept. How could they? I was so ashamed.

And then a myriad of thoughts crashed into my mind. Dominic's quiet response when we had discovered evidence of a tryst at the boathouse and thought it Evergreen. His tolerance of her appalling words to Billy. His inattentiveness towards me last night. Had it been a façade from the very start?

I had been so easily deceived. Indeed, though I had little experience with men, I was no imbecile. I read people well enough. But Evergreen? My blood boiled as I thought of her efforts to be kind and how she used me to entertain herself whenever she pleased. No wonder she was so snide with me—she wanted Dominic for herself, and I was getting in the way.

As my tears quickly gave way to rage, so my fury mounted. I turned over onto my back and stared at the ceiling. My fingers twisted the pendant I still wore about my neck, but it brought little comfort.

Dominic Wolfe had stolen my heart, and now ignited my vengeance. I would not be humiliated, nor would I be used for his pleasure any longer. As for Evergreen? She thought she had my friendship, but now she would receive my wrath. I would never forgive either one of them.

Chapter Twenty-Five

DOMINIC CALLED AT THE HOUSE the next morning, but I had already instructed my uncle that I was unwell and wished to see no one. I heard them talking and then Dominic's retreating footsteps. But I cared not. I planned to immerse myself in work and let this pass.

As the morning went on, I found myself still plagued by thoughts of our investigation into the death of Jareth Flynn. What of Billy's situation at the gaol? Could I honestly forget all I had learned these past weeks because of a foolish flirtation? No. I could not. My feelings were but a mere trifle in comparison to the danger Billy Wolfe faced should he go to trial. Therefore, regardless of my opinion, I would continue with my enquiries.

That afternoon, I folded up Evergreen's dress, wrapped it in paper, and set out for Hollyfield House. Other than the fact the dress was not mine to keep, I wanted no reminder of an evening which had held such promise yet had been ruined by the subsequent betrayal of two people I considered friends.

I planned to drop off Evergreen's gown without speaking to her. As luck would have it, I turned from our street onto Lake Road and bumped into her maid, Peters. The young woman had done such an artful job of arranging my hair for the evening at the Mountjoy's. She recognised me immediately and we exchanged greetings. I asked if she was returning to the House anytime soon. Peters said she was on an errand to the post office. I showed her the package I held, and she offered to stop by and collect it on the way back. I leapt at the chance to avoid going to Hollyfield. I told her my address and went back home to await her arrival.

She did not take long. With a little persuasion, I encouraged her to come inside and share some tea.

"This is right nice of you, Miss Jillian." She beamed, taking another biscuit.

"'Tis the least I can do, Peters. I have never had my hair arranged before. It was a treat, and I appreciate your work."

"Well, I thought you looked very pretty in the gown, miss. I do believe Miss Evergreen was a little put-out with that. She don't like competition."

"I doubt very much if anyone could outshine your mistress. She looked stunning in her sari."

"She does like her clothes, that one." Peters continued. "I've never seen one woman go through so many dresses. Though she is generous an' gives away the old ones to those of us workin' at the house."

"That is kind," I said flatly. "I am sure you are all most grateful."

"We are." She looked sheepish. "I think she does it 'cause she feels guilty."

"Guilty? What do you mean?"

"Miss Evergreen can be difficult at times. She has a cruel tongue—if you get my meanin'."

"Oh, yes. I understand. I have been on the receiving end of that myself. It is like getting stung by a whip."

Peters nodded. "Lots of the girls up at the house,

well they don't care for her. They like the gents well enough, but Miss Evergreen can be very demandin'."

That was putting it politely. "How long have you been Miss Evergreen's maid, Peters?"

"About a month now." She helped herself to another biscuit.

"Is that all?" I was surprised.

"Yes, miss. The last one left after one of my lady's 'tempers'. I expected the position to be a tough one, but the money is good, so I took it. Right after I started at Hollyfield, Miss Marabelle died. I didn't know much about her other than the staff said she never required her own maid. By all accounts, she was a very unhappy person. She and Miss Evergreen never saw eye to eye, about anythin'."

"I noticed they were not close," I commented, egging her on.

"You can say that again. The night of the lecture there was a such a carry-on. It was my first time to dress Miss Evergreen for a formal evenin', and she was in a right old mood. Miss Marabelle, well, she'd barged into the bedroom and they had a nasty set to."

"What about?" I asked.

"I don't know 'cause they asked me to leave. But it was somethin' about Mister Perry and his foreign friend. By the time I was called back in, I barely had any time to get my lady ready."

"Well, you did a fine job, Peters. I remember how lovely she looked that night." And I remembered that Marabelle had lost her life as well.

The subject changed to other topics until finally, Peters thanked me for the refreshment, took the parcel containing Evergreen's dress, and went on her way.

After she had gone, I went out into the back garden and sat down on the kitchen doorstep to think. I reached into my mind to find a missing piece of information I knew had to be there somewhere.

I started at the beginning—the day I had been knocked down in the village by the LaVelle carriage. Slowly I retraced all the events which had taken place since Jareth Flynn's death—Billy's arrest, his shocking parentage, Marabelle's fall, Louisa's confession, Evergreen's relationship with Flynn, and finally Perry and Marik's secret affair.

Evergreen still had the strongest link to everyone. Her relationship with Flynn was more than a flirtation if the accounts given by Billy and Jem were to be believed. And what of the boathouse? Evergreen had been seen there with Flynn, by the children. It was there we had found his watch. With her past reputation, surely there could be no doubt there was more to her involvement with the blacksmith than she was willing to admit. But could Evergreen be a killer? I doubted that very much. Her spiteful nature was evident, yet it was a huge leap to go from cruelty to cold-blooded murder. So, who had killed Jareth Flynn? And had Marabelle fallen to her death or had she been pushed?

And that brought me to Dominic. He had been dismayed the day we went to the boathouse. I distinctly remembered the look on his face when he realised the place was being used for a lover's tryst. As my thoughts replayed the sight of Evergreen kissing the man I cared for, disgust swirled in the pit of my belly, and my anger began to smoulder.

UNCLE JASPER WAS GOING FOR A walk on the hills and

Mrs Stackpoole told me she would accompany him. She was busy making sandwiches and packing a small picnic basket. I determined their friendship was growing stronger by the day. As soon as the cheerful pair left the house, I waited a few minutes after their departure and then got myself ready to go out.

I had stewed all night over what I should do with my many conflicting emotions because of Dominic. But I could not allow my personal feelings to sway me from doing what was right. I set off for Hollyfield, and this time I did not notice the lambs in the fields or hear birdsong. I was too intent with what I wanted to say to Evergreen LaVelle.

I waited for her in the conservatory. This was not by my request, but hers. I sat on the same wicker chair as before and reflected upon my first time here when Dominic was painting her portrait. Back then, I had felt so differently. I remembered the interesting conversation with Marik and how much I enjoyed his company. It was strange now, thinking of his relationship with Perry. They ran such risk of being caught and punished. I could not imagine how it was to love someone and not have the freedom to express it publicly.

"I am surprised to see you here this early in the day, Jillian. It must be important?"

She appeared before me in another lovely dress, this one the colour of hazelnut. As always, I was taken aback by her impact. If nothing else, Evergreen was a beautiful woman—at least on the exterior. She sank into the chair opposite mine and raised a brow. "Well?"

"I wish to speak with you on a personal matter," I stated bluntly.

"I see." She stared at me with her pretty eyes, yet there was no warmth there.

"What was Jareth Flynn really to you?" She opened her mouth to speak, but I continued. "And before you say anything, I would have you consider this. You were seen with him, Evergreen, by more than one person. So please, tell me the truth."

She got to her feet and paced back and forth in front of her seat. "I do not see what business it is of yours, Jillian. What I do with whomever I please has nothing to do with you."

"Perhaps," I agreed. "Except this person was brutally murdered and found close to where you live. A boy's life hangs in the balance should he be convicted. I believe it my duty to make a point of helping where I can. Besides." This time I raised a brow. "Why should you care if you have done nothing wrong? Unless you have something to hide?"

She sat back down and fixed me with an angry glare. "You have a lot of nerve, Jillian. But then that's probably what I admire the most about you." She sighed. "Jareth Flynn and I were lovers." She paused and threw me a glance, no doubt expecting to see a look of shock on my face which would have pleased her. Her expression showed disappointment because I did not even blink. She smiled. "He was a handsome fellow. Quite the ladies' man in Ambleside, ask Louisa." Again, she stopped to watch my reaction and was left wanting. I decided to take a little stab myself. "I know all about Louisa," I said confidently. "Mr Flynn had a lot of secrets." I was alluding to what I knew of his blackmailing habits, for now I was convinced he must have also been blackmailing Perry, or Marik. I took a bold step. "Was Jareth Flynn blackmailing you because of your affair?"

She audibly gasped. "Good grief, Jillian, how dare you suggest—"

"I think it likely, actually," I replied. "I am aware of your indiscretion in London and the reason Victor packed you off to the country, as you shared that with me. But to engage in yet *another* affair with someone far beneath your position, why I am sure your father would have been furious. Perhaps even disinherited you?"

Her face was livid. I believe if Evergreen could have, she would have slapped me. She was enraged, two pink dots shone on her cheeks. And that was all I needed to know. She did not have to corroborate my accusation—it was written all over her lovely face.

I stood up and, without another word, left the conservatory. As the maid shut the door behind me, I walked away from Hollyfield letting out the deep breath it felt like I'd been holding throughout the entire conversation. Evergreen was no pushover. It had taken all my resolve to maintain a steady demeanour and not become intimidated by her forceful disposition. I smiled, a little of my pride restored. I had succeeded.

Now I understood why people were victims of Jareth's blackmailing endeavour. Evergreen, Louisa, Marik and Perry. What a devious individual the blacksmith had been. In some ways, it was understandable someone wanted him dead and killed him. But it was never Billy Wolfe. The person responsible for killing Flynn could be commiserated with in part, because they certainly had motive—Flynn was a miscreant and despicable blackmailer. Yet the murderer had stolen Billy's knife with the sole intention to kill Flynn and frame an innocent young man. It was contemptible—incriminating a boy who could be convicted and subsequently hung for something he did not do? It was unforgivable.

But which person did I seek? And what about Marabelle? I still had not accepted her death as an accidental fall. How on earth did she factor into this tangled mess, and who would want her dead?

I walked back towards Ambleside, ruminating over what I already knew. I still had much to understand—yet something told me I was getting closer.

As I turned up our street, someone stood waiting outside the front door. Too late I realised it was Dominic.

Chapter Twenty-Six

HE SAW ME AT THE SAME TIME and immediately headed my way. I hesitated, wanting to escape—I was not yet ready to speak with him, for I still smarted. But he called my name, and there was nothing for it but to wait for him to approach.

"Jillian. Where have you been? I take it you are feeling better?"

"What do you mean?" I had no idea what he referenced and then remembered my excuse for avoiding him yesterday. "I am well. Why do you wish to see me?"

"To ask if you would join me for a short walk. It is a fine morning, and we have much to discuss. Will you come?"

In truth, I did not want to walk with him, I was still disgusted, full of regret. I wanted to spit my accusations in his face. Tell him I was no fool and berate him for giving me false hope. Tears pricked my eyes, but my fury dried them instantly.

"Fine," I relented. "I shall walk with you, but not far. I have much to attend to before Uncle returns later." I did not look at his face. I could not.

If he noticed the distance in my voice, he did not comment upon it. He joined step beside me, and we made our way down the street toward the village.

"Jillian," he began. "I want to clear the air between

us. I know you are angry with me because of the behavior I displayed at the Mountjoy's. But you must let me explain what has been going on before you convict me and toss me aside."

He was more intuitive than I had credited him being. Consequently, he had my attention. I was extremely interested in what he would say and how he proposed to extricate himself. I glanced over at him none too kindly. "Go ahead. I cannot wait."

He threw me a wary glance. "I am innocent until proven guilty. Remember that."

I nodded acquiescence.

"These past weeks have been surreal, and I have often found myself in a state of despair. The nightmare that began with Billy's arrest, has spread like a thick fog, saturating my mind until I do not know if I come or if I go." He ran his fingers through his dark wavy hair. "At each turn, there is conflict. To accuse one is to devastate another. My head has spun so much I am dizzy."

"Can you be more specific?" I said bluntly, not giving him an inch—he deserved it.

"When we found evidence at the boathouse that day, I was astonished. I knew should Víctor learn of his daughter's discretion he would be beyond devastated. So, I asked Evergreen to meet me, and I told her what I suspected. She was furious, and at first denied it all, but eventually owned up to having met the man once or twice."

"She lies." The words burst from my lips.

Dominic looked at me. "I know." He went on. "As you discovered more of Flynn and his other liaisons, I believed Evergreen's role in the entire affair must be greater than I first imagined. I became worried and also torn. I have a brother in the gaol while his half-sister conceals the fact she was involved with a murder victim. I was conflicted, but also concerned for Victor to bear this knowledge. I confronted Evergreen once again, but this time she decided to use a different tack, she began to flirt with me."

I stiffened, and Dominic looked at me quickly. He continued. "When I was very young, Evergreen bestowed upon me my very first kiss. To a poor young farm boy, she was a princess. I was completely smitten with her from that moment on, though she had no feelings for me other than wanting my homage. However, as the years passed and I grew up, I finally understood the kind of woman Evergreen was then and is now. She has relied upon her gender and beauty her entire life. She has effortlessly collected young saps, myself included, along the way.

But Evergreen has no moral compass, no concern for any but herself. When she decided to set her cap at me once again, it was not difficult for me to ignore her advances—I understood her intent. She sought to control me by seduction. But Jillian, I am no longer the foolish young boy from years ago. I have no interest in the woman beyond that of friendship. Besides." He stopped and reached to take my hand. "My heart is already taken."

I saw the earnest affection in his eyes, and still I pulled my hand away sharply.

"I have seen how she impacts you, Dominic. I have watched your expression change when she enters a room. She is lovely, and I cannot blame you for having your head turned…"

"No, Jilly." He gave a deep sigh. "You have it wrong. I admit my feelings toward Evergreen are complicated, but only because I have seen through the veneer of her character. I have been troubled, and I realise I should have explained my feelings to you. But where to start? Since we met I have worked the farm, seen Billy at every opportunity while also becoming involved with you, and trying to protect Victor. I am at a loss to juggle everything in my head. I have tried to behave as though all is well, especially when I am with you. Our time together has been the only thing stopping me from going mad—you have to believe that."

"I do not," I said flatly.

He was undaunted. We reached the church, and he indicated we should sit on the bench. I did so but kept a great distance between us.

"The day of the Mountjoy's dinner, Evergreen told me she had something of importance to tell me. She came to the farm and said the reason she hated my brother was that he had molested her on more than one occasion."

I gasped. "No, that is ridiculous!"

"Yes," he said mournfully. "I agree." He turned to me. "But regardless of what I thought, she meant to tell Victor and then the constable. If she had done so, Billy's fate would have been sealed."

"She is a manipulative and wicked girl," I said. But now I began to understand Dominic's strange mood the night of the dinner. He had been distant, so cold. And I had immediately assumed it was all about me.

"Evergreen tormented me with her threats the entire evening. I was distracted and angry. Unsure of what to do next. When I looked for you and found you already gone, I realised I had offended you. But Jillian, I was in no state of mind to worry over that. I was consumed with fear for my brother. The following evening, Evergreen came to the farm. She told me she planned to tell Victor very soon, and then he would stop helping with Billy's case. I argued with her. I called her every foul name I could think to call her. She responded by trying to kiss me. It was as though the passion of our rage seemed to fuel her desire. I was revolted."

I faced him. His pallor had whitened, and his eyes were sad.

I took his hand. "Dominic, I was there."

He gave me a puzzled look. "Where?"

"At the farm. I had come to see you because I was worried. You were so indifferent to me at Mountjoy's dinner, and I was upset. The next day I sought you out to confront you, to ask if you were finished with me. I saw you with Evergreen, and I saw your kiss." I watched his response carefully. His expression changed to relief. "Then you also witnessed how strangely she behaved, and how I pushed her away. It was too bizarre, Jillian. And now I do not know what I should do about any of it."

I did not tell Dominic about my reaction to the kiss, how I had flown from the farm in misery. I was gratified he assumed I witnessed the entire event and behaved as though he had nothing to hide from me. I took this as a great comfort. It had all been a misunderstanding, yet I had learned much.

"I have just visited Evergreen," I said. "And I told her I knew of the relationship she had with Jareth, and that others saw her with him. She is very angry with me, but I care not. Evergreen knows far more than she lets on, Dominic. I fear her role in Flynn's demise goes further than we realise."

"What do you mean?" He frowned.

"I believe Evergreen knows who killed him."

Chapter Twenty-Seven

DOMINIC AND I SPENT THE remainder of the day together at Wolfe Farm. I helped him clean out the chicken coop and muck out the stables and the barn. The physical labour must have been good for me, because by the next morning, my demeanour had greatly improved. Certainly, our disagreement had taken some of the shine from the relationship we had so recently begun. Yet traversing through our conflict and misunderstanding would hopefully serve to give us a stronger foundation.

Today we planned to see Victor and tell him everything we knew. Dominic still had many misgivings, not the least what Evergreen would do with her fabrication of Billy molesting her. But I had convinced Dominic that, at this point, it was better to be honest with Victor. Although it was a great deal of bad news and would grieve the man to learn of it—he was much more robust than Dominic realised. His successful career certainly emphasized that.

We met on Lake Road. Our moods were sombre, which was to be expected on such a solemn occasion. We walked together but were lost in our respective thoughts as we approached the house. Dominic planned our arrival to coincide with Victor's breakfast. As a rule, he would be the first to rise, and we would therefore catch him alone.

Victor exclaimed surprise at seeing us together and so early in the day. But before long we sat with him as he finished his eggs and kedgeree, and accepted a proffered cup of tea from the footman before he left the room.

As the door closed behind the liveried man, Dominic cleared his throat. "Victor. Though I hate to do this, I have many things I must tell you, and none of them good."

The older man paused from eating and his green eyes narrowed. He looked like a tiger ready to pounce.

"Then you'd better get started."

Dominic relayed all we had both learned, in a precise and orderly fashion. I found myself impressed at his capacity to make good sense of it all, and he wisely maintained his composure throughout the entire ordeal. He recalled each of our discoveries. His only omission was though he conceded Marik to be a victim of blackmail, he did not reveal why. We had agreed Marik and Perry's relationship was for them, and only them, to speak of.

It was a long speech and, thankfully, Victor did not interrupt, not one single time. His self-control appeared effortless, but I knew the man had to feel devastated, even angry. When Dominic was finished, Victor rose and went to the sideboard, where he poured himself another cup of tea. He then rejoined us at the table where we both sat in silence.

"Well, Dom." He spoke after a moment. "That is indeed much for me to take in. I am quite astounded and impressed you and Jillian have deduced all that you have. It appears you work harder than our local constabulary.

We remained quiet. It was Victor's turn to talk.

"You know, building my business has taken much from me over the years. It has been hard work, and I readily admit I have not done it alone. Countless people have helped me succeed, yet it has come with great sacrifice." He took a sip of his drink. "I have worked long hours and given much priority to my career and ambition. I have buried a wife and two infants, and now it is blatantly apparent that I have neglected my son and daughter.

"I brought my family back home to England after the loss of Emma, because staying in India without a mother proved too painful for the twins, especially Evergreen. I hoped both the stability and the influence of our British family would aid my children after losing their mother so young. Yet I believe my absence has rendered me oblivious to signs that all was not as it should be." He sighed, and I felt such empathy.

He continued. "When Evergreen committed her indiscretion—though it was not her first—I thought it best to bring her here, away from the temptation of London and under the watchful eyes of Marabelle, my wife's cousin. I knew it was not an ideal situation, but at least it would offer some structure, short of sending the girl away, which I did not want to do. But as time has passed, I have been increasingly aware that Evergreen has—" he struggled for the word. "Some difficulties adhering to rules, especially those dictated by her class in society. I have long overlooked her problems because, in truth, I have always feared she might be more like her mother than I suspected."

Dominic and I looked at one another. I knew his puzzled expression was the same as mine must be.

"Evergreen's mother was of a nervous disposition. I believe there was some thread of it in her family, yet it would not be noticeable to most. Emma struggled with many things in life. She was shy of strangers, and then alternatively too forward with others. She was prone to fits of anger and then might cry for days. Emma was somewhat of an enigma. But I ignored any misgivings I had and buried myself in my work.

"In our first three years of marriage, we lost two sons to cholera. It is my belief Emma had not the time to recover emotionally before she was with child again. This time she gave birth to the twins, Perry and Evergreen. After their arrival, Emma's depression became all-consuming, and her interest in the children was simply absent. It was a most trying time for all involved, culminating in her fatal overdose of laudanum before the twins' second birthday."

He stopped for a moment, and I thought he must have travelled back to that time in his mind. There was such sadness in his story. I thought of his young wife, Emma. How unhappy she must have been to feel as though taking her life was the only choice.

"Perry and I adjusted to moving back very well. We brought Marik with us, so I am sure it helped my son having as good as a brother to share things with. But for Evergreen, well, it was quite challenging. There were a succession of friends who marched in and out of her life. Yet none stayed long—I fear they saw in her that which I could not."

He stopped short as the sound of conversation approached. The dining-room door opened, and Perry and Marik walked in, closing it behind them.

"Dom, Miss Farraday," Perry said pleasantly.

"What brings you here so early?" He must have comprehended the atmosphere in the room and seen our serious dispositions. "Is something amiss?" He addressed his father. "What is it?"

"Would you and Marik join us please, Perry?" Victor requested. Perry looked swiftly over at Marik's worried frown. They seated themselves across the table from Dominic and I and then glanced to Victor for clarity.

"Son, why was Jareth Flynn blackmailing you?" His words were quietly spoken, yet their impact was as though he had shouted them.

"Flynn?" Perry looked puzzled. "What on earth are you on about, Father? I barely knew the fellow. Don't think I ever spoke to him more than once. Why ever would you think he was blackmailing me?" Perry's voice was incredulous. He was telling the truth. "What's this about?"

Victor sighed. "We have evidence and information which proves Flynn was blackmailing several people in the area, and you are among them."

"That is ridiculous." Perry was outraged. "I have never heard anything so preposterous. Do you think I am lying?" He rose to his feet, his face red with indignance.

"Your father is right," Marik said softly.

Perry stared at him. "What do you mean?" He sat back down.

Marik looked to the head of the table. "Victor, Perry has no knowledge of this, I promise you. Jareth Flynn planned to approach him, but I intercepted and told him he would have to deal with me instead."

Perry was aghast. "You never said—"

"...I did not want to worry you."

"Why was he blackmailing you?" Victor addressed them together. Marik's black eyes quickly shifted to Perry, whose face flushed—his blue eyes, so like his sister's, shone bright with emotion. Neither answered.

"Did Flynn discover you were lovers?" Victor asked, and the room went completely still. I could not look at them. I was an intruder to something too personal, too private. I kept my eyes downcast and wished I were somewhere far away. I had no desire to embarrass Perry or Marik.

"Come on, Perry. For once, can my family not be honest with me?"

Perry looked up at his father, his face both a mixture of sadness and defiance. "How long have you known about us?" he said quietly.

Victor shook his head. "Years," he said softly. "I was but waiting for you to tell me."

I glanced at Marik. He held his head high and did not flinch as Victor turned a cat-like gaze in his direction. "And what of you, Marik. Do you have nothing to say?"

"I love your son, Victor—with all of my heart. Because of that I tried to protect him from Flynn. That despicable man would stop at nothing, and so I paid money for his silence. I just wanted to buy time so that I could determine the best course of action. But then he was killed. I would be lying if I did not say I felt immense relief when I found out he was dead. I thought our troubles were finally behind us."

"Not if you were the person who killed him," Dominic growled. "Because it was not my brother."

"I have not killed anyone," shouted Marik.

"You have no alibi," Dominic replied and watched the Indian's face widen in surprise.

"You were overheard speaking to Evergreen about your fears of being suspected of something suspicious," Dominic explained. "You certainly had a motive."

"Perhaps I did have good reason to want the man dead," Marik said icily. "But I did not kill Flynn, though I would shake the hand of the person who did with heartfelt thanks. Flynn was scum. He feasted upon the secrets of others like a rat gnawing a carcass. The day he died, Perry and I were in Hawkshead, with some of our—friends."

"Then you do have an alibi," Victor commented.

"Not one we could share with a constable," added Marik. "Unless we wanted to admit to our relationship."

"And be imprisoned," I said. They turned to look at me as though just realising I was there. "It is a terrible dilemma for them both," I continued. "Escaping the condemnation of one crime would lead to the punishment of another."

"Just so." Marik sighed. "But I am glad it is finally out. I have been worried sick with it all since the cad turned up dead."

"Evergreen knows of your relationship, does she not?" I asked them both. They nodded, though Perry reluctantly.

"Do not be angry with her, Father," he pleaded. "She has been a good sort about it from the start."

"Did she also know Jareth was blackmailing you, Marik?" I had to know.

"Yes," he admitted.

Perry looked at him with surprise. "You told her, yet not me?" There was hurt in his voice.

"She wanted to help. Evergreen loves you, Perry," he explained.

I turned to face Dominic. "We should take our leave now, and let these good people finish their conversation." I got to my feet.

Dominic stood also and glanced at Victor. "I will be at the farm for the rest of the day. Please do not hesitate to come if you have need of anything. This is not finished."

There was no response.

I said nothing but slowly followed Dominic from the room.

"POOR VICTOR," DOMINIC SAID, AS he put the kettle on the stove.

I removed my coat and hung it on a peg before joining him. I passed Dominic the empty teapot. "I am relieved Victor already suspected Perry and Marik. At least he didn't have that as a shock. But what he shared about his wife was most sad."

"Yet it explains a great deal about Evergreen, does it not?" he said, placing tea leaves into the pot. "Do you think she might be afflicted with the same illness as her mother?"

"It seems likely given the propensity Evergreen has with her moods. Victor might want to seek help from a medical man. Surely there are methods or medications which can help someone with that type of affliction," I suggested.

"Victor has the means and resources to find out," said Dominic. "You know, though their visits were infrequent over the years, I've often thought Evergreen a complex person. She has many wonderful qualities, but beneath them lays something immoral." He finished making the tea, and we sat down at the table.

"What do you think will happen now?" I asked.

"Victor will need time to reflect on everything we told him. Then I imagine he will come and speak to me, and then to the solicitor, Kemp."

"I would expect the evidence of blackmail would give more credence to Billy's case. Don't you think?"

"Yes," Dominic agreed. "The problem is Louisa Mountjoy will never admit her secret, and if Victor exposes Flynn's blackmailing Perry and Marik, he runs the risk of both men going to gaol. If he mentions Evergreen, her reputation is gone forever. He has so few choices and none of them are good."

"It is unfair," I declared. "We have learned so much, Dominic, yet we are no closer to freeing Billy than we were at the beginning. If Victor does not tell Mr Kemp, what shall you do?"

"I cannot remain quiet." Dominic's voice was grave. "Victor must choose his own course—but I'll not let my brother hang for the sake of the LaVelles' reputation."

Chapter Twenty-Eight

I HAD NOT YET DISCLOSED ANYTHING to Uncle Jasper. He was happily ignorant of Dominic's and my investigations, and I preferred to keep it that way. Therefore, when the LaVelle carriage stopped at our house the next morning with a note from Victor requesting my immediate presence, he grew curious. I concocted a quick story about my offering Victor an opinion on the organisation of Hollyfield's library. This seemed to pacify the dear man, but only after I had assured him I was not going to start working for the LaVelles.

As the carriage turned down the driveway to the house, I hoped everything was all right. Yesterday's conversation with the head of the LaVelle family had been incredibly personal, and I still felt uncomfortable having witnessed it. What did Victor want with me? Perhaps Dominic was there too?

When I was shown into the study, I was alarmed to see Evergreen sitting in one of the leather armchairs. She quickly got to her feet and bestowed me with a beaming smile.

"Jillian. I am so pleased you came." There was no trace of animosity in her voice. It was as though our most recent heated discussion had never taken place.

I held my ground. "I am not come to see you, Evergreen. 'Tis your father who sends for me."

"Nonsense." She grinned again. "It was me. I took the liberty of signing his name. I knew you would not come if it was at my request."

I glared at her with no thought to spare her my irritation. "That was deceitful, Evergreen. I am not at your beck and call whenever you have the desire to have company."

She arched a brow. "Is that so, Jillian? Yet you are happy enough to be at my father's." It was a well-aimed shot, and it had the desired effect.

"What is it you want?"

"I wish to speak with you on a variety of subjects. I believe you have misunderstood many events which concern me. I considered us friends and I would welcome the opportunity to clarify where there might remain a misunderstanding."

I bit the inside of my cheek. What should I do? Make one concession and hear her out? I thought of Victor's revelations. My own mother had been the centre of my world. It was from her nurturing that I had learned how to navigate my life. Evergreen was far less fortunate. Motherless, with a father bent on a successful career, she might have had plenty of financial resources behind her but not the emotional support every child needed.

"All right," I conceded. "What is it you wish to say?"

She looked over my shoulder and out to the hall. "Not here. There are too many prying eyes and ears. What I wish to discuss is delicate in nature. Let us take a turn outside. It will be more private."

The day was already warm and the weather perfect for a stroll. Evergreen led me away from the house down the path to the boathouse and the lake. The gardens were thick with early summer blooms, Dahlias, Asters, and Roses. Their fragrance hung in the air.

"Thanks to you and Dom, Perry and Marik's secret is finally out," she began. "'Tis a relief if you ask me. The boys have been mad for each other since they were old enough to read. Father is being rather decent about it as well. Shame he never admitted knowing anything earlier. It would have saved a lot of bother and that idiot blacksmith could have been sent packing."

"I doubt that for a moment," I replied. "Your father would not have been able to protect them. Flynn would have told the authorities, and Perry and Marik would have been arrested."

"You are right, of course." We had reached the boathouse. Evergreen walked around to where the boat was docked. "But then you have been right about so many things, dear Jillian. Come." She gestured to the boat. "Step in. Let us go out on the lake."

I frowned. "I am in no mood for a jaunty sail, Evergreen."

"Don't be ridiculous," she snapped. This was the Evergreen I was most familiar with. "I am to meet with Peggy Nash. Surely you know of her by now? The old crone sent word for me to come. She insists she has information of great import to share."

"That is most cryptic," I exclaimed. "But what has it to do with me?"

"Dominic," she said his name and then smiled. "Peggy wants to tell me something about Dominic and Jareth Flynn."

I grew suspicious, "Then why do you not tell her to come here to Hollyfield?"

"She refuses to come anywhere near the house," Evergreen said impatiently. "She demands I go to her. She says she knows something about Billy's knife too."

What on earth could the old woman know? She had already told me of Billy's innocence, though she was not able to give him a strong enough alibi. But had Peggy found more proof? My instinct was to let Evergreen go on alone. But part of me mistrusted what she would do should Peggy have anything which could help Billy's case.

"We should tell Constable Bloom," I stated. "Let him take care of this."

"No," she spat. "The hag won't talk to anyone but me. I am sure she expects me to reward her with a coin or two. Now," she unfastened the rope tethering the boat. "Do you join me, or not?" Evergreen stepped into the boat and held out her hand. "Peggy camps in a small bay, and though we could go on foot, it would take all morning."

"How did she contact you? And why would you suddenly care about helping Billy? You are the one who has been happy to see him in gaol."

"True," she admitted and gave a shrug. "I think him a simpleton, and I have never liked the brat. But after the long talk I had with Father last night—well, let us say he has persuaded me to think a little differently. If he can show compassion to my brother, then I can make an effort to do the same with Billy. I received word from one of the gardeners early this morning that Peggy had been on the grounds yesterday. Apparently that is when she asked him to pass the message along." She blew out a breath. "Look, Jillian, I am going whether you come or not. It may be a complete waste of time, but I will not find out anything by doing nothing."

I was not entirely convinced, but I decided to give her the benefit of the doubt. After all, what would it hurt? I took her hand and stepped into the boat. Evergreen gestured for me to sit on one bench seat while she took the other which faced me. She pushed against the side of the dock and the current took us slowly out of the boathouse. Evergreen grasped the oars and, once we were free, she began to row.

"You are not seasick I hope? I never thought to ask."

"No," I replied. "I'm a Devonshire lass. I grew up by the sea."

"Do you miss living there?" she asked.

"Sometimes. But after my mother died, there was nothing to stay there for."

"Rather like me and India," she commented. "I loved it there. But once mother died, there was no reason to stay." She sighed heavily. "I have never been happy in England."

"I am sorry to hear it," I said kindly, and I meant it.

"Oh, Jillian." She chuckled. "You are such a liar."

I had not anticipated that response. I was astonished.

Evergreen laughed. "You should see your face—'tis quite a picture." She was no longer smiling, and her eyes held malevolence. "You have enjoyed yourself since you came to Ambleside, Jillian, but at great cost to me."

"What are you talking about?" My pulse picked up speed.

"I wish the damned coach had run you over the day we met, for you have done nothing but bring me strife since you set foot in my house." She pulled hard on the oars, heading straight for the centre of the lake.

And then all at once, everything started to make sense. "You are not taking me to see Peggy, are you, Evergreen?"

Her pretty eyes gleamed with malice. "Of course not. You really are quite stupid, Jillian—or perhaps gullible is the better word."

"And you have no intention of ever helping your *brother*, Billy."

Her face flushed red with indignation. My using the word 'brother' hit the mark. Instantly agitated, she scowled.

"As far as I am concerned that imbecile can swing. Imagine having a half-wit for a brother?" She laughed, and the sound was maniacal. "With him out of the way, Dominic can return to London and his painting. We can be together, and I shall introduce him to society. He'll make quite a name for himself."

I did not take her bait. "You are completely mistaken." I responded, forcing my voice to remain calm though my heart hammered against my ribs. "Should anything happen to Billy Wolfe, Dominic would never leave the farm. He would be too heartbroken."

She stopped rowing and glowered at me. "And how would you know? I've loved Dominic for years, since I was a child! You've spent a handful of weeks with him. That does not equate to your knowing him better than I. Dominic has always been in love with me."

"You are wrong. You mistake the infatuation of a boy for the passion of a man. The only person Dominic loves beyond measure, is Billy. And do not forget,

Dominic knows much of what you have been up to. Would he ever forgive a woman who contributed to the incarceration of his brother? Think about it. After all, do you not feel that way about Perry? You would do absolutely anything for him, wouldn't you?"

And then the penny dropped. The little scrap of information that had rested just out of reach in my brain finally revealed itself. It was love—everything that had occurred had happened because of love.

"You killed Flynn. Didn't you, Evergreen? You discovered he was blackmailing Marik and Perry, and you had to protect your brother."

Her expression did not change. She stared at me as we floated aimlessly out into the middle of the vast lake.

I continued, "You were seeing Flynn, meeting him at the boathouse. But when Marik confided that Flynn was blackmailing him, threatening to expose he and Perry's homosexuality, you decided to get rid of him. How did you manage it?"

Her face remained impassive—and then she grinned. Not the smile of the person who had bought me tea and crumpets all those weeks ago when we first met. Or the girl who laughed as we shopped for hats in Kendal. The woman who faced me in a small boat, isolated upon the waters of Lake Windemere, smiled at me like the madwoman she was.

"You think yourself so damn clever, don't you, Jillian? So clever that you have come out here alone and your fate rests in my hands." She paused, as though considering her options.

My mind raced ahead, composing what actions she planned to take and what I could do? Yet though I was frightened, I was sick and tired of her games. It was time for her to tell me the truth.

"Not as astute as you believe yourself to be, Evergreen." I taunted. "You think yourself infallible, yet ultimately you have been bested by a mere blacksmith."

That got her. Her upper lip rose in a snarl, I had managed to land a hit to her fragile ego.

"Flynn, was an utter moron," she said. "But he was a wonderful lover. So passionate, so handsome. I knew he was a rotten scoundrel when he couldn't wait to tell me all about Louisa. She had fallen for the man—the stupid sap. Yet I'll admit, it was deliciously fun stealing him away from her." Evergreen arched a brow. "I didn't care one whit about Jareth. He meant absolutely nothing to me, other than a welcome distraction to my boring existence here in this godforsaken village. He was just an amusement, someone to play with. Until he became a liability."

She tilted her lovely face up at the sun and sighed with pleasure. "I do so love it out on the water." She looked back at me. "When I ended our liaison, Flynn threatened to tell my father about our affair. Well, I could not have that, could I? Especially after London. But really, it was all Marabelle's fault. She started the whole mess."

"Marabelle?" A shiver passed through me.

"Yes. The self-righteous bitch. She had caught Marik and Perry together, in *flagrante* and planned to tell Father. She threatened Marik and demanded money. The woman was obsessed with becoming the matriarch of the family. Marik told me what had happened, and so I confronted her. I said, in return for her silence, I would help ingratiate her with my father. That I would encourage his attentions towards her if she kept the boys' secret.

"It would have ended there, except Jareth Flynn spotted Marik and my brother at the waterfall one evening while on his way to meet me. He planned to approach Perry with his demands, but Marik intercepted and dealt with him instead. I met Marik in the woods, and he gave me Flynn's blackmail letter. I tore it up and tossed it away."

My mind conjured up the image of the pieces of note Billy had found and hidden.

"Marabelle was keeping her end of our bargain. My only problem was with Flynn. He might expose Perry's love for Marik and tell Father about his previous involvement with me." Evergreen gave a sigh and smiled at me. She was enjoying herself. Now she had started I could see she could not stop. It was as though she had bragging rights. She was insane.

"I sent for Jareth. I told him I missed him, that I couldn't stand being without him. I even went so far as to suggest I would tell Father I wanted to marry him. The arrogant bastard actually believed me." She laughed derisively. "As if I would sink so low. On the day we met up, Billy Wolfe saw us together in the woods. I told Jareth we'd been spotted, and of course, he chased after Billy to scare him away."

"And then you tried to frighten him too, didn't you? You went to the shed to scare him, and that is when you stole his knife."

"My, you are the clever one, aren't you? No wonder I wanted to be your friend." She looked so pleased with herself. "Yes, I took Billy's knife, and the next time Flynn came to meet me, I stabbed him. It was ridiculously easy. I dragged him out to the water and left him there."

"Did you know Peggy found him?"

"Of course. That nosy old witch. I saw her from the boathouse, but she didn't see me watching."

"Flynn was still alive you know."

She shrugged, "Not for long."

"And the knife?"

"I kept it for a few days, and then placed it in the woods. I took one of the gardeners with me looking for a handkerchief I said I had lost. I knew he would find the knife."

"That was very clever. And I suppose you hid Flynn's wallet in Billy's room at the farm as well?"

"Yes," she chuckled.

"You thought you had taken care of everything—saved Perry and Marik and yourself from Flynn. But there was still one other who knew the truth about your brother."

"Greedy bitch," she spat. "Marabelle was furious that Father had been too preoccupied with Billy to pay her any attention. She began to get a little too full of herself."

I remembered her maid's comments about Marabelle and Evergreen's argument. "Did Marabelle threaten to expose your brother on the night of the lecture?"

"Now who's being clever?" Evergreen laughed out loud. "Oh, Jillian, you should have seen her face when I pushed her off the balcony. It was the only time I ever thought her funny. She dropped like a stone—and right in front of you too!"

And there it was. My suspicion confirmed. Good God, Evergreen LaVelle was stark raving mad. How could I not have seen it? Indeed, how could any of us have missed it?

I wanted to get away from her and alert the authorities. "Evergreen. We should return to shore now. Let us find Victor and get you help."

There was the laugh again. "I need no help. Look what I have accomplished already. Do you honestly think I would have told you everything if I was planning to let you go?"

"Evergreen," I said as firmly as I could, trying to conceal the anxiety galloping through my body. "We must speak with your father. He can try to sort this mess out. You have already killed two people."

She stopped laughing, and her entire expression changed to an evil leer. "Two people? Why dear Jillian, I intend to make it three!" In a flash, she raised an oar and brought it with a resounding smack against the side of my head. An immense pain rushed through my ear. Evergreen made a guttural sound and raised the oar up to hit me once again. But this time I was ready. As the paddle reached me, I held up my forearm and deflected its course. It bounced hard against my bone, and I cried out in terrible pain, but I had parried her attempt to render me unconscious. Reaching over, and with all the strength I could muster, I wrenched the oar from her grip and threw it into the water. She paused in surprise, then roared in anger and lunged for me.

My dress ripped open as she clawed at me. Grabbing a handful of her hair, I pulled it so hard that her head snapped back. The look of utter madness in her wide eyes terrified me, but my desire to survive far outweighed anything else. I kept her head back and with my right hand formed a fist and brought it up to punch her soundly under her chin. She collapsed back onto her seat, but I knew she was not finished. As she landed, I released her hair, climbed behind her, pinned my arm around her throat, trapping her head. She flailed, desperately trying to get purchase, then clawed at my arm. I could only hold onto her for a moment longer. Suddenly I knew what I must do to keep the advantage. With what remaining energy I had left, I placed my other arm about her waist, and pulled us both into the water.

She went straight under. I let her go while I struggled to loosen my skirt and petticoats and pull off my shoes before my clothing weighed me down. Then I swam below the surface to find her before it was too late.

The lake was deep, but as the weather was fine and the wind calm, the current was not strong, though the water was murky. I could see Evergreen well enough. She was in a complete panic. Her arms and legs kicked and flailed, but the weight of her sodden gown was dragging her to the bottom of the lake like an anchor.

When I reached her, I grabbed her arms, and at first she fought me. Then suddenly she went limp, and I was able to gain purchase and hold her, kicking my legs to force us upwards. As we broke the surface, I spluttered and coughed. More from exertion than anything. Evergreen was still, and I realised she must have fainted from fright and lack of oxygen. I put my arm around her neck to keep her head above the water, and I used my legs to propel us back to the boat.

I did not attempt to climb back in but hung onto the

side of the boat with one arm while supporting Evergreen with the other. I desperately tried to mobilize my legs and move us in the direction of the shore. It was exhausting. I prayed for enough strength to get back to dry land.

I worked hard, but our progress was poor. My strength slowly began ebbing away, and it was not long until the exertion of it all took a toll. My legs had turned to lead. The arm I had crooked around Evergreen's shoulders became numb, and my fingers could barely grasp the side of the boat. My head pounded from where she had clobbered me with the oar, and I felt as though I could be violently sick.

What should I do? If I let Evergreen loose, I could try and get back into the boat. But the girl was still out cold, and I knew should she go under, I would not have the energy left to save her from drowning.

How much time passed? I do not know. But I hung on, desperately hopeful to see another boat, yet none were forthcoming. It was still early for recreational sailors and too late for the fishermen to be out.

And then I became vaguely aware of a faint voice in the distance. Was someone calling my name? Was I delirious? I had been soundly hit in the head, after all.

I heard it again, and this time I looked around and all but cried with joy. Thank goodness! It was another boat, and there was Victor and Dominic, frantically rowing to reach us. I tried to call out to them but could not find the breath. My grip on the side of the boat loosened, my head spun, and all the fight left my body.

Chapter Twenty-Nine

"HOW DO YOU FEEL?" DOMINIC sat by my bed, holding my hand, concern etched across his furrowed brow. I was surprised to see him, but he said he had slept downstairs on the sofa in the parlour. That explained why his hair looked as though something had tried to nest in it.

"I am well. Please stop worrying." The doctor had pronounced me fit enough to return to my uncle's house last evening. Victor had offered his home, but I wanted nothing more than to leave Hollyfield.

Uncle Jasper had flown into a panic at the sight of me, but dear Mrs Stackpoole stepped in as nurse and shooed him away. I was plied with warm drinks and soft food. Under doctor's orders I was to be kept awake for the next eight hours to ensure I would not fall asleep and never awaken. I did not understand exactly why, but it was something to do with where I had taken the blow to my head. After such time, I would be out of any danger.

In the middle of the night, Mrs Stackpoole had finally stopped talking, turned out my lamp and told me I could now rest. I had fallen into a deep and exhausted sleep and not woken until mid-afternoon at the sound of Dominic and Mrs Stackpoole entering my chamber.

I pulled myself up into a sitting position. Mrs Stackpoole wrapped a shawl around my shoulders for propriety's sake, declaring my door must remain open as she discretely withdrew.

"Oh, my head throbs," I complained. "Evergreen is surprisingly strong at wielding an oar." I gave a weak laugh.

"'Tis not funny." Dominic chastised. "She could have killed you. Thank goodness you are a strong and intelligent woman. Any other would have dropped into a dead faint, fallen out of the boat, and drowned. I am immensely proud of you putting up a good fight. I'd warrant Evergreen had not expected that."

"I did warn her I was a Devonshire girl," I said smugly. "My grandfather was a fisherman, and I spent much of my childhood on his boat." I thought for a moment. "I did not ask you earlier, but when you rescued me, how did you know I was in danger? Your timing was impeccable."

"That was all down to Jasper. Victor and I were in the village when your uncle and Mrs Stackpoole spotted us. Jasper asked your whereabouts and had you returned home. Victor did not know what the professor alluded to. When Jasper explained the LaVelle carriage had come to collect you with a message from Victor himself, he denied sending the request and it was then your uncle realised something underhanded must have occurred."

"That was lucky indeed." I wondered how I should have fared if they had not arrived in the nick of time. "Where is Evergreen now?"

"At a women's gaol in Preston—they have declared her quite mad. I believe she has been declining for several years. But it will all be determined later. Do not worry, Jilly." He could tell I was sympathetic, though she deserved none of it. "Evergreen is Victor LaVelle's daughter, and he will not allow her to be mistreated." His eyes darkened. "Unlike Billy, *she* will not face the gallows—though why her mental state is excused while his was not, seems unfair."

"How is Billy?"

The smile returned to his face. "Ecstatic. He understands he will be coming home. We do but wait for the pardon to be signed by the magistrate, sometime later this evening. He will be back on the farm tomorrow."

I sighed. Billy would be free once more. Thank goodness everything had turned out so well for the brothers. "You will be glad to have him home again, I think." I squeezed Dominic's hand.

He leaned over and kissed me gently on the lips. When I opened my eyes, it was to look into his.

Dominic smiled. "You are safe and, once my brother is back at the farm, I shall never want for anything again."

WITHIN A FEW DAYS, I WAS CLOSE to feeling more like myself once again. I was careful, for if I did too much, my head would begin aching. This would diminish as the swelling subsided, Uncle Jasper said, repeating the physician's words. Until then, I was not allowed to work.

Dominic came to visit every day but had yet to bring Billy. He wanted to wait until I was ready to go to Wolfe Farm. Then, he promised, he would cook an excellent dinner, and we would all celebrate together. This sounded fine to me. It was wonderful to see the worry gone from him and hear happiness in his voice once more.

Today, Uncle Jasper had gone out for his first ramble since my accident, and left me under the watchful eyes of Mrs Stackpoole, who, I noticed, looked extremely well. Her skin glowed, her eyes sparkled, and there was a continual smile upon her face. I was delighted she and my uncle made one another happy. It was obvious the woman was in love.

I reflected that, though love completed the lives of Uncle Jasper and Mrs Stackpoole, even Dominic and myself, look what the emotion had done to the LaVelle family. Evergreen had killed for it. Perry and Marik had lived false lives to hide it and poor Marabelle Pike had died for it.

In the afternoon, Mrs Stackpoole left to go to the library and pick up some books for me to read as I could do little else while convalescing. She left me on the back lawn, sitting on a thick blanket enjoying the sunshine. I watched our wet washing on the line dance under the warm, summer breeze, and was lulled into a sleepy trance. The click of the back door opening roused me, and someone stepped outside. It was Victor.

"Hello, Jillian. May I join you?" He came down the path, and I gestured to the blanket.

"Be my guest. Though I cannot guarantee its comfort, nor that the grass underneath is not damp."

"I'll take my chances," he said and sat down beside me.

I looked over at him. Somehow, sitting on a blanket in our back garden diminished Victor's dynamic presence—he appeared more ordinary, more human. I noticed his face had thinned and he looked drained. Was it any wonder after the recent events he had dealt with?

He gave me a warm smile. "Dominic tells me you are much recovered."

"Yes, I am. Between him, Uncle Jasper and Mrs Stackpoole, they have worn me down to the point I want to be well so I can get away from them and have some peace and quiet."

He nodded. "Well, I am glad to see you have blossomed under their care."

I studied him. "How are you, Victor? You have had more than your fair share to tolerate these past few weeks."

"I am well enough," he said unconvincingly. He turned his gaze on my face, and his attention was intense. "Jillian, I have come to see you to do more than check on your welfare. There is a delicate matter I wish to discuss with you. This may not be the most appropriate time, but due to many other concerns I have at the moment, would you be agreeable?"

I was puzzled. "Of course." The man had been nothing but civil since our first meeting.

"First of all, thank you for saving my daughter's life."

I opened my mouth to speak, and he held up his hand. "Please. Let me speak my mind, and you may address what I say once I have managed to get it all out." He smiled so I would not be offended. "After what Evergreen has done to so many, regardless of her mental state, you did not have to rescue her from drowning. Though she put you in mortal danger and tried to kill you, your clemency was remarkable. You would have been well within your rights to let Evergreen die. Yet you did not. You gave compassion where she had shown you none, and I will be forever grateful." He sighed. "Evergreen will remain in custody until next month. At which time she will be taken to Ticehurst House, a private asylum in Sussex."

"I am sorry to hear that."

"Do not be. Evergreen has been spared the horrors of imprisonment and a hangman's noose. She will live in a reputable place. 'Tis no madhouse like Bedlam. I have money, therefore Evergreen, unlike so many unfortunates, can live out her life being well cared for. Once she is settled, I will be allowed to visit her. So, you see, she is luckier than most. But you have nothing to fear from her ever again, for she will never be freed." He paused. "And now another matter."

I frowned. "Yes?"

He glanced at the pendant I had worn since the accident. "Your moonstone. May I see it?"

I pulled the cord over my head and handed it to Victor.

He held it in his palm and studied it intently. "I recognise this stone," he said gently. He held it up to the light. "Do you see the tiny flaw, just here where the light catches?" He pointed. "See? Right there?"

I squinted to focus better, and yes—there it was. "I do, though I had not noticed it before. Does it have significance?"

"It does not decrease its value or beauty, but rather makes it a unique piece." He handed it back to me and I slipped it over my head.

"Many years ago, I bought that very pendant from a merchant who had imported it from India. It was a parting gift for the woman who had stolen my heart." He turned his face to stare into mine. I digested his words and slowly began to comprehend his meaning.

"You?" I stuttered. "You knew my mother?"

"If her name was Gwen Jackson, then yes. Gwen was a beautiful girl I met in Devon, not long before I was to leave for India."

I covered my mouth to trap the sob which threatened to spill.

Victor touched my shoulder. "I was there to study with one of the prominent shipbuilders, and just after I arrived, I met your mother."

I was utterly speechless.

"I was honest with her. I told Gwen I could not remain in Devon as there was an appointment waiting for me in India. I was engaged to be married to Emma Symington, and her father had paid for both my studies in Devon, and my subsequent passage onto India. But try as we might, we could not stay away from one another. When it was time for me to go, I gave Gwen the pendant as a keepsake of what we had shared."

"Oh Victor. How could you have left her?" I said. "You must have broken her heart."

He closed his eyes, as though he could not bear to look at me.

"Yes, she was heartbroken—and so was I. But I had a signed contract with the Symingtons, one I could not breach for fear of legal action. The family had invested a great deal of money in my education and training. Money I would never be able to repay. After I married, I was to take part-shares in the company and start a new branch, dealing specifically in steamers."

His shoulders sagged. The memories were difficult for him. "Jillian, I was young, I had ambition, and the last thing I'd expected was to meet a young Devonshire lass and fall madly in love." His fingers rubbed at his temples as though the thought brought him unbearable pain. "When I left Devon, I debated whether I could renege on my agreement with the Symingtons. I resolved to hire a lawyer to read my contract once we made land and see if there was a way to wriggle out of it. But on the voyage out there, I fell sick with cholera. I was fevered for many days, and, by the time I arrived in India, I was too weak even to walk. It took several months for me to regain my strength, and by that time, our wedding was planned, and everything had been settled."

I said nothing.

"Sometimes, I like to think that if I had not fallen so ill, I would have left the ship at one of the ports and rushed home to be with Gwen."

I blinked and felt a tear roll down my face. "Did you ever write to her, my mother?" I looked over at him, and he hung his head. "Once, before I married. But she never replied."

I gave a loud sigh. This was much to take in. My emotions were so conflicted. I wanted to be angry with Victor, for he had broken my mother's heart and left her for another woman. A wealthy woman who had eventually taken her own life and bequeathed her mental illness to Victor's daughter. And look what damage had been done. Yet, there was another part of me who understood how life could be. That sometimes we were not able to have that which we desired. Timing was everything. If they had met but a year earlier…

"I am not angry with you, Victor," I said softly. "I grieve for you both. And though I know my mother had a wonderful life with a good man, I am sure there was always a part of her which belonged to you."

Victor wiped his eyes with the back of a hand and smiled at me. "Gwen must have been so proud to have you as her daughter."

"I hope so."

He gave a long sigh and then looked at me with a strange expression on his face.

"Jillian. There is one more thing I must tell you before I leave you to yourself." As he spoke, he loosened his cravat and began unbuttoning his shirt.

Instinctively, I shifted away from him. "Victor, what on earth are you doing?" I jumped to my feet.

He also stood up, never taking his eyes from mine. "When Dominic and I pulled you from the lake, your clothing was sodden, your dress gone, and what little you wore was torn." He pulled open his shirt and there, on the left side of his chest was an oblong-shaped strawberry birthmark.

I stared, frozen to the spot as I looked at the same mark I bore on my body.

And then his green eyes met mine, and I realised through my tears, that I had been looking into a mirror every time I had looked at Victor's face.

Victor LaVelle was my father.

Epilogue

It was a glorious day for a wedding. There was not a cloud in the sky, nor a whisper on the breeze. I stood outside the church in my new apple-green dress, with Dominic by my side. I had not felt this happy since my mother had been alive.

As the bells chimed merrily, the married couple burst through the doors with beaming smiles across their faces. Everyone cheered and hurrahed, throwing handfuls of rice to sprinkle over the bride and groom. Uncle Jasper looked so handsome in his new grey suit, and his blushing bride, Miss Prunella Stackpoole, now Mrs Jasper Alexander, looked radiant in a lilac gown, a bouquet of violets in her hands.

They were helped into the LaVelles' open carriage, which was festooned with garlands of flowers for the occasion, and set off for Hollyfield House, where a grand picnic awaited in their honour.

"Thank goodness Uncle Jasper has finally found something he likes even better than lichens," I remarked to Dominic as we walked from the church down Lake Road. We were not alone, for most of the village had been invited to the festivities. Throngs of people headed in the same direction.

"He does look delighted," Dominic said.

"Wait for me!" Came a voice from behind, and we

slowed our gait until Billy caught up with us. He looked joyful, his eyes shining with the prospect of a picnic and no doubt some games. He took my free arm, and I walked between the two Wolfe brothers.

"I'm so hungry," Billy complained. "Jilly, will there be cake?"

"Lots," I said with a chuckle. "And mince pies, sausage rolls, all kinds of wonderful food."

"She won't be there, will she?" Billy asked, as he often did since he had come home from the gaol.

"No, Billy," Dominic reassured him. "She won't ever be there again, so there's no need for you to be scared."

Victor had done my uncle proud. The entire garden at the rear of Hollyfield House was filled with tables laden with pastries, fruits, ales, and all manner of delicacies. A maypole stood in the centre of the lawn, and a small group of musicians entertained the guests. There would be a dance after dusk. It was a wonderful gesture from the LaVelles and an excellent tonic for a village still healing from the tragedies of the past three months.

Dominic sent Billy off in search of cake and then asked if I would walk with him down to the water. It was not my first time back to the boathouse since my run-in with Evergreen. I had thought it wise to conquer that fear right away. Evergreen had made such a devastating impact on so many lives over the spring and early summer and I was loath to give her any power going forward. My future was to be my own.

We strolled down to the shore and then away from the boathouse until we came across a small bench. Without speaking, we both sat down, and a few seconds passed before Dominic broke the silence.

"Well, Jilly. Are you ready to start this new chapter of your life?" He referred to my uncle marrying Mrs Stackpoole.

I sighed. "Though it will be different, yes, I am ready. So much has changed since I moved here. It seems I have gained many relatives all at once." I thought for a moment. "Accepting Victor as my father is still challenging, and I wonder if I shall ever grow used to the idea of it?" My relationship with Victor in his new parental role was in its infancy. Victor was slowly coming to terms with the fact he had been friends with my Uncle Jasper and somehow never realised their true connection. This was easily explained, for Uncle Jasper was my mother's uncle, and they did not share the same surname. Not to mention that when Victor had stayed in Devon many years earlier, my uncle had long been gone from the county.

"You know, Victor really wants you to live at Hollyfield House," said Dominic. "He has mentioned it to me on more than one occasion."

I shook my head. "I can never do that. It is not my home, nor will it ever be." And that was the truth. For in my heart, dear Thom Farraday would always be my true father. For he had nurtured me, cared for me and loved my mother with all his heart.

But my living arrangements were still unsettled. Uncle Jasper had insisted I would always have a place with him. He reminded me daily that I should take my time to get used to the new arrangement with Mrs Stackpoole, who I now called 'Aunt Prue', and my developing relationship with Victor. It was the right solution for now—at least until I knew what I wanted to do with the rest of my life.

Dominic chuckled. "Just think, Jilly. If I had been more forward with you, I would have guessed your true identity much sooner."

He was right. Had Dominic ever seen me in my undergarments, he would have immediately recognised on me, the very same birthmark his brother Billy had on his chest. Apparently, Perry bore the same dominant marking as well. No wonder Evergreen had gaped at me when I tried on her gown prior to the Mountjoys' dinner party. I had sealed my own fate without even knowing it.

"'Tis strange to gain a father, and two half-brothers at my age," I remarked. I acknowledged Perry and Billy, but would never own Evergreen as a sister, not after what she had done.

"I do miss seeing Perry and Marik," Dominic said. "Though I know their life will be far better in Florence. At least there, they will not be persecuted for loving one another."

"Indeed. Perhaps one day they might even feel safe enough to come back and visit us," I said wistfully.

Dominic put his arm around my shoulders and we both fell silent while lost in our own thoughts. The gentle sound of lake water lapping on the shore was calming, and faint threads of music wafted through the trees from the gardens.

I thought about my parents, and how much they would have liked Dominic, and Billy too. I thought of Victor—that he had lost a wife to mental illness and now a daughter as well. That his eldest son must live exiled in another country, while his youngest afflicted son could never join Victor in the family business.

Which left Victor with me. It was ironic he would lose one daughter and gain another. How strange life could be—how fickle was destiny.

I was roused from my thoughts when Dominic raised a hand to gently cup my chin, turning my face towards his. His amber eyes burned into mine, and just looking at him took my breath away.

"Jilly, the day I bumped into you at the Ambleside Post Office, I had a feeling you were going to be someone special," he said softly. "Though little did I know just how significant."

I smiled.

His thumb brushed across my lips. "Thank you, Jillian Farraday. Thank you for coming into my life and staying there through all the turmoil. For keeping me from giving up and for saving my brother—our brother's life. I can never repay you, not ever." His eyes clouded with emotion. He took a deep breath. "Jilly, I am very much in love with you."

Before I could respond, he bent his head to mine and kissed me. His lips were firm, yet tender. And the chaste yearning within me bloomed into a bud of passion, saturating each cell of my body until I was consumed with feeling, with love.

He ended the kiss and pulled back without moving too far away. I was powerless to speak. My mind still processed his declaration while my heart filled with longing.

"Jillian, there is one more favour I would request from you, though you have done so much for me already."

I frowned. Then I saw him smile and I instantly relaxed. "Yes Dominic, what is it?"

"'Tis much to ask," he said, his eyes shining with merriment.

I groaned. "I do not wish to have my portrait painted, Dominic."

He laughed. "No Jilly. That is not the favour. It is much more adventurous than that. I have decided to travel to Italy, and I want you to come with me."

I gasped. "Italy? Why, this is news to me. When did you decide to go away? How can you leave the farm?"

"Whoa," he placed his finger against my mouth. "Slow down. You ask too many questions at once."

I apologised but asked another anyway. "Will you go to Florence and see Marik and Perry?"

"Yes. I have long desired to see that fair city, for it boasts art collections unrivaled anywhere in the world. As for the farm, once the crops are harvested, there is no reason I could not be gone for a short time."

I considered the offer. Why should I decline? I had never travelled, other than from Devon to Cumbria. The prospect of being abroad was both terrifying and wildly exciting.

"Well?" he asked. "What do you say? Will you go with me?"

"Of course!" I beamed. "'Tis an excellent notion. It will be good for Billy. After all he has endured he…"

"No, Jilly." Dominic said sternly. "Billy will remain here with Victor. I do not want to go on this particular trip with our brother."

I did not comprehend. "Dominic, that is unfair. How can you not take Billy?"

"Please be quiet for just for a moment," Dominic said with a smile. Then he looked into my eyes with such love. "Jillian Farraday LaVelle, I ask you to travel to Italy with me, for our honeymoon."

And as he waited for my answer, the sound of happiness surrounded us as the dancing at the wedding party began with merry music on the air.

I placed one hand over Dominic's, the other around the moonstone where it rested against my neck, and I looked into his beautiful eyes.

"I love you, Dominic Wolfe," I whispered. "And I will go anywhere in this big wide world, as long as it is with you."

About the Author

Jude Bayton is a Londoner, who currently resides in the American Midwest. An avid photographer and traveller, Jude enjoys writing about places close to her heart. To keep up with her latest releases and her monthly blog, subscribe to at judebayton.com

Find Jude Bayton at:
judebayton.com
Facebook: Jude Bayton
Twitter: @judebayton
Email: author@judebayton.com

Other Books
By Jude Bayton
The Secret of Mowbray Manor

The Secret of Mowbray Manor
By Jude Bayton

Sunday, November 9, 1890
Dorset, Southern England

COMPLETELY ALONE, I glanced about the deserted platform, grateful for a dim light from one solitary gas lamp. My grip tightened on my small valise and suitcase. Swanage Railway station appeared as devoid of life as a ghost ship on the English Channel. I hastened to find an exit while my eyes chased shadows from the flickering, weak lamp. My mind battled the impulse to bolt, but I steadied my nerves, though it took every ounce of my composure not to run.

Outside the station and engulfed in darkness, I saw no other buildings, which fed my growing sense of unease. My eyes scoured the area, hungry for the welcome sight of Mowbray Manor's carriage. I had been assured someone would meet me. Discouraged, I set my bags down upon the sodden ground, pulled up the hood of my cloak to block the bite of November wind, and considered my predicament.

Wispy ribbons of fog floated like waifs through the dark canvas of night, while the moon sulked behind drab clouds like a child hiding in its mother's skirts. I shivered and pulled my worn cloak tighter. What if no one came?

An owl hooted, its companionable call a welcome reprieve from my silent isolation. And on I waited, it seemed for an age. My back stiffened as I stood so erect and scared, and the blood in my veins turned frigid. I grew weary. Then a low rumble upon the ground broke the quiet, and a faint light materialized. As it swayed through the gloom, I felt immense relief. I was rescued.

The carriage creaked to a halt a few yards away, and the driver climbed down from his stoop and approached. An older man, stocky of build, his face coarse and bearded, inclined his head, yet avoided looking at me directly.

"Good evening, sir," I stammered. "Are you come from Mowbray Manor?"

The man grunted a low, unintelligible response and reached down to take my belongings. They did not weigh much, for my possessions were few, and he tossed them into the cab with ease.

"Get you in then," he mumbled gruffly and gestured for me to follow the course of my bags. I needed no further encouragement.

I quickly relaxed into the worn leather of the cab as the hackney traversed the road to Mowbray Manor. My body warmed slowly as my eyes grew heavy from a long day of travel, my healthy constitution no match for the torrent of uncertainty which plagued my mind.

After a time, our gait slowed, and we turned into a driveway. Although the dark windows of the carriage were closed tightly, a scent of saltwater permeated the atmosphere, and I inhaled deeply. Now wide-awake, I pressed my nose against the cold damp glass, and my eyes strained through the blanket of night to see my destination. Fortuitously, the clouds parted to allow a sliver of moonlight to shine down, and my breath caught in my throat. Mowbray Manor stood regal and imposing. Though wrapped in folds of gossamer fog, its austere mass pushed through the obscurity, as though even the elements could not veil its majesty.

With the same unfriendly manner he had displayed earlier, the coachman delivered me and my belongings unceremoniously before the front steps. I stood rooted to the spot. My gaze traveled upward, followed the grey rock of the building that rose before me like a monolithic stone giant. With trepidation, I picked up my bags, ascended the steps, and stopped at Mowbray's gargantuan oak doors. My hand shook as I reached for the bell-pull, and its trill ring pierced the quiet of evening. Footsteps approached from within, and my emotions became conflicted. I yearned to be inside a warm safe-haven, yet felt anxious that I had arrived at my destination where I knew not one soul.

The heavy door swung open to reveal an elderly man, white-haired and somberly dressed. His clothing was dapper enough to be a gentleman's, but his diminutive bearing at once declared his status as servant. He did not ask me to come in, but I basked in the light which flowed invitingly behind him.

"Good evening, miss." His voice, eloquent yet disdainful, conveyed a tone which intimated that I should be stood at the servants' entrance. This impression was likely based upon my lack of finery. I looked as I was—poor.

I steeled myself. "Good evening. My name is Kathryn Westcott, and I am come to see Lady Clayton." His eyes flickered momentarily. He was no doubt surprised by my accent. He had obviously expected my speech to be that of a common girl.

The old man nodded. "You are late," he said without ceremony and gestured for me to enter. He closed the door behind me, and my relief was instantaneous now that I was out of the damp night air. I set my bags down and stared at the butler.

"Wait here," he commanded and walked away through the foyer down a well-lit hallway. As soon as he departed, I quickly examined my surroundings.

Several gas lamps were affixed to the walls, their sconces radiating soft yellow light which illuminated the scene before me. The space was immense, the floors made of polished marble. Two large pieces of statuary stood sentry either side of a staircase wide enough for a small carriage to pass between its carved bannisters. A majestic crystal chandelier hung like a stalactite, suspended from the painted fresco ceiling which depicted the heavens and what surely were gods, though which beings I could not say. Its magnificence exceeded my expectations.

A low murmur of voices escaped as a door opened and closed in the distance. The returning footsteps of the butler drew near. He stopped and extended a gnarled hand.

"This way if you please, Miss Westcott."

I glanced down at my valise and suitcase. The old man noticed my consternation and nodded to leave them where they stood. I took a deep breath and followed him down the hall.

As we entered the drawing room, its sudden warmth engulfed my cold bones, though my nerves still chattered. Inside the room, thick Aubusson carpets cushioned my step, and lavish fabrics and ornate furniture surrounded me. Yet I absorbed none of it in my present state of mind. The butler announced my name and, at once, a figure rose from a winged-back chair placed close to the blazing fire. As she approached, my eyes slaked across the woman's face, the elegant arrangement of her white hair and the length of her silken-clad figure. My feeling of uncertainty now I finally saw her in the flesh completely consumed me. Until this precise moment, the woman had been surreal, a fictional character in a popular novelette. Yet here she stood, the woman I had come to loathe through the words of her daughter, my dearest friend, Aramintha.

In a flash, I absorbed her features. The harsh jaw, thin lips, aquiline nose. Her skin like pale chiffon, soft with delicate creases, which changed the topography of her face. A striking woman, even in her sixties, she must surely have been a beauty in her youth.

"Ah, there you are, Miss Westcott." Lady Blanche Clayton inclined her head. "Good evening. I trust you had a pleasant journey?" She stood a few steps from me, and our gaze met evenly. She did not offer me a seat. I smiled and nodded, observing the cordial expression on her face, yet her eyes were cold and grey as stone.

"Thank you, my lady. I did indeed." I willed my voice not to betray the depth of my discomfort. "I apologize for the lateness of the hour. The early train was canceled."

She waved a gloved hand. "'Tis of no consequence. Our housekeeper, Tricklebank, has your room prepared and will bring you a light repast." Lady Clayton turned away and went to a small ivory table. She grasped a small bell and rang it sharply. I watched her every move. The profile of her aristocratic face, the silver threads of her elegantly coiffed hair. Immediately the drawing room doors opened, and the elderly butler entered.

"Your Ladyship?"

"Baxter, show Miss Westcott to her room." She inclined her head toward me and gave a thin smile. "We will speak again in the morning at ten o'clock. We can go over your duties then."

Dismissed, I turned away and followed the butler from the room, elated that the first part of my plan had succeeded. Lady Blanche Clayton had absolutely no idea who I really was.

I AWOKE WITH THE strange sensation I might still be dreaming. I lay cocooned within a large canopied bed, my body swaddled in linen sheets and warm wool blankets, my head cradled like a baby on soft feather pillows. I smiled with guilty pleasure, and then sat bolt upright as my mind cleared. Was I really at Mowbray Manor? Drowsy layers of slumber fell away as my thoughts arranged themselves in proper order. I glanced about the chamber. The morning light shone through chinks in the curtains, which offered clarity previously denied by lamplight last night.

The room was indeed pleasant. Sumptuous pink cabbage roses papered the walls, a busy backdrop to the multitude of small, framed paintings which depicted all manner of pretty birds. The mantel over a white fireplace was festooned with swarms of tiny china ornaments. At one side of the hearth stood a large wardrobe, painted white with gold trim embossing its doors, and on the other side, a writing desk situated beneath a generous window.

Curious to see what lay outside, I rose to pull back heavy damask curtains. Light swept into my room and painted the walls with bright honey. The winter sun was substantial, and I squinted until my eyes adjusted, only to be rewarded with a most spectacular view.

The grounds were impressive. A carpet of velvet, green grass was bordered by flower beds filled with a riot of heavy-laden rose bushes, the last blooms of the year. The center of the lawn appeared to be dissected by a narrow oblong pond, its somber steel-grey water littered with listless lily pads which floated aimlessly across its glassy surface. Beyond the gardens, my eyes were drawn to a remarkable landscape. For there in the distance lay the dark indigo of the English Channel, shimmering beneath the sunlight like molten sapphires. I could not help but be taken aback by the majesty before me, saturated with the delight of it, and then I thought of my darling, dearest Aramintha.

At Brampton Ladies College destiny had presented me with an education at the mere cost of my pride. All but a servant in status, I was given room and board in exchange for my abilities as a tutor. To the girls of the college I seemed inconspicuous, to its staff, insignificant. Yet to Aramintha Clayton I was a person, an individual whom she endowed with the generous gift of her friendship.

Aramintha had been my salvation. She alone had rescued me from drowning in a sea of loneliness when she plucked me from seclusion and called me all but sister. Indifferent to my social status and unconcerned with my lack of fortune and prospects, in Aramintha, I discovered purpose. My ambition had been solely to pursue knowledge and a good education, but Aramintha showed me the many possibilities within my reach should I acquire both.

"Miss Westcott?" Fingers lightly rapped on my door and roused me from thought.

"Come in."

Miss Tricklebank, whom I had met briefly the night before, entered my chamber holding a small tray in her hands laden with a pot of tea, boiled egg, and slices of hot buttered toast. She placed it down upon the desk and seemed surprised to see me still in my night attire.

"I trust you were comfortable?" she asked politely, her dour expression reminiscent of the headmistress at Brampton, stern and rather chilly. Her frown rippled with disapproval as she observed my disheveled state, my unbraided hair.

"Most comfortable, thank you, Miss Tricklebank." I glanced at the tray. "I would have come down to the kitchen—"

"It is customary to take breakfast the first day in your room. You may join the rest of the staff at luncheon and meet everyone then. It will be a full day, Miss Westcott, I can assure you." She smoothed down her stiff black skirts and absentmindedly patted the back of the brown bun in her hair. "Her ladyship will see you at ten o'clock."

As soon as the door closed, I set about my meal as though starved. I had never before been so spoiled with my breakfast served thus. I ate, my mouth savoring every bite, while my eyes feasted upon the scene from my window.

It was as I sipped my last drop of tea that I saw him. He strode towards the pond and then stopped as though taken by something which lurked in the water—a tall man, with the breadth of a laborer yet garbed as a gentleman. I could easily make out his form, his black, tousled hair, yet no other detail as he was too far from my vantage point. My mind conjured up the list of characters I had come to know from Aramintha's colorful stories and entertaining letters. I ran through the names in my head and landed upon his, for who other could it be than Benedict?

Aramintha had often referred to her half-brother as the devil in a sea of angels. For he alone had been the only child of Sir Nigel not gifted with the Clayton golden hair, blue eyes *or* the family name. She had said the late Lord Clayton's bastard son was half Romany gypsy, which would account for his swarthy complexion and raven hair. In truth, though I could not see much of the man, he did cut an imposing and formidable figure.

Suddenly his face turned, and he looked directly up at my window. I gasped and leaned back in surprise. Had he seen me watching? I composed myself and chased away my embarrassment for being so foolish. On this my first day at Mowbray Manor, I must settle down and keep my wits about me. I should dress and go downstairs, for I was to meet Lady Clayton within the hour.

I ENTERED THE DRAWING room escorted by the formidable Baxter to find Lady Clayton seated at her writing desk. But upon our arrival she placed her fountain pen down, then turned to look at me waiting self-consciously in my worn workaday dress. The butler departed, and she rose majestically from her seat and moved to a velvet settle.

"Miss Westcott, please do come and sit." She

gestured to an intricately carved armchair, one of a matched pair which faced the sofa. I did as she bade, and rested my hands in my lap, my back ramrod straight as though I sat before a queen. Again, I was struck at the ethereal beauty of the older woman, the paleness of her complexion, the silver hair. Her ice-blue eyes assessed me, the cheapness of my dress, the cut of my collars.

"I trust your room was adequate?" The tone of her voice implied she expected an answer to the positive.

"Indeed, Lady Clayton, thank you, it was most comfortable."

"Splendid. Now I should like to discuss your position here. I was most satisfied with your credentials, though it is unusual for a young woman of your—" she paused to select her words, "…station, to have attained such a high level of education."

Attending a ladies' school without wealth or a position within society was highly uncommon. Therefore, her query seemed understandable. In my quest to be engaged as teacher to the youngest member of the Clayton family, I had intentionally withheld my relationship with Aramintha. My education at Brampton alone gave me the entrée required to join her staff. Lady Blanche would have been mortified to know her privileged daughter had been the best of friends with a personage as low in the social order as myself. But she would never make that connection. In our correspondence Aramintha had always called me Miss Victoria, after our Queen. She loved subterfuge, and it had been the easiest path to conceal a friendship her mother would have forbidden. Now I was glad of it, for I was determined to discover what had happened to my dearest friend.

"I count myself fortunate indeed to have an education, Lady Clayton. My father placed great value upon it. He considered knowledge the best security for my future. He did not wish me to be vulnerable nor dependent on any other but myself."

"I see," she muttered. Her tone suggested she did not. "I am sure you will prove worthy enough to instruct my son. Gideon is a bright boy, yet somewhat high-spirited, though no more than most thirteen-year-olds. My decision to educate him at home may change as I fear he has proven himself to be cleverer than his prior tutors. Not in scholastic endeavors, but rather with his stubbornness and cunning."

Aramintha had regaled me with many stories of her little brother. I was forewarned, and therefore forearmed. "Gideon and I will make the best of it, Lady Clayton."

"One hopes so." She raised her eyebrows. "You understand his past tutors have been men. This will be a trial period for the first month to see how you progress. Do I have your agreement?"

"Indeed."

"Good. Benedict will make the appropriate financial transactions based upon our contract." She rose with a rustle of fabric. "Follow me, and I will take you to the schoolroom and introduce Gideon."

THE CLASSROOM WAS SITUATED at the top of the house, along with what I presumed to be Gideon's bedroom, a nursery and a playroom. Lady Clayton led me down a short corridor into a spacious chamber, decorated with charts, maps, and diagrams of an educational nature.

The front wall was covered in a black chalkboard, with three large desks facing towards where the teacher might conduct lessons. A young blond boy occupied the centre desk, and upon our entrance, he glanced up from his writing. I barely managed to conceal my sudden intake of breath as the boy stared at me with Aramintha's face. But for his gender, he could be her replica, the same pale blue eyes, butter-yellow hair, full mouth and upturned nose.

"Gideon, here is your new tutor, Miss Westcott," Lady Clayton spoke sharply. The boy rose to his feet, his fingers still rested on the desk as his gaze fastened on my face. I moved forward and held out a hand in greeting.

"Good morning, Master Gideon, it is a pleasure to make your acquaintance." He blinked at me but ignored my proffered hand, which I quickly dropped. I smiled, but his expression remained impassive, his demeanor far less attractive than his looks.

"Come, Gideon, where are your manners?" Lady Clayton's face crumpled with displeasure. "Introduce yourself to Miss Westcott at once."

"Good day to you, ma'am," he said begrudgingly and then sat back down.

Lady Clayton sighed. "Gideon can be rather sullen at times." She observed with a glance at me, her light eyes harsh. "I trust you will be able to manage him?"

"Indeed, Lady Clayton." My voice conveyed more confidence than I felt.

"Then I shall leave you to it," she stated flatly, and without further ceremony, Lady Clayton left the room.

I went to the chalkboard and retrieved a long piece of chalk, wrote my name, the date and then turned to my unhappy student.

"Well, Master Gideon, I look forward to us working together. To begin, we should discuss the lessons you have had in the past and determine where we shall start."

He was completely unresponsive. His pale eyes shimmered with obvious disdain; his chin tilted in defiance. Gideon Clayton was an angry boy. But why?

I tried again. "Master Gideon, I am in no doubt you are displeased with my coming. It is usual to feel this way when a new tutor arrives. Perhaps—"

"We have just met," he interrupted. "Therefore, how can you profess to know anything whatsoever about me?" His voice balanced on the cusp of breaking, teetered between boyhood and maturity, but the tone was clear. Gideon Clayton was irritated.

"True enough," I agreed. "But in my experience, it is natural to feel animosity towards an individual who implements a change in routine. I am here to teach. My intention is not to upset you nor cause any discomfort. However, I shall engage you in lessons to earn the salary your mother pays me, monies which ensure my survival. Lady Clayton insists you are to be educated, and if not by me, she will bring in another to teach you, or perhaps even send you away. If your objective is to make my task difficult, you only prolong the punishment by making new acquaintances each time a replacement tutor arrives." I looked straight at the boy who sat listening to my every word.

"Master Gideon, I am here to teach, and that is all. This can be a relatively decent experience, or you can render it more painful. The decision is yours. Please make it."

He seemed astonished. The expression upon his face spoke volumes. The boy had apparently never been challenged and seemed surprised by my frank words. I cared not. The most important relationship between pupil and teacher had to be respect. We would make little progress if the sulky boy did not accept me.

I recognized the precise moment Gideon allowed the tension to leave his shoulders. He leaned back in his chair, still unsmiling, but less combative.

"Now," I said. "Let us discuss how far you are come with your various studies."

THE LUNCH GONG SOUNDED. Time had passed quickly. Gideon and I had examined his previous tutor's work and registered where my instruction should begin. Still reluctant to converse, he answered my questions with the barest of responses. At least his diminished pout was enough to encourage me our relationship might improve a little by our next meeting. I dismissed Gideon until after luncheon and went down to the kitchen.

I walked into a hive of activity downstairs, due to the preparation of dinner for a certain Mr. Reginald Plumb the parish Vicar, and his wife. I had met several of the kitchen staff after breakfast when returning my tray, but now felt somewhat at a loss. Fearful of causing any strife, I avoided Mrs Oldershaw the cook, and instead asked a young kitchen maid where to partake of a bite to eat. She directed me to the servants' dining room off the kitchen, and there I enjoyed a slice of crusty fresh bread and a hunk of cheese.

Contemplating my plans for the afternoon, I opted to take Gideon outside for a nature ramble. Doing so might provide a better opportunity to get to know the boy away from the stern confines of the schoolroom. Gideon was dour to be sure. Cherubic in appearance, yet as sullen as a fish. I searched my catalogue of memories to conjure past conversations with Aramintha when she spoke of her family, but found little of him there other than his escapades. I had not learned much about the boy, but it would not take long to form my own opinion, and quickly.

The remaining brother I had yet to see was Gabriel, the current Lord Clayton. This sibling was a frequent subject of Aramintha's. Her elder by ten years, when she spoke of him, her eyes would grow misty with affection, her words revering as she described his admirable qualities, his handsome stature and pleasant ways. Perhaps I would meet him before the day was out? I considered the half-brother I had seen from my window that morning, Benedict. Of him, Aramintha had said little, yet the impression given suggested he remained somewhat aloof from the rest of the family, though why, she had not commented upon. For a bastard son to keep polite distance from the legitimate children of nobility was not considered unusual. Aramintha had told me Benedict was astute, adept at managing the Clayton estate for the legitimate heir, Gabriel. I had always surmised from her tone she cared well enough for Benedict yet adored Gabriel. I contemplated her opinion. Would mine be the same?

GIDEON AND I SPENT THE better part of a chilly afternoon traversing a well-trodden footpath. We walked along the green clifftops of the Purbeck hills while the frigid sea pounded sandy beaches far below.

The air felt damp yet invigorating, and we were both wrapped in our respective thick outer garments. The salty wind stung my cheeks like kissing bees, and my lungs hungrily sucked in the fresh, clean air, so vastly different from London.

As we travelled, I attempted to coerce Gideon from his unwillingness to make conversation, and after a time he begrudgingly began to relent. Initially, we discussed items we studied along our trek, flora and fauna, then identified the variety of seabirds wheeling in the skies and the colorful, comical puffins who inhabited the terrain. But more than anything, I desperately wanted to learn about the Clayton family.

I finally plucked up enough courage to steer the conversation away from our lesson. "Tell me, Gideon, do you spend much time with your siblings? I understand you have a sister and two brothers?"

He did not falter in his step. "Not really. I only have one brother, Gabriel. Benedict is half-brother to me, and he works for the estate." He continued to walk. I kept abreast of him, my heart picked up speed.

"And what of your sister?" I endeavored to keep the tremble from my voice. "Is she at home often?"

Gideon stopped abruptly, catching me off guard. His solemn face turned to mine. His skin was ashen.

"My sister is dead."

*****

Visit Jude's website (judebayton.com)
to find out where you can purchase your copy of

The Secret of Mowbray Manor

Made in the USA
Monee, IL
10 July 2023